Summer
at the
Dog & Duck

Jill Steeples lives in a small
market town in Bedfordshire
with her husband and two
children. When she's not writing,
she enjoys reading, walking,
baking cakes, eating them and
drinking wine.

Summer
at the
Dog & Duck

JILL STEEPLES

ⓐ

First published as an ebook in 2017 by Aria,
an imprint of Head of Zeus, Ltd.

First published in print in the UK in 2017 by Aria.

9 7 5 3 1 2 4 6 8

A catalogue record for this book is available from
the British Library.

ISBN (PB): 9781788541008
ISBN (E): 9781786691798

Typeset by Divaddict Publishing Solutions Ltd.

MIX
Paper from
responsible sources
FSC® C020471

Printed and bound by CPI Group (UK) Ltd, Croydon, CR0 4YY.

Head of Zeus Ltd
First Floor East
5–8 Hardwick Street
London EC1R 4RG

WWW.HEADOFZEUS.COM

For Phyllis and Stella

With love

Summer
at the
Dog & Duck

One

'Come on, Digby, let's get a move on, we haven't got all day.'

Digby looked up at me, his ears pricked, and immediately walked on at a faster pace, his tail wagging as if understanding my every word. That nice smiley lady off the telly had assured me that spring had well and truly sprung, and she wasn't wrong. Little Leyton was feeling positively balmy this morning. I wriggled out of my fur-trimmed anorak and hung it over my arm.

We'd been out for over an hour already, walking our usual route across the fields and down the back lanes and now we were heading back along the High Street towards the pub. I breathed a sigh of contentment, a smile spreading involuntarily across my lips. The pub – *my pub*, who would have thought it? There were days when I could hardly believe it myself. After all the upheaval of last year, when we first discovered the pub was up for sale and the future of the village inn had looked uncertain for a long time, I still had to pinch myself sometimes to truly believe that I was actually running the Dog and Duck now.

Crossing the road, a car tooted its horn and I span round to look, my heart lifting at the sight of Max Golding's distinctive Jeep, which drew to a halt at the kerbside. The driver's door was flung open and he jumped out.

'Good morning! How's my favourite landlady?'

'Very well, thank you. And how's my favourite hotshot property developer?'

Max nodded, giving consideration to that idea, before his mouth curled in amusement, clearly approving of the description. He came towards me and slipped his hands around my waist, pulling me in for a kiss.

'Yep, good. Much better now,' he said, his voice dropping an octave.

Butterflies danced in my stomach. I called it the Max effect. Something to do, I suspected, with his broad frame, mussed up hair and dark eyes that danced with intent, eyes that were watching me closely now. We'd been dating properly for a few months now, yet still he had the power to make my heart beat faster in my chest, and my skin tingle in anticipation.

'Time for a coffee?' I asked, mentally shaking myself free of the giddiness.

He glanced at his watch and grimaced. 'I'd love to, but I've got a conference call at eleven, and a few other things I have to see to before then. We're still on for Friday though?'

'Yep, can't wait,' I said, quashing my disappointment with a smile.

Just then another car, a little blue jaunty number that I didn't recognise, pulled up behind Max's Jeep, and the passenger door window eased open and the driver leaned across the seat to speak to us. 'Hello, Max, Ellie!' The woman's voice was warm and friendly.

I did a double take.

'Sasha!'

I don't know who was more surprised, me or Max. The last person I'd expected to see this morning was Max's ex-girlfriend, looking as indecently fresh-faced and naturally glamorous as I remembered. She'd left the village last autumn when she and Max decided to go their separate ways after a five year long relationship. It had been an amicable split, so Max had told me. Even so, when we got together soon afterwards it was something of a relief to know that his lovely ex was out of the way, having returned to her life in London. I'd barely given her a second thought since. But, sadly, now here she was… and she hadn't grown any less gorgeous in the meantime.

'Lovely to see you both,' she beamed. I only wished I shared her enthusiasm at reconnecting, but, in truth, I was struggling.

'You too,' said Max, as charming as ever. 'Although this is something of a surprise. What brings you to Little Leyton?'

'Ah, long story,' said Sasha, her gaze flickering across to me for the briefest moment. 'In fact, I'm glad I've run into you, I was hoping we could have a chat. There was something I wanted to discuss, if that's okay?' This was very much intended for Max, and not for me, I quickly realised.

'Sure thing,' said Max. 'I'm tied up for the next hour or so, but I'll be free later if you want to pop down to the manor.'

'Great!' breezed Sasha.

Great, I repeated silently through gritted teeth, while smiling sweetly. Time enough for Max to entertain his ex, but not enough time for a coffee with me. I see… As if reading my mind, Max's arm slipped around my waist and he gave me a gentle squeeze, by way of compensation, I supposed. If Sasha was perturbed by Max's show of affection towards me, she certainly didn't show it.

My gaze drifted off down the High Street towards the pub where I noticed someone standing beneath the recently renovated sign of The Dog and Duck; a man peering through the glazed pane of the front door.

'Look, I'm going to have to go,' I said, curious now as to whether I had a delivery, although infinitely more curious as to what Sasha might want to discuss with Max.

'See you later,' said Max, giving me a kiss on the cheek.

'Lovely to see you, Ellie,' said Sasha, from her car, lifting her hand to wave at me. 'We must catch up soon.'

'Yes,' I said, giving her a little wave in return. I tugged gently on Digby's lead and scurried off towards the Dog and Duck, wondering if Sasha and I actually had anything to catch up on. She wasn't a local girl and I'd only met her a couple of times when she'd still been with Max. As far as I knew, he was the only thing we had in common and I didn't much fancy swapping notes on that particular subject.

'Good morning,' I said, rushing up to the man who now had his head pressed up against the bay window of the pub. 'Can I help you?'

'Ah yes, well I was hoping to get a drink around here, but...'

'No, no, we're open,' I said brightly, taking a glance at my watch. It was only just gone opening time. Sod's law that this man, who I'd never seen before, had caught me out today. 'If you hang on, I'll go and open up.'

I ran round the back with Digby, my fingers fumbling with the keys to open the door. Usually, I enjoyed the quiet of the early mornings, before the first of the customers arrived.

It gave me a chance to get myself organised, and to get my head straight too, and after my unexpected meeting with Max and Sasha today, my mind was all over the place.

'What can I get you?' I asked, once I'd unbolted the front door and ushered the man inside. Digby gave his sniff of approval before wandering off and slumping on the rug in front of the fireplace.

'I'll have a pint of Best please.'

'Ah...' Wasn't that just typical? We'd been so busy yesterday that by the end of the evening all the barrels had run dry. Dan was coming in early today to change them over, but clearly not early enough for this particular customer. 'I'm really sorry; the draught beers are off at the moment. They'll be back up later.'

'Oh.' I saw the disappointment on the man's face and heard the disapproving tone in that one little word. 'I'd better have one of the bottled beers then. I'll try this one,' he said, pointing to the list of craft beers on the blackboard. He planted himself on a stool up at the bar, and looked all around him. My gaze followed his and it was only then I noticed the mop and bucket resting against the old oak beam. Denise, our cleaner, had phoned in sick this morning, so I'd had a quick whizz around instead. Only after a few minutes of half-hearted mopping, I'd got distracted, which was often the case when I was cleaning, and had decided that a walk outside with Digby was a much better proposition. I'd planned on picking up where I'd left off when we got back, only I hadn't anticipated my early morning customer. 'This place has had a bit of a spruce up since I was last in,' he said now, 'although that was probably a few years back.'

'Yes, we're under new ownership. A full refurbishment

was carried out just before Christmas.' I poured the beer into a glass and handed it across. 'We've tried to keep the essence of the pub as it's always been though.'

The man nodded and turned his gaze to appraise me. 'You must be Ellie Browne then?'

'Yes...'

'I've seen the write-ups in the local press. I remember Eric well, of course. He was a decent bloke. Ran a good pub.' He paused for a moment to look me up and down. 'To be honest, I was expecting someone older.'

'Everyone does,' I said, breezily, ignoring the slight. I dashed round to the other side of the bar to collect the cleaning paraphernalia, but I failed to notice the low stool that I'd moved out of the way earlier, and which was now very much in the way, tripping over it and catapulting into the bucket, sending the contents spilling everywhere.

'Shit! Oh bugger. Oops... sorry!' I said, suddenly remembering my customer, who was looking down at the water pooling around his lovely brown brogues. He grimaced and lifted up his feet and placed them on the bar rest of the stool while I mopped up around him.

In three months of running the pub I'd grown used to the comments from people surprised that a woman in her twenties might have the audacity to think she could run a pub. Honestly, what were they expecting? That I'd get rid of the old wooden seats and bring in a bunch of bean bags, and do away with the real ales and turn the pub into one of those dry bars that were apparently all the rage these days?

Still, the people that mattered most to me had complete and utter faith in my abilities. Max Golding, the new owner and saviour of the pub – not to mention stealer of my heart –

was the one who'd asked in the first place if I would consider running the Dog and Duck. He'd stepped in to buy the place when rumours were rife around the village that the pub might be sold, leaving the old inn to an uncertain future. At the same time, Eric, the landlord, who I'd known since I was a small girl, had decided to retire, creating a vacancy at the pub that urgently needed filling. Along with my doggy daycare business I'd been working several shifts at the pub anyway - I'd worked there on and off for years - and along with most other people in Little Leyton, I wanted to see the Dog & Duck continue as it had always done. With Eric's encouragement and the support of my family and friends in the village, I'd taken on the role and hadn't regretted the decision for one moment. Now as I sloshed the mop up and down, I was determined not to let this man's throwaway comment rattle me.

'Do you have any pork scratchings?'

'Um...' Oh, double bugger! They were on my list of items to collect from the cash and carry later today. 'We've got crisps and peanuts.'

'Doesn't matter,' said the man, unconvincingly.

What was it they said? You can't please all of the people all of the time, and I suspected this could be one of those times.

'Right, well thanks very much,' said the man, pushing his half-finished beer back across the bar and shaking out his feet in an exaggerated manner. Totally unnecessarily, I thought. 'I'll come back some other time, when you've got your draught beers on.'

'Yes, please do,' I said with a smile, but I was left with the distinct impression that he was one very dissatisfied customer.

'Crikey, someone's an early bird.' Dan came through the front door for the start of his shift, passing the customer on his way out.

'Yep, you don't know him, do you? Came in for a pint but was a bit disappointed to find all the draught beers off.'

Dan looked at his watch and shrugged. 'Better get those barrels changed right away then. Didn't really catch a look at the guy though.'

'Dan? Can I ask you something?'

He stopped, one hand on the cellar door and turned to look at me. 'Sure. Fire away.'

'Tell me honestly. Do you think I'm the right person to be running the pub?'

'What!? Where the hell has that come from?'

'Oh, I don't know. I just sometimes wonder if the regulars miss having Eric around. If they wouldn't want someone more blokeish behind the pumps?'

Dan chuckled and shook his head. 'Well, I don't think you'd ever fill the blokeish remit. You've not had any complaints, have you? The locals love you. Everyone's just pleased that the Dog and Duck is still here, running as it's always been. For a while there, we didn't even know if Little Leyton would get to keep its pub. You were the perfect choice, Ellie, and you're doing a great job.'

'Thanks Dan,' I said, warmed by his words. I picked up a tea towel and began polishing some glasses. 'I was just having a moment, that's all.' A moment brought on by Sasha's sudden reappearance, I suspected, and only made worse by my unexpected and awkward customer this morning.

'Look, don't let that bloke bother you. He'll probably never come back again.' Dan paused, a smile toying at his lips. 'Unless of course he was from the Good Pub Guide…'

'Oh… my… gosh… He couldn't be, could he?'

Dan shrugged. 'Hmmm, well they do tend to make a habit of popping in at the most unlikely times.'

'Oh great,' I sighed. 'That's just bloody brilliant.'

'Hello lovely, get me a triple vodka, on the rocks please!'

Thankfully, before I'd had chance to consider whether my early morning customer had actually been from one of *the* most influential pub guides in the business or was just a grumpy middle-aged man, Polly waltzed into the pub and slumped down on a stool at the bar.

'Oh, you're having a bad day too then?' I asked.

'Yes, I really am, and it's not even lunchtime yet! I suppose I'll have to give the vodka a miss; a coffee will have to do. I've left Jacqui in charge of the shop.'

I smiled. Polly, one of my best friends, and proprietor of Polly's Flowers, which just so happened to be next door, was a frequent visitor to the pub, usually popping in when she knew it would be quiet to have her favourite tipple of an orange juice and lemonade, or if she was pushing the boat out like today, a coffee, and the opportunity to catch up on all the news.

With Dan down in the cellar, I put two large cups on the tray of the coffee machine and pressed the button for two cappuccinos, handing Polly her cup when it was ready, before sitting down on the stool opposite her with my drink.

'So, come on then, what's gone quite so wrong today?'

'That's just the thing. Nothing in particular. I got in early to do the orders, and was absolutely fine putting together the bouquets and wreaths, and then just as I was putting cellophane over the last order, some stupid song came on

9

the radio and that was it, I was gone. Within moments tears were running down my cheeks and I was one hot snivelling mess. "Johnny Remember Me," would you believe? As if I needed any reminding.'

I groaned. Bloody Johnny Tay.

'Honestly, Ellie. I thought I was over him. I've been doing really well these last few weeks, trying my hardest to put him out of mind and then all it takes is one silly tune and I'm right back there to when it happened.'

'Oh Polly.' I leaned over the bar and wrapped my arms around her neck. 'It's just a wobble. You were bound to have some along the way. It's good to have a cry. Get it out of your system and then move on again. You've been doing brilliantly well.' Polly gave a rueful shrug. 'I thought so too, but if I'm being honest I miss Johnny so much. I still don't understand what happened.' She sighed heavily. 'One minute we were getting on fantastically, talking about a future together, and the next thing he's telling me he isn't sure what he feels anymore and that he needs some space. What did I do so wrong?'

'You didn't do anything wrong, Polly. You have to get that thought out of your head. This wasn't about you. It was about Johnny. He had a midlife crisis – it just came a bit early that was all, more like a quarter-life crisis, I suppose. You have to remember that he's spent his whole life in this village, he didn't go away to university or take a year off to go travelling around the world, and I think he just thought if he didn't do something now, break out of his rut, then he might never do it.'

Polly's mouth curled in disapproval, and I wondered if I didn't sound as though I was sticking up for Johnny. 'Funny how he chose that particular moment to escape, just as things were becoming more serious between us, when we had so much to look forward to.' She swirled her coffee in its cup and my heart twisted at her obvious sadness.

Their romance had been a bit of a whirlwind admittedly, they started dating and within a couple of weeks were inseparable, so we were all shocked when Johnny upped and left suddenly. No one more so than me. That last conversation I'd had with him, the day before he headed out of Little Leyton with only his rucksack on his back, had played over in my head so many times. Could I have said or done anything to prevent him from leaving?

'It's just something I have to do, Ellie,' he'd told me. 'I've not planned this, but with a brand new year ahead, I've just got this burning desire to get away, to see what else the world has to offer me.'

It was so unlike the Johnny I knew and loved. We'd been friends since school and even had a bit of a fling when we were teenagers, but I could never have seen this coming. 'But what about Polly? I thought you two were good together.'

'We are. She's a great girl and the last thing I want to do is hurt her, but...' He'd paused, raking a hand through his hair. '... The time isn't right for me. I need to get away. I'm not sure I can trust my feelings anymore. When you think about it, it wasn't that long ago that I was feeling the same way about you.'

The intensity of his gaze upon mine had made me uneasy.

'Oh Johnny, that's not what this is about, is it?' It was my only regret about coming back to Little Leyton, falling into the easy familiarity of Johnny's arms that first weekend. In hindsight, it had been a stupid thing to do and telling him that we had no future together as a couple was one of the hardest things I'd had to do. To be honest, I was relieved when he and Polly got together shortly afterwards. It got me off the hook, or so I'd thought.

'No.' He'd shrugged. 'Well… I don't know.'

Which had done nothing to ease my conscience at all. Now as I looked across at Polly, I felt a pang of guilt that I'd played some small part in Johnny's sudden wanderlust.

'Look Polly, I wouldn't spend any more time obsessing about it. You'll drive yourself mad. Johnny's gone off to make a new future and, however hard it is, that's what you need to do too.'

'Hmm, I suppose you're right.' She wiggled on her stool, straightened herself up and gave me a rueful smile. 'It doesn't seem the same around here now though, with Johnny gone. And Eric. And your parents.'

'I know, it feels like the whole bloody village has deserted us!' I laughed.

My parents had left about this time last year – just after I'd returned to the village, although I felt sure that had no bearing on their decision – when my dad took up a new job in Dubai. It was only meant to be for nine months, but they'd both taken to the ex-pat lifestyle so well that when the company offered to extend Dad's contract, they'd jumped at the chance. Then Eric, who had always been like a second father to me, had decided he wanted to travel the world too after hanging up his tea towel over the pumps at The Dog and Duck for one last time.

'Please tell me you're not making plans to disappear to the other side of the world?' said Polly, only half-jokingly.

'No way, I've got too much to do around here.'

Returning home last year after being made redundant from my job in the city, I'd found solace in a simpler way of life, working shifts at the Dog and Duck, and running my own doggy day care business. It had only ever been intended as a temporary move – it was hardly as if I could make a career out of pulling pints and walking dogs – but then, just before Christmas, I was faced with a decision. Should I return to London and take up the frankly amazing job I'd been offered at a top-notch corporate firm, with a salary to match, or should I follow my heart and stay in the village and take over the running of the pub?

My decision was made a whole lot simpler when Gemma, one of my dog-walking clients confided in me that she wouldn't be able to keep her dog, Digby, the black Labrador, who I walked on a regular basis, because her husband had lost his job and they were moving into smaller, rented accommodation. Without even thinking, I'd offered Digby a home with me. A sign, if I'd needed one, that Little Leyton was where my future lay.

'So,' said Polly now, 'enough about me, and my miserable love life, how's things with you? How's it going with the delectable Mr Golding?'

Hmm, and of course there'd been other more enticing reasons making me want to stay in the village. *The Max effect.*

My hand reached down to ruffle Digby's coat, who'd wandered over to my side, and I felt warmly appreciative that these days I had not just one, but two dark and handsome men in my life.

'Fine, we're both so busy of course. We're not getting to see much of each other at the moment, but, yeah, it's good.'

More than good in fact. Admittedly, our relationship hadn't got off to the best of starts and there'd been some wobbly moments along the way, but we'd now found a new deeper level of understanding. Initially I'd been wary and suspicious of the man I'd met when I was wading about in the river on his estate trying to rescue Milo, the escaping Cockapoo, one of many fond memories from my dog-walking days. I hadn't known then that I was trespassing on Max's land, only that the tall, good-looking stranger had an immediate and startling effect upon me. There was something about him that infiltrated my skin, and it wasn't just the water flooding my wellies at the time, it was something else, something that I simply couldn't ignore.

Later, finding out that he had a gorgeous girlfriend installed at Braithwaite Manor, his impressive home, and that he was making enquiries about buying The Dog and Duck, only added to my innate distrust of the man. Rumours were spreading around the village that Max wanted to buy the pub and convert it into a luxury home, making a quick profit, and I was determined not to let that happen. As it was I'd had no reason to doubt Max's intentions, he turned out to be the village's knight in shining armour when he stepped in to save the pub from an uncertain future.

'Oh, look at you,' Polly joshed, nudging me out of my daydreaming, 'one mention of Max's name and you go all soppy.'

'No, I was just thinking that was all. I bumped into Max earlier, outside, we were having a chat when Sasha turned up.'

'What?! Max's ex?'

'Yeah, did you ever meet her?'

'No, although I saw her a couple of times. Very attractive girl. Brunette. Tall and leggy.'

'Yeah, that's her,' I said, not really appreciating Polly's enthusiastic description, even if she was right on every count.

'Hmm, so what's she doing back in the village then?'

I shrugged. It was a question I was asking myself too.

Two

'Thanks for the coffee, Ellie! See you later.'

Picking up the dirty cups, I took them out to the kitchen and loaded them into the dishwasher, my mind mulling over recent events.

At least Polly had left in better spirits than when she'd arrived, but I hoped her cheery facade wasn't for my benefit only. All these weeks and I thought she'd been handling the break-up with Johnny well. What a rubbish friend I was! I'd been so wrapped up in the pub, and with Max, that I wondered, with a twist of guilt, if I hadn't given Polly the time she'd needed. I would need to make it up to her.

Dan wandered back up from the cellar, a crate of Belgian beers in his hands.

'All done,' he said, with a smile.

'Great, thanks for that. You see, if only that customer had come in an hour later he could have discovered just how wonderful our beers are.'

'Honestly, don't give him a second thought. There'll always be that one tricky customer.'

Dan was my cellar-man and right-hand man and I honestly didn't know what I'd do without him. We'd been workmates at the pub for years, first sharing shifts together when I was still a teenager, and I'd been worried when I took over as landlady that he might resent the change in the status, but I should have known better. Dan didn't have an ounce of malice in him, despite the multitude of tattoos and piercings possibly suggesting otherwise, and took everything in his stride.

'How's Silke?' Silke was Dan's girlfriend and they lived together on a narrowboat on the canal just five minutes away, which meant he was always on hand for any emergencies at the pub, although I tried my hardest not to take advantage of his good nature.

'Yeah,' he said, nodding. 'Good.'

'Right,' I said, glancing at my watch, 'I should get off to the cash and carry, and then I'll be back for the lunchtime rush. I need to check on George too. See how he's getting on.'

'George?' said Dan, his brow furrowing. 'Now, let me guess. A Dalmation? A Retriever? Or that scruffy Bitsa you had in here the other day?'

I laughed. 'No, George isn't a dog. And for your information, that scruffy Bitsa is called Shirley, and she's absolutely adorable.'

Dan curled his lip, looking wholly unconvinced. Since Christmas, Dan had accepted, with remarkable good grace, the steady flow of canine visitors to the pub. With a heavy heart, I'd had to make the decision to cut back on my doggy day care duties. With the responsibility of the pub, I just didn't have the time, but that hadn't stopped me from helping out my friends – because that's what my clients had become – when I could. Milo, Holly, Rosie, Amber, Shirley and many others dogs were frequent visitors to the pub, staying for a couple of hours, or for the day, joining Digby and me on our daily walk across the fields.

It wasn't in Dan's job description to care for my four-legged friends, but he took it all in good part, even managing to keep his cursing down to the bare minimum when they got under his feet behind the bar, tripping him up and sending beer spilling out of the pint glasses he was serving, but I liked to think it all added to the cosy atmosphere of The Dog and Duck.

'So who is George then?' Dan looked perplexed.

'Oh, he's the new tenant who's moved into Mum and Dad's house. I haven't met him yet, so I just wanted to pop in and introduce myself and see how he's doing, ask him if there's anything he needs.'

'Ah right, and absolutely nothing to do with the fact that you're just dead nosy about who's living in your old home?'

'Whatever are you suggesting?' I said, laughing at Dan's perceptiveness. 'Just being a friendly neighbour, that's all.'

Outside, the sun had broken through the cloud and the air felt warmer than it had earlier this morning. The grey stone of the buildings in the High Street were lifted by the bright cheerfulness of daffodils poking their heads up from the pavements. Across the street, I spotted Dave and Janet, a couple of my regulars, who were walking hand-in-hand deep in conversation. Mrs Shah from the newsagents poked her head out from her shop and gave me a cheery wave as I passed, and I could see the distinctive sight of Rosie's little tail bobbing in the distance as she walked alongside Mrs Elmore. I took a deep breath, feeling renewed gratitude that this was where I'd chosen to make my home. Really, there was no place better.

When I reached the gate to No. 2 Ivy Lane Cottage, I wavered for the briefest moment, my gaze running up and down the stone cottage that had been our happy family home for so many years. It felt strange to be here as a visitor, unable to walk up the path and put my key in the door, and let myself in. To find Mum and Dad waiting for me inside. This was someone else's home now, and I supposed I ought to get on and introduce myself. Tentatively I rapped on the brass knocker.

When there was no reply I tried again.

After knocking for the third time, with increasing impatience and force, I was about to turn around and head off into town when the front door was flung open with gusto and a man, broad and tall and clearly disgruntled at being disturbed, filled the threshold.

'Yes?' he barked.

'Sorry to disturb you, but…'

'Look, if you're selling something, I'm really not interested.'

'Oh no no, I'm not selling anything. I'm looking for George Williamson.'

'Yep.'

Ah right. Suddenly this seemed like a very bad idea. This wasn't how I'd pictured Mr George Williamson in my head at all. I'd imagined a man in his fifties or sixties with kindly eyes and a cardigan. Not an irascible, but undoubtedly good-looking man in his thirties, wearing cargo trousers, a fitted T-shirt and with mussed-up hair. Without a woolly in sight. I took a deep breath.

'I'm Ellie Browne. This is my house, well my parents' actually, but they're abroad at the moment. I just wanted to check that you've settled in okay or see if there's anything you might need. I've brought you a cake.'

I thrust the round tin containing the homemade Victoria sponge into his hands. Homemade by Betty Masters at The Bluebell Tea Rooms, that was, and not by me, but it's the thought that counts, although I was beginning to wish I'd never had this particular thought. George looked at the cake in his hands and then at me, looking ever so slightly non-plussed.

'Thank you. That's, um, kind.'

'You're very welcome. Have you settled in okay?' I asked, looking over his shoulder, feeling a sudden protectiveness for our lovely family home. Only a few months ago I'd been living here, although to be honest it had always felt strange without Mum and Dad being around, and far too big for me rattling around on my own. When I took over the pub it made sense to move out and into the living quarters upstairs. It was no great hardship, as the extensive renovations Max had carried out just before Christmas meant that the kitchen and bathroom were all shiny and new, and all the bedrooms had been given a fresh lick of paint.

'Yeah. Great,' he said, his hand hovering on the door, as though he might slam it shut in my face at any moment.

'If there's anything you need to ask me about, like the appliances, then just let me know. The Aga can be temperamental at times, but it's fine when you get used to it. There's an instruction booklet in the top drawer of the dresser and—'

'Don't worry, I really don't think I'll be doing a lot of cooking.'

'Ah, okay. And you should know that the power shower in the main bathroom can take a long time to warm up, but—'

'The shower's fine. In fact, everything's fine.' He pulled his lips tight in a smile. 'It's just that I'm rather busy.' There was a pause, before he added. 'Working. Sorry.' And then, as if remembering his manners, 'But this is lovely of you, thank you.'

'Right then, well I'll let you get back to your... work,' I said, rather hoping that George might fill in the blank for me, but clearly not picking up on my questioning tone. 'The offer's there though, if there's anything you need just shout. You'll find me at the pub, The Dog and Duck. Just down the road.'

'The pub? Well, I shall definitely pop in some time. When I'm less busy.'

Okay, never let it be said that I couldn't take a hint. I was clearly stopping this man from doing whatever it was he wanted to be doing. Still, at least I'd made the effort and extended the hand of friendship to the latest incomer to the village. What I had to remember was that not everyone was cut out for the friendly intimacy of village life. There'd been a time when I couldn't wait to leave Little Leyton, to escape the cosy confines of a place where everybody knew your business. It had been refreshing to move away to the big city, to live and work in a place where no-one knew the first thing about me, a place where I could be anyone I wanted to be. Admittedly, I'd eventually grown disillusioned with the anonymity and lack of community spirit in London, but I realised village life wasn't for everyone.

I closed the wrought-iron gate of No. 2 Ivy Lane Cottages behind me, my gaze lingering over the pretty house. Perhaps George Williamson didn't want to be my new best friend, I thought with a sigh. Disappointing, but I supposed I would have to forgive him that. As long as our new tenant paid his rent promptly and kept the house in good order, then that was all that mattered.

Three

On Friday, after a busy lunchtime shift, I was just scrubbing the hearth, doing my best Cinderella impression, when I heard a familiar voice fill the snug, sending a warm sensation flooding through my limbs.

'What's a man got to do to get a drink around here?'

I turned and pushed myself up off the floor.

'Max!'

Even after all these months it still took me by surprise just how startlingly attractive he was, reminding me of the first time we'd met. It had blindsided me then. And every single time since. I walked into his open arms, that familiar one-sided smile on his lips that spoke directly to my insides.

He cupped the back of my head with his hand and kissed me.

'God, I've missed you.'

'Me too,' I said, tidying my hair behind my ears, feeling back-footed by the intensity of Max's unexpected presence. Our date wasn't until this evening and I'd been so looking forward to it – when I'd had the chance to primp and prettify myself for the occasion. Now, I glimpsed down and wiped away the dust that had collected on my jeans. 'Are you staying for a drink?'

He glanced at his watch. 'Maybe a quick one. A gin and tonic?'

'Sure.' Round the other side of the bar, I fixed his drink and poured myself a glass of water, looking up to meet his gaze. 'Are you busy then?' Silly question, I knew when that was Max's default mode. Even though his schedule was manic, he still managed to find the time to call or text me and just hearing his voice would lighten up my day, filling that gap until I could next see him again. Now he was here, without warning, and my poor heart, galloping in my chest, was still catching up with that fact.

He raked a hand through his hair in a move so natural he could have no idea the impact it had upon me. 'Yep. That new development I'm working on has run into problems. The usual stuff, suppliers not meeting delivery dates, subbies letting me down, cashflow issues. I think I've pulled it back on track now, but it's made me realise I need to have more of a hands-on approach with this project.'

I bit on my smile. In the months since I'd come to know Max, I'd quickly realised he didn't work any other way. He was a very successful property developer, but liked nothing more than getting stuck in on a project at a grass roots level, helping out his sub-contractors and getting his hands dirty. It was one of the many things I adored about Max, his passion and his dynamism, his enthusiasm for getting the job done.

When the renovations were being carried out on the pub it was Max who worked through the night, stripping and painting the woodwork and laying new floors, just so that the pub could re-open on Christmas Eve. It was his surprise Christmas gift to me. I'd been devastated when he'd told me that he was closing the pub down just before Christmas, in fact I'd stormed off and vowed never to speak to him again, but what I hadn't known was that he was working all hours to ensure the pub could reopen in time for the Christmas celebrations, just as I'd wanted.

Max might own the freehold to the pub, but he didn't get involved in the running of the pub at all. 'This is your territory,' he'd told me, when we'd first signed the paperwork. 'You're far too good at what you do for me to be interfering. That's not to say, I'm not here if you want to bounce some ideas off me or need any advice.'

Those words from Max had reassured me, knowing he had absolute faith and trust in me to run the pub the way I wanted to. As far as Max was concerned business was business and our personal relationship, well that was something else entirely. I didn't want to look too far ahead, but for the moment we were happy, even if we didn't get to spend that much time together. Something I'd learned over the last couple of years was that it's not always best to make too many plans. Sometimes it was better to just go with the flow and see where life took you. That was the approach I'd adopted ever since I'd been back in Little Leyton and, so far, it had worked a treat.

'When's the completion date?' I asked.

'This project? End of the month, but I've got another development lined up straight afterwards. To be honest, I'm not feeling it at the moment.'

'Really? Why?'

He shrugged nonchalantly. 'Not sure. Sometimes I feel as though I could do without the hassle. You know what it's like, it's full on, and for the first time I'm thinking I might like to live a simpler kind of life.'

'Oh, Max. Are you kidding? You'd hate that. You thrive on what you do.'

'Yeah, I suppose you're right. Although there are other, more important things in life than working seven days a week.' His gaze lingered on my face for a moment too long, and a little shiver ran down my body.

'Well listen, if you ever need a less stressful job, I can always find you something to do here in the pub. Washing up, collecting glasses, that kind of thing.'

'Ha! Thanks for that. I'll bear it in mind, but I could never work with you, Ellie. You'd be way too much of a distraction.' He paused, running his hand along my forearm, from across the other side of the bar. 'Look, Ellie, I'm going to have to cancel dinner tonight.'

'Oh really?' I felt the disappointment like a physical pain. 'You're blowing me out again?' I said lightly, trying not to show it.

'Yeah, I'm really sorry, but something's come up.' An image of Sasha's smiling face flittered into my mind and I felt a pang of alarm. 'Family stuff. Apparently all's not well in Spain and Katy has been causing all sorts of problems. I've got to dash off and collect her from the airport'

'Your sister?' I asked, ashamed at the huge amount of relief I felt.

'Yeah, there's been a massive fall-out. To be honest, I'm not sure what's been going on, but Mum was in a real state, crying down the phone, saying she can't cope with Katy anymore. Something to do with Alan, I think.'

'Katy's boyfriend?'

'No, Mum's husband. He and Katy always used to be close so I don't know what's gone quite so wrong.'

'How old is Katy now?'

'Um...' Max screwed up his face, trying to work it out. 'Seventeen, maybe eighteen?'

'Hmm, well it can be a tricky age. Perhaps she's just asserting her independence. It's natural for teenagers to want to rebel against their parents.'

'Yep, I guess, although I'm not sure Mum sees it that way. Katy's supposed to be at school, doing A levels, or whatever it is they do out there, but she's left and is refusing to return. She's saying she doesn't want to live with Mum and Alan anymore, and is giving Alan a whole lot of grief. She's acting up, staying out to all hours of the morning and coming home drunk. I think Alan's put his foot down and said something has to change. Mum's worried sick and feels caught in the middle.'

'Oh, that doesn't sound good,' I said, grimacing.

'Exactly, that's why I agreed to have Katy come and stay for a couple of weeks.' He shrugged. 'Mum begged me to so I could hardly say no. Not that I'm sure I'll be a lot of help. I don't have a great deal of experience with stroppy teenage girls, and Katy and I have never spent any length of time together before, so it'll be interesting, if nothing else.' He lifted his palms to the air, looking hopelessly out of his depth.

It was lovely to think that Max wanted to help out his sister, even if it might mean us having even less time together. Still, I was sure it wouldn't be for long and I was excited at the prospect of meeting Katy as he hadn't introduced me to any of his family yet.

'Well that's probably all that's needed,' I said. 'A change of scene and a bit of distance between Katy and her mum.

I bet, a couple of weeks spent in Little Leyton and she'll be dying to get back home again.'

'Yeah, well that's what I'm hoping. To be honest, I'm going to be pretty busy these next few weeks, but she can make herself comfortable at home, do whatever it is teenage girls do. She's not been to the house before and it will give us a chance to get to know each other.'

'Well if there's anything you want me to do to help out then just let me know.'

'Thanks Ellie. I'm really sorry about tonight. I'll make it up to you some other time. I promise.'

'Don't worry. I understand. You need to be there for your family right now.'

Max downed his drink and flashed a rueful smile. He rarely spoke about his family. As far as I knew he hadn't seen any of them in the time since I'd known him. Max's father died when Max was still a teenager and his mother had quickly remarried and moved to Spain with her new husband to make a fresh start, taking Max's little sister Katy with them. Max hadn't said as much, but I'd got the impression he wasn't particularly close to his family. The only person that Max spoke about with genuine affection was his grandfather, Noel, who I'd known long before I'd met Max. It was the reason Max had come to Little Leyton in the first place, to take care of his grandfather in the final weeks of his life. Sadly Noel, who had been a regular at the pub, always sitting in the rocking chair next to the fireplace, a chair that was now affectionally referred to as Noel's chair, passed away soon afterwards, leaving a hole in the hearts of the villagers who'd grown fond of the old man, and an even bigger gap in the heart of his grandson.

Funny to think I'd ever doubted Max's motives for wanting to buy the pub, when all he'd wanted was to keep the Dog and Duck running, in respect to his grandfather's memory. I looked across at him now, feeling a warmth spread round my skin.

'Families, huh?' he said, with a shrug.

'I know,' I replied, smiling at his obvious bemusement, 'but it sounds as though they need you right now.'

'Come here.' He beckoned me over to his side of the bar and I walked around into his arms, relishing the sensation of his strong embrace, resting my head on his chest, soaking up his delicious male scent. Outdoorsy, fresh, all-masculine, all-Max. He ran his fingers through my hair, looking at me imploringly. 'I know I'm guilty of not giving you enough time at the moment, Ellie, and I feel bad about that.'

'There's no need, we're both busy.'

'Yes, I get that, but I don't want our relationship to suffer as a result. I know we both have our other commitments, but once Katy goes home we ought to make more of an effort. What do you reckon?'

Relief swept through me hearing Max talk like this because I'd had a niggling worry ever since Sasha had turned up the other day, wondering why she was here and what she wanted. I'd been planning on mentioning something to him, but given what he'd just said, and the way he was observing me with those dark intense eyes, I figured her visit couldn't have been important and was probably not worth bringing up now.

So, *what did I reckon?*

With Max's face so close to mine, it would have been hard to disagree, but then again why would I have wanted to.

'Definitely. I've been thinking the same.'

'You have?'

I hadn't wanted to push it with Max, but I had to admit it was frustrating only seeing each other occasionally, snatching moments together when we could. As brief and delightful as those moments were, they always left me feeling slightly bereft and longing for more.

'Well, it's good to know we're of a similar mind.'

Could we really be of a similar mind? Did Max really feel the same way as me? I still didn't know. Ever since Max had volunteered to be my co-driver on the charity run to France last year when Eric needed to pull out after breaking his ankle, I'd felt a sense of gratitude towards Max and a deep connection too. I'd been horrified at first at the thought of being stuck with the sexy, but hugely intimidating newcomer to the village in a van on a trip to the continent, but I'd had no need to worry. Being with him had felt so natural and my feelings for him grew quickly, feelings I'd had to keep a lid on when I found out he had a gorgeous girlfriend installed at Braithwaite Manor. When Max later split up from Sasha, our relationship was given the chance to flourish, but ever since then there had been a small part of me holding back from completely letting go. Wasn't it time to let go now?

Four

After Max left, I popped round to the flower shop next door where Polly was perched high up on her stool at the worktop, seeing to some paperwork. She smiled as she looked up to greet me.

'What are you doing tonight?' I asked.

'Um, let me consult my very busy social calendar.' She ran a fingernail down her order pad. 'Yes, as I suspected, absolutely nothing. Why do you ask?'

'Great. Fancy going out for something to eat at that new pizza place in town?'

'Well in the unlikely event that Daniel Craig is going to waltz through that door and whisk me away from all of this, then yes, I'd love to,' said Polly, her face lighting up.

I didn't take many nights off work and having already organised cover at the pub for my date with Max, it seemed a shame to see the evening go to waste. Besides, it had been far too long since Polly and I had a proper catch-up, I realised, as I sat across her from the table in the restaurant later.

'So where's Max tonight then,' Polly asked, as she topped up my glass from the bottle of Prosecco in the ice bucket.

'Well, he's had to go off to the airport to collect his sister, Katy. Between you and me, she's been having a few problems at home, so she's coming to stay with Max for a little while.'

'I didn't even know Max had a sister,' said Polly. 'I guess you'll get to meet her then?'

'I hope so. I haven't met any of his family yet, well apart from Noel, but that was before I even knew Max. I'm not sure he's terribly close to Katy. She's about twelve years younger than him and they didn't spend a lot of time together growing-up. Obviously they've seen each other a few times over the years, but I think only for fleeting visits. To be honest, Max doesn't talk much about his family.'

'Oh right. Well, he'll have no choice but to get to know his sister now,' said Polly wryly.

'Exactly. In a way it's a good opportunity for them all to build some bridges. Although I think Max is a bit apprehensive about how it will work out. As he says, he's not used to dealing with teenage girls.'

'Well, at least they'll be doing it in style, up in that lovely manor house in Little Leyton, he could take in a whole minibus full of orphans if he wanted to. I've always thought what a shame it is that it's only him rattling around inside there.

'I know,' I chuckled. 'It does seem a bit mad.'

I'd thought the same the first time I'd visited the manor. I'd been overwhelmed by the scale and grandeur of the place. With over ten bedrooms, state-of-the-art appliances, oak woodwork throughout and acres of landscaped gardens outside, it was like something from a glossy magazine. I'd wafted around the place, waltzing up and down the vast sweeping staircase with a flourish, imagining myself to be a movie star from a bygone age. It was a stunning house, a showpiece, but lacking in that one vital ingredient, that something indefinable, that turns a beautifully constructed house into a warm and welcoming home.

'Anyway, how are you doing now?' I asked her.

Polly lifted her chin, her eyes narrowing as though not having the faintest idea what I was talking about.

'You were a bit down the other day,' I reminded her. 'About Johnny?'

'Johnny who?' she said sharply, before a smile caught on her mouth. 'Oh, I'm sorry about that. I was a right old misog that day, wasn't I? I shouldn't have offloaded on you like that.'

'Don't be daft. We're friends. That's what I'm here for. I know I might seem preoccupied with the pub at times, but anytime you need to talk, I'm here for you.' I leant over and placed my hand lightly on hers. 'I mean it, Polly.'

'Thanks, Ells.' She sighed, intertwining her fingers together. 'I know Johnny and I hadn't been together that long, just a matter of months really, but I thought we had something special, something that might go somewhere. I could never have imagined he would just up and leave the way he did.' She lifted her gaze from her fingers. 'He broke my heart, but what can you do?' she asked, a weak smile forming on her lips. 'I can't waste any more time pining over him. As much as I might not like it, Johnny's moved on and that's what I have to do too.'

'Easier said than done, eh?'

'In this village, it is. Sometimes I wonder where I'm going to be in five years' time. If I'll still be preparing bouquets for other people's wives and girlfriends, without ever finding someone special of my own.' She flapped her hand against her chest. 'It's that feeling of being left behind. As if life is something that's happening to everyone else, while I'm still waiting to even get on the bus.'

'Oh, Polly, it will happen to you too.'

She gave a shrug. 'Funny thing is, I didn't realise I was even looking for it until Johnny, and now I know how lovely it is to have someone to share those simple things in life with, I know I want it again.'

'Yep,' I nodded, mulling over the truth of Polly's words. 'I suppose deep down it's what everyone hopes for, to find that special person to spend the rest of their lives with.'

'Well you're all right,' said Polly, rallying. 'You've got Max.'

'Yes, but it's still early days for us. Who knows what might happen?'

'Nah, you two are solid. He adores you. You only need to see the way he looks at you to know that.'

A warm feeling flooded my stomach. Deep down I knew Max was my 'one'. I could only hope he felt the same way too. If Polly had noticed, then maybe I ought to start believing it was true.

'Well, look. Maybe it's time for you to start dating again. To test the water,' I said. 'Nothing too serious. Just to get out there and start having fun again.'

Polly gave me a doubtful look. 'The last time I went on a date was before Johnny and that was with the carpet man. Remember him? And how fantastically that went?'

We both sniggered at the memory. It had been a double date, of sorts. Johnny and I had gone along for moral support, which was just as well really because it turned out that the carpet man could bore for England. We'd made our excuses as quickly as we politely could and after dispatching the carpet man the three of us ended up in the Dog and Duck laughing about Polly's lucky escape. It wasn't long after that Polly and Johnny got together...

'By the way, did you find out what Sasha was doing back in the village?'

'No, I didn't like to ask, Max was a bit preoccupied with all this business about Katy. I expect it was something to do with work, Sasha's an interior designer and I know she's worked on a couple of projects with him before. Max would have said if it was anything else.'

'Ah right,' said Polly, nodding.

I mean, it had to be work, right? What else could she possibly want with Max?

*

Walking into the pub on a Friday night was a life-affirming experience. As soon as we pushed our way through the heavy front door, we were greeted by a warm buzz of conviviality. Lively conversation, laughter and the sound of people enjoying themselves wrapped around us in a welcoming hug.

Usually, I'd be behind the bar, in the thick of all the action, serving pints, clearing glasses, exchanging banter with the customers, not stopping for a moment to draw breath, but to be able to take a moment in the hubbub of all this activity to see the place through a customer's eyes was lovely. I thought of Eric, off now on his travels, and how delighted he would be to see the pub he'd given so many years of his working life to, still thriving and serving the community of Little Leyton as it had always done.

'Go and find a seat and I'll grab us some drinks.'

Polly headed off into the bustle and I turned towards the bar, spotting my best friend, Josie, pulling pints. I made a beeline for her. Josie was Eric's daughter and had grown up in this pub. She probably knew more about running the place than I did, and I was so happy when she'd decided to come back to work after having her baby. If I had any problems I could always ask Josie what she thought and invariably her advice was spot on.

'How's it been tonight?' I asked her now.

'Busy,' she said, smiling. 'Just as we like it, but nothing we couldn't handle. It's just beginning to thin out now. Actually, I'm glad you're here because I need to have a word with you sometime when you have a moment?'

'Sure. Polly and I are going to share a bottle of Prosecco. Why don't you come and join us before you leave? That's unless you have to get back and rescue Ethan?'

'Not likely,' said Josie laughing. 'He needs to do his turn occasionally.' Ethan was Josie's husband and covered babysitting duties for little Stella on the evenings when Josie worked at the pub. 'I'll be over in a bit.'

With the bottle of Prosecco and a couple of glasses in hand, I weaved my way through the crowds – no easy feat when I was stopped by every other person wanting a chat, such was the life of a landlady – before finding Polly sitting at a table in the back bar. She'd been joined by Victoria Evans, the young woman who worked on the local newspaper.

'Hi Victoria, how's things?'

'Good. I wanted to catch you actually, I've got some good news for you.'

'Really?'

'Yes. We've had the list of shortlisted pubs in the county come through for the Potters Pub Guide and The Dog and Duck is on the list!'

'Of course it is!' said Polly, pouring the wine into the glasses and raising hers in the air. 'There'd have been a national outcry if it wasn't.'

'Oh gosh, that's brilliant,' I said. 'And such a relief too. Can you imagine not making the shortlist this year, now I'm in charge. That would have been terrible.'

'We're going to publish the list in this week's edition of the paper and then we'll do a feature on each of the pubs in the following weeks in the run-up to the announcement of the overall winner.' Victoria leaned into my side and whispered in my ear, 'You would be our winner, obviously, but for the sake of fairness we thought we had to feature the other pubs too.'

'So how's the winner actually selected then?' Polly asked Victoria.

'Well the shortlist is drawn up from customer nominations and then the overall winner is selected by representatives from the pub guide. They make unannounced visits to the pubs and rate them against a checklist of standards to come up with the best pub in the county. So you'll need to be on high alert for any mystery visitors.'

'Oh shit!'

'What?' Both Polly and Victoria turned to look at me. 'I think it might be a bit late for that. I had a guy in the other day. I didn't think much of it at the time but I didn't make the best impression.' I shook my head, remembering the disastrous visit. 'He came in early for a pint, but none of the draught beers were on, and then he asked for some pork scratchings. I didn't have any. Then to make matters worse, I tripped over a bucket of water I'd left in the middle of the floor and spilt it all over the man's shoes.' I let out a big sigh, before taking a restorative glug of Prosecco. 'I'm not sure I would have ticked any of the boxes on his wretched checklist.'

'Oh... well maybe it didn't go as badly as you thought,' said Victoria, trying to make me feel better, I knew.

'Yeah, or it might not even have been him. Perhaps it was just a random punter. That's the thing about a mystery visitor, they're mysterious!'

I gave Polly a doubtful look.

'Why all the glum faces?' Just then Josie came over and joined us at the table, picking up the bottle and filling her glass, after topping up mine and Polly's.

'Oh we were just discussing the Potters Pub Guide awards. I think I may have blown our chances this year. Your dad always did well in the awards, didn't he?'

'Yeah, I think he picked up a few medals over the years. I know he was always dead chuffed when he received the news.' Josie must have noticed my stricken expression because she quickly added, 'But honestly I wouldn't spend any time worrying about it. The pub is doing just as well as it's ever done and that's all that matters. You don't need a silly gong to prove anything.'

Maybe not, but I did feel a sense of responsibility to uphold the good reputation of the pub. To think that people might be saying it had gone downhill since I'd taken over filled me with dread.

Still, if tonight was anything to go by, then I had to be doing something right. The place was full to the gills with happy punters.

'Anyway, no more moping,' said Josie, banging her hands on the table, 'because I've got some news. We've finally got round to arranging little Stella's christening. It's going to be on the 14th of June at St Cuthbert's and you're all invited.'

'Isn't that the weekend of the summer fair?' Polly asked me.

'No, we've pencilled in the following week, the 21st, but nothing's confirmed yet. We're having a meeting here soon to finalise the details.'

'Oh, perfect then,' said Polly.

'I can't wait,' I added. We all doted on Stella and couldn't get enough of her squidgy cuddles.

'Well, I've chosen that weekend because Dad will be over. It's a shame your mum and dad won't be here, Ellie, but one of Ethan's friends has offered to film the service for us so I can send it to your mum so that she won't feel she's missing out completely.'

Our families had always been close, and that bond had only grown stronger when Miriam, Josie's mum, died when Josie was still a teenager. Eric had done his best, but struggling with his own grief, had floundered at times. Mum had stepped in to provide support and a listening ear to Josie for those times when she really needed a mother figure to confide in. When Josie became pregnant, Mum was delighted; I swear she couldn't have been happier if it had been me who had been expecting. And the way I looked at it, it got me off the baby-making hook for a few more years at least.

'What a lovely day it will be,' said Victoria.

'Yes, I can't wait and what I wanted to ask you, Ellie,' said Josie, grabbing hold of my hand from across the table, 'is if you'd be Stella's godmother?'

'What!?' I had to double-check her expression to make sure I'd heard her correctly. 'Me? Really? Do you mean it?'

Josie's face lit up in a smile, before she broke into laughter. 'Of course, I mean it! Who else was I going to ask? You've been my best friend since forever and I can't think of anyone who would make a better godmother to my daughter.'

A tight ball of emotion rose in my throat. 'Oh my gosh! I wasn't expecting that.' I swallowed hard, feeling deeply touched that Josie had asked me. 'Honestly, I'd be thrilled to be godmother to your gorgeous daughter.'

Josie stood up and leaned over to give me a tight hug.

I allowed the smile that had been hovering on my lips to spread across my face. It only confirmed to me that coming back to Little Leyton had been the best decision I'd ever made and it certainly put into perspective any silly niggles about pub awards.

'Well I think this calls for another bottle of fizz to celebrate,' said Polly, never one to miss an opportunity.

Another bottle of Prosecco was ordered and the four of us, me, Polly, Josie and Victoria, sat around the table catching up on the gossip. Josie was in the middle of telling us about Stella's crawling antics when Polly seemed to develop a sudden and urgent body twitch.

'Psst Ellie, over there.' She was flailing her head in the direction of the bay window, clearly agitated.

We all turned round, looking over our shoulders to see.

'Stop it!' she hissed. 'Don't make it so obvious.'

'What are we actually looking at?' asked Victoria, perplexed as the rest of us.

'That man over there, sitting on his own, with his laptop. Look at him. I reckon he could be your mystery man from the pub guide.'

'What on earth would make you think that?' I asked, unable to see the man through the throng.

'Watch him. He keeps looking at his beer and then jotting something down in his notepad.'

'You never know, he might just have come out for a quiet pint,' I said, shaking my head despairingly. 'That is allowed here you know.'

'Yeah, but I've never seen him in here before. Have you? And why would you bring a notepad?'

'I've no idea. And to be honest, I can't really see what he looks like. I reckon we should all stop staring. I'm trying to attract new customers, not put them off from coming.'

All this talk of mystery pub visitors was making me decidedly nervous. I would have to make sure I was on top form from now on, just in case Polly was right in her suspicions.

Victoria had dropped her head to one side, peering in the direction of the man, clearly giving the matter some serious consideration. 'I don't think he can be your pub guide man though,' she said, 'he's far too good-looking.'

'What's that go to do with anything?' said Josie, laughing.

'Think about it, someone who goes round the county drinking all those different beers is going to be middle-aged, portly and beardy. Not young, cool and lethally sexy.'

'Oh God, now you come to mention it, the man who was

41

in the other morning fell into that category.' Three eager faces turned to look at me. 'The middle-aged and portly one,' I added.

'Mmm,' said Polly with a sigh. 'Whoever he is, he is very, very hot.'

Polly and Victoria were gawping as though they'd never seen a good-looking man before, although in fairness it probably was a rare event for the Dog and Duck.

'Hey, look out,' said Josie, 'he's coming this way.'

We all giggled and sat up straight in our chairs, like a bunch of silly schoolgirls caught out on some misdemeanour.

'Oh gawd,' I said, getting a proper look at the man for the first time, before dropping my gaze. 'That's no mystery man, that's George Williamson.'

'Who?' The rest of the girls asked in unison.

'Oh it doesn't matter. Just stop staring or else he'll notice.'

Only he didn't. He just waltzed past us on his way to the loos without even so much as a glance in our direction. A few minutes later, on his way back again, I stepped into my role as landlady and called out his name, wanting to give him a proper warm welcome to the pub.

'George?'

He stopped, turned, gave a megawatt smile to his newly formed adoring fan club, before his gaze alighted on mine. 'Oh hi. It's Ellie, isn't it?' Ten out of ten for remembering my name.

'Yes, that's right. Lovely to see you in here. Are you settling well into the cottage?' 'Yes, it's absolutely fine. Everything I wanted. So peaceful and quiet.' I smiled, noticing that George seemed so much more affable this evening. I'd obviously caught him at a bad time the other day. 'Oh, and thanks for the cake by the way, it was delicious. You're a great baker.'

I swelled with pride, until remembering that I hadn't actually made the cake, which was only brought home to me by the surprised expressions on my friend's faces.

'Well actually it's...' Heck, what did it matter. '... One of my favourite recipes,' I quickly added, which wasn't strictly a lie. 'I'm so glad you liked it. Let me introduce you to a few of the locals. This is Polly, who owns and works at Polly's Flowers next door. This is Josie who works here. She grew up in this pub, she's the daughter of the previous landlord, and this is Victoria who works on the local newspaper.' I turned to my friends who were hanging on my every word, well that's what I told myself, at least. 'This is George Williamson who's just moved into No. 2 Ivy Lane Cottages. You'll find us a very friendly bunch. There's a poster over on the beam next to the bar which shows all the events running here. There's usually something going on most nights.'

'Hello,' he lifted his hand in acknowledgments to my friends. 'And thank you. I'll take a look, although really I'm here to work so I won't have a lot of time to get involved.'

'Of course,' I said, wondering again just what it was he did for a living. 'No pressure, but you'll be most welcome when you do have a spare moment.'

'What do you think of the pub then?' Polly piped up.

'Yep,' said George, nodding his head as he looked around him. 'It's great. Just how you'd want a village pub to be.'

'Oh good, and the beer is just as you'd like it too?' she probed.

A mild hint of panic darted across George's eyes, but he did a good job of retaining his good-natured composure, addressing Polly with a smile. 'The beer was very good, yes.'

'Did you try the pork scratchings?'

I shoved my foot into Polly's leg beneath the table, but she was totally oblivious and steamed ahead regardless, with all the subtlety of a sledgehammer.

'The pork scratchings,' she insisted. 'I can recommend them. Or there're crisps and nuts, if you prefer. There's always plenty of choice here.'

'That's good to know, but I just came for the beer... which was great. Anyway,' he said, looking desperate now to escape as he took an exaggerated glance at his watch, 'I ought to be making a move. It's been great meeting you all.'

Poor man, probably thought we were all completely loopy.

'Well there you go,' said Polly, once he'd gone. She banged her hands down on the table, looking as though she'd uncovered the missing piece in a murder investigation. 'He's clearly not the pub guide man, but whoever he is, he's very, very lovely.'

Five

'I should leave. You'll be wanting to go to bed.'

I'd locked the door on the last of our customers and only Josie remained, but she wasn't looking as though she wanted to go anywhere.

'Well, I'm going to have a coffee,' I suggested. 'Do you fancy one?'

'Oh please,' she said, looking relieved as she slipped off her coat again.

'You do know it was your dad who got me into this bad habit. After a busy shift we would lock the doors and have a sneaky coffee, usually with a dash of something alcoholic in it.'

'I know, I remember us doing that too. It's those little things that I miss so much.' Josie's face slipped, her tone wistful.

'Oh me too. But it's not long until the christening now and he'll be home and it will be as if he's never been away. Should we hold him hostage and make him promise not to go off gallivanting again?'

'I might have to do that,' said Josie, laughing wryly.

'Everything is all right, isn't it darling?' I asked her. 'I don't know, you've seemed a bit subdued tonight.'

'Yeah, I'm all right. Just missing Dad, I guess. Having Stella is the best thing that's happened to me, but sometimes it's hard, not having Mum around or Dad close by. Ethan's parents are great, but it's not the same.'

'Oh, Josie, I can imagine.' I reached across the table and took her hand, interlocking my fingers with hers. 'There are certain times in your life when only your mum will do, and it must be really hard doing this without her.'

'Yep,' she sighed, resignedly. 'It is. I know it's been over ten years, but I miss her more than ever now. And it makes me so sad thinking how much she's missed out on.'

'Well, what you have to remember is how proud she would be to see the fantastic job you're doing. She might not be here in person, but her spirit and personality lives on in you and Stella.'

'Thanks, Ellie, that would be nice to think so. Ethan can't understand why I'm suddenly feeling this way. He doesn't really get it.'

'Well, you know what it's like, men can be a bit dense at times.'

'You're not kidding. I know it's not really his fault, but it annoys me how my life has changed beyond recognition and he just carries on in his own sweet little way. Going to football practise a couple of times a week, meeting up with his mates, popping in on his parents whenever he wants to. While if I want to do anything it's like a military operation, because wherever I go, apart from here of course, Stella comes with me.'

'Well if Ethan's not doing his fair share then you need to tell him. He probably doesn't even realise what it's like for you.' Ethan was a sweet lad, but could be a bit thoughtless at times.

'You're probably right,' she said, letting out a heartfelt sigh. 'Don't take any notice of me. I'm just having a moan.' She shook her head and shoulders as it to get rid of the negative thoughts. 'I wouldn't really change anything for the world. I know how fortunate I am to have a gorgeous little girl, great friends, and a good husband, even if he can be a bit gormless at times.' She laughed and looked at her phone to check the time. 'I ought to get going. With any luck they'll both be sleeping when I get home.'

'Will you be all right, walking home by yourself? I can see if I can get you a taxi, if you like?'

'No, don't be daft. I'll be fine.'

'If you're sure? Look, you know I'm always here if you need to let off steam. And anything I can do to help, then just say. Babysitting duties, husband-wrangling, wine-pouring or cake-providing. All of those things.'

'You know I might just take you up on that,' she said, laughing.

'I'm so bloomin' chuffed to be Stella's godmother.' It still hadn't really sunk in yet. 'It never even occurred to me that you might ask.'

'Well, like I said, there's no one else in the world I would rather have.' She enveloped me with a hug. 'Thanks Ellie. For listening. For being there. Not sure what I'd do without you.'

Just then there was a loud banging on the front door and we both turned to look at each other, startled.

'Sorry, we're closed,' I called out.

'Ellie, it's Max. Can you let me in?'

Quickly, I went across to the main entrance and unbolted the lock, pulling open the door.

'Sorry to turn up so late, but I saw the light on, I hoped you might still be up. Oh hi,' he said, addressing Josie.

'I was just on the way home,' she explained, 'so I'll leave you two to it.'

'Really, there's no need. I can't be long,' said Max, 'so if you hang on a moment I can give you a lift home, if you need one.'

'It's no problem. I was going to walk. It's not very far.'

'No, really, don't be silly. It's on my way.'

'Ooh thanks, Max, that's very kind.'

'Is there something wrong?' I asked, wondering what this midnight visit was in aid of. 'Did you collect Katy?'

'Yes, she's at the house now, but she left one of her bags in Spain, the one that contained all her toiletries and make-up. This is a disaster akin to the end of the world apparently. Who knew?' He rolled his eyes, and shrugged. 'She tells me she won't be able to sleep if she can't take her make-up off. And all sorts of terrible things will happen to her spots. Not that I can see any spots, but it seems quite important to Katy. I suggested soap and water, but that didn't go down very well at all. I don't suppose you can help me out, can you?'

'Of course,' I said, laughing. 'Hang on a minute and I'll go and grab some things.'

Upstairs, I found a spare make-up bag and filled it with some sample beauty products I had lying around in my drawers.

'These should see her through to the morning,' I said, handing them over to Max, 'but I've got to go into town tomorrow so I could always pick up some bits for Katy if you let me know what she needs.'

'You are my lifesaver, Ellie,' he said, clasping my face in his hands and kissing me. 'Do you fancy coming down for breakfast tomorrow. You'll probably have more of a way with Katy than I do, and honestly, you'd be doing me a massive favour.'

So, early the following morning, with Digby at my side, we crunched across the gravel leading to Braithwaite Manor, Max's magnificent country home. I'd been here on several occasions now, but still the sight of the imposing Georgian building was enough to set off butterflies in my stomach. We walked round to the back entrance where Holly and Bella, Max's rowdy Irish setters, were waiting enthusiastically to greet us, sweeping up Digby in their excitement, the three dogs dashing into the garden, their tails wagging furiously.

'Oh, am I pleased to see you,' said Max, relief peppering his words. 'Come in.' He slipped an arm around my waist and pulled me into his side, the tempting aromas of fresh coffee, frying bacon and the essence of Max competing for my attention. No competition. I'd pick Max every time.

'How's it going?' I mouthed.

'She's not up yet. She was pleased with those bits you provided though. I guess it must be strange for her coming here where she doesn't know anyone. We're just tiptoeing around each other at the moment.'

'Has she said anything about what's been happening at home?'

'Nothing. To be honest, she's barely said a word.'

I sat down on one of the oak carvers at the farmhouse kitchen table, cupping my hands around the mug of coffee

49

Max had handed me. 'She's probably just exhausted. Sounds as though she's had a lot going on recently. A few days' rest and recuperation and I bet she'll be back to her usual self.'

'I hope so. But I can't help feeling I'm out of my depth here. I'm used to dealing with mouthy subbies and demanding clients, I know exactly what to say to them, but teenage girls, even if this one happens to be my sister, are a mystery to me.'

I smiled at Max's obvious bemusement. 'Don't worry too much about it. Let Katy lead the way. I'm sure she'll talk to you when she's good and ready, it will all work out fine, you'll see.'

'Oh…'

We hadn't heard the bare-footed approach of Katy who was now standing in the threshold to the kitchen looking at us warily, big brown eyes darting from me to Max, as if she might disappear back where she came from at any moment. A furry onesie with bunny ears swamped her tiny frame.

'Katy! I was just going to give you a shout. Breakfast is almost ready. Come on through. This is Ellie, my girlfriend. We have her to thank for coming to the rescue last night with the toiletries.'

'Hi,' she said. 'And thanks.'

'Hello Katy, no problem,' I said, standing up to greet her, before making a quick decision not to go in for the welcoming hug as, with hers arms wrapped tight around her chest and her gaze averted to the floor, I was getting the district impression she wasn't ready for such social niceties. Shaking hands wouldn't have worked either, so instead I wrapped my arms around myself, mirroring her body stance. 'It's great to meet you.' In all honesty, I was still replaying

Max's words over in my head, '*Ellie, my girlfriend*.' It had the most delightful ring to it.

'What happened to Sasha?' she asked, her question cutting like a knife through my daydreaming.

'We split,' said Max, matter-of-factly. 'You knew that? Last year sometime.'

'She was cool,' said Katy, before padding over to the fridge, helping herself to a glass of milk and pulling out a chair at the table.

I nodded. Well, she had a point. Sasha was pretty cool. I still hadn't discovered what business she'd had with Max the other day, but now probably wasn't the time to ask.

'Come on, get stuck in,' he said now, bustling around the table. 'Before it gets cold. There're pancakes, bacon, blueberries, maple syrup. And some scrambled eggs, if you fancy them. Just help yourself.' He dropped knives and forks into the middle of the table with a clatter, before pulling out a chair to join us. The dogs had returned from their romp around the grounds and were mooching around between our legs on the lookout for any stray crumbs.

'Well, look at all this,' I said, trying much too hard, I knew, to inject some goodwill into the kitchen. 'Usually I make do with a coffee and a slice of toast, so this is a proper treat.' Katy was half-heartedly running her fork through some eggs, pushing them around her plate. 'This is your first time at the manor, isn't it?' I asked her. 'What do you think?'

'It's all right,' she shrugged.

'Only all right?' I said, forcing a laugh. 'I think Max has done an amazing job. Braithwaite Manor is the most beautiful house I've ever been in.' He'd put his heart and soul into restoring the old property, it had been a real labour of love for him over several years and he was rightly proud of the transformation. It saddened me to think that the first member of his family to step over the threshold could be so utterly underwhelmed.

'I didn't realise it would be in the middle of nowhere,' she said as though she'd landed in the wilds of a remote island.

'It's not that bad. There's a bus that goes into town, every couple of hours I think, and there's a big shopping centre, with a cinema and theatre, and loads of bars and restaurants. You can get a train into London from there too, it only takes about forty minutes. We've got the best of all worlds here and Little Leyton definitely has it charms.' Although judging by Katy's reaction, I suspected they were lost on her. 'Admittedly we don't share the same amazing climate as Spain, but apparently we're due a heatwave this year.'

'Well, that would be something to look forward to,' said Max.

'It gets far too hot in Spain,' said Katy. 'That's something else I don't like about living there.'

'Oh well, I do hope we have a good summer,' I said, ignoring Katy's allusion to the fact that there might be a whole long list of things she didn't like about Spain. 'The highlight of the Little Leyton social calendar is the summer fair,' I told her. 'It's always such a brilliant day with lots of different events like a coconut shy, a children's carousel, Punch and Judy show, face painting, a dog show. And then there're all the friendly competitions that everyone can get involved in; best fruit cake, best sponge cake, best vegetables, biggest marrow, that sort of thing. This year we're having an evening bash as well.'

Katy stopped, her fork midway to her mouth, and I

detected an almost imperceptible roll of her eyes. Thinking about it, I probably hadn't sold it that well. It was hardly the height of cool to a cosmopolitan teenager.

'It really is exciting as it sounds,' said Max chuckling, not really helping my case.

'It is!' I protested. 'It's wonderful, just like something from an episode of *Midsomer*.'

'Don't they all get murdered in that?' said Katy.

'Um yes.' I said, realising it probably wasn't the best example. 'We do try and avoid murdering each other, but having worked with the summer fair committee before, I can see how these things happen.'

Max was still chuckling. 'Look Katy, don't worry. You'll be pleased to hear you'll be back in Spain by then so you'll be spared the delights of the Little Leyton summer fair.'

Katy pushed her plate away, with more force than she intended, as the remains of her eggs scattered over the white tablecloth.

'Don't worry,' I said, jumping into action and scooping them up on to my empty plate and taking the dishes over to the sink.

'I've only just got here, Max,' she accused him. 'And already you're wanting to send me home again. I knew you didn't want me here. Not really.'

'Katy, it was a joke. I didn't mean anything by it.'

'Well, I'm not going back to Spain. No way. I don't care what you say or what anyone says I'm never going back there.'

I ran the hot tap filling the sink with water and suds, anything to distract from the tension now crackling across the kitchen table.

'What's happened, Katy?' Max edged his chair closer to hers, his voice warm and comforting, but I suspected she wouldn't want to open up with me there. They needed time alone together, one on one.

'Look, I'm going to go, leave you two to chat together.'

'No, don't,' said Max, reaching out his hand to me.

'Don't leave because of me,' said Katy sulkily.

'Well,' I said, uncertain what to do now, 'I'm sure whatever has been going on is just a misunderstanding and it will blow over. I remember when I was a teenager I was always having big rows with my parents, and storming out of the house, vowing never to return.'

'You really have no idea,' said Katy, in a withering tone.

'There's no need to be rude,' said Max, chastising her. 'And besides, you'll have to go back at some point, Katy.'

'No, I won't. Not if I don't want to. You can't make me. None of you can.'

'Oh Katy, Mum's worried about you. She only wants what's best for you. For you to be happy. It might not seem that way to you, but it's the truth.'

'Huh, I doubt that very much. She only worries about keeping Alan happy. She might think the sun shines out of his arse, but I don't...'

'Katy, please!'

'... and I don't see why I should take any notice of him anyway, he's not even my father. They don't want me there. And you don't want me here either. Well that's fine, I'll go somewhere else.'

'No one's saying they don't want you here. Believe you me, if I hadn't wanted you to come I would have said so to Mum. You're welcome to stay but you just need to give some thought to what you're going to do next. That's all. You must have something in mind?'

'No, not really,' she said, dropping her defiant gaze as I heard the distinct wobble to her voice. 'But I'm an adult now. I can do exactly what I like.'

'You're hardly an adult, Katy. You're seventeen, for …' Max just stopped himself from saying anything further, but his frustration, which he'd been doing well to keep a lid on, filled the air.

'Well maybe now's not the time to have this conversation,' I said lightly, trying to defuse the bubbling tension.

'I should have known,' said Katy to Max. 'You're just like Mum and… that idiot husband of hers! I don't know why I expected anything different.' She pushed back her chair, scraping the legs against the floor, the ear-splitting sound making me wince. 'Don't worry, I won't stay around here where I'm not wanted.'

'Don't be ridiculous. Where on earth would you go?'

'I could go anywhere I wanted to, just watch me.'

Max flashed me a glance. I don't think either of us was in any doubt that she meant every word she said.

'Look, Katy,' said Max, his tone more conciliatory now. 'I'm not being difficult, honestly. I'm just trying to understand. Talk to me. Tell me what this is all about. Something bad must have happened for you to quit school without finishing your exams, it doesn't make sense. Mum always says what a good student you are and what good grades you were achieving. It's madness to turn your back on all of that. Isn't it, Ellie?'

'Max has got a point,' I said, really wishing I wasn't party to this conversation.

'Decent qualifications are more important than ever these days. Ellie's got a degree and an accountancy qualification. Once you've got something like that no one can take it away from you.'

Katy span round from the window where she'd been gazing out over the garden. 'Well, it didn't do you any harm, did it?'

I stood at the draining board, drying the crockery with a tea towel and twisting my mouth in an attempt to stop the smile playing on my lips.

Max had never hidden the fact that he'd hated school and left as soon as he could. He'd gone straight out to work, picking up jobs on building sites, learning a trade that would hold him in good stead for his future, very successful, career.

'That's different. I wasn't academic in the slightest. But you are. Don't think that any of this has come easy to me,' he said, gesturing around him, 'because it hasn't. It took me years to gain this level of success. I'm not sure if I was starting out today that I would even have a chance of achieving any of this. I'd probably need all sorts of qualifications now.'

'You don't need to worry about me, Max. I'm really not your problem. I'll be out of your way as soon as I can and then you can forget I was even here.'

'Don't be like that, Katy. Of course, I'm going to worry about you. I'm your brother. And I know you may not think so, but I am on your side here.'

Katy chewed on the side of her fingernail. Her highly charged emotions filling the space around us.

Up close, she looked even younger than her years. Her pale skin and freckles belied the fact that she'd spent her formative years growing up in Spain. Now with the morning

56

sun filtering through the kitchen windows it caught the warm coppery highlights of her hair. Where Max was tall and broad, Katy was tiny, with not an ounce of fat on her bones, but there was something in the way they held themselves that gave away the family connection. And there was no doubt that beneath her fragile appearance, Katy shared the same strong and determined personality of her brother.

'I'm going out,' she said decisively, heading for the back door.

'Where?' asked Max, unable to hide the concern from his voice.

'Just out. For a walk. That is allowed, isn't it?'

'Well don't be too long. Why don't you take the dogs...'

The door slammed shut before Max could finish his sentence.

'Katy!' he yelled, turning to dash after her.

'Don't, Max.' I grabbed his arm, pulling him back towards me. 'Let her go. It'll do her good to get some fresh air. There'll be plenty of time for talking later.'

I just wasn't sure whether Katy would be prepared to listen.

Six

'Hmm, that went well,' said Max, giving a wry smile, as he watched his sister march off down the drive. 'I handled that completely wrongly, didn't I?'

'No, I don't think so. Perhaps she's not ready to open up just yet. She's probably feeling completely overwhelmed by everything that's happened and the realisation that she's actually away from home now.'

'Well, I wish she'd come with an instruction manual because I honestly had no idea what to do there.'

I laughed, relieved that the tension had swept out of the building, alongside Katy. 'Come here,' I said, beckoning him into my arms. 'She'll come round, you'll see. At the moment she thinks everyone's against her and she's coming out fighting. Give her a few days and then, when emotions are a little less high, sit down with her and see if you can talk things through properly.'

'Yes, you're probably right. Thanks for coming, Ells,' he said, planting a kiss on my forehead. 'I can't tell you how far out of my comfort zone all this is. You being here made all the difference.'

'Did it? I kind of felt in the way a bit. As though I was intruding on personal family business.'

'No.' Max shook his head. 'Not at all. I was so pleased you were here.' Max squeezed my hand. Everything seems much more manageable when you're around.' His gaze lingered on mine for a moment.

Max wasn't one for huge outpourings of emotion but occasionally his words came unexpectedly, touching me deep down inside with their sincerity and honesty.

'So what did you make of Katy then?' he asked me.

I couldn't help but like her. 'She seems like a great kid, beneath all that attitude. Obviously she's hurting inside and that's so sad to see.' Honestly I just wanted to wrap her in my arms and tell her everything would be all right. Although I'm not sure how well that would have gone down.

'I'm beginning to get an idea of how things must have been in Spain for Mum and Alan. Katy's going through, what shall we call it… a difficult phase. And to be honest, I'm not sure what the answer is.' He let out a heartfelt sigh. 'I guess we'll just have to see how it goes and hope we can work out something between us. Anyway, enough about my little sister.' He tipped my chin up with his finger. 'Do you have to rush back or can you stay awhile?'

'Sure, I can stay. Andy and Dan are opening up today. We could take the dogs out, if you like. We might even bump into Katy out there.'

'Really? I had something else in mind. We should make the most of this unexpected opportunity, don't you think? It's been far too long.'

I laughed, taking a step backwards from his embrace. My body was willing, but my head was all over the place, full of thoughts of Katy and then… Sasha. Where had that come from? And why now, when I could have been cosying up to

Max instead? 'Oh, I meant to ask you. How did it go with Sasha the other day?'

'Sasha?' Max was clearly as puzzled. 'Yeah, yeah, it was fine.' He pulled me closer again.

'Good,' I said, brightly, breathing in his scent, trying not to be distracted by his proximity. As easy as that would be, now I'd bitten the bullet and dared to mention Sasha, I really wanted to get to the bottom of her recent visit.

'Soooo,' I hung on to that vowel just long enough to convince Max I wasn't that interested in Sasha really, I was just being polite in asking. 'What was it she wanted then?'

'Um...' Max was having trouble focussing on my question, as his eyes concentrated intently on my face. 'What did she want? Advice. She's thinking of moving, so we were talking about property prices, renting, that kind of thing.'

'Ah right.' It made sense now. Sort of. Max held a huge portfolio of properties. He would definitely know about that sort of thing.

'But why are we talking about Sasha, when all I'm interested in right now is you and me and...' He stroked his finger around my jawline, down my neck, and along my collarbone, and in that instance all thoughts of Sasha, and Katy, drifted from my mind. His kisses, sweet and attentive, unlocked within me the memory of his touch, every nerve cell in my body responding in warm anticipation. 'Come on, let's go upstairs,' said Max, taking my hand and leading me out through the kitchen door into the magnificent galleried hallway. He closed the door to the kitchen behind him. The dogs would be happy mooching around in there, before no doubt collapsing in a heap in the plethora of soft and squishy beds in the utility room.

Walking up the grand sweeping staircase, the splendour of Max's house always took me by surprise. The high ceilings, the oak woodwork throughout, the central glittering chandelier and the many original and bold pieces of modern artwork on the walls lent an opulent yet classy look. Could Katy really be so unmoved by the gorgeousness of these surroundings or was that all part of her teenage bravado?

Upstairs, our hands interlinked, Max led the way into the master bedroom, closing the door with his foot behind him. He took my face in his hands, his dark eyes full of hungry intent.

'Oh Max, do you think we should?' I said. 'What if Katy comes back?'

'You worry too much. We'll hear her if she comes back. Besides, we have no reason to be tiptoeing around. This is my house. We can do what we want to do,' he said, clearly amused. 'And we can be quick,' he said, his eyes challenging me seductively, 'if that's what you'd prefer?'

His kisses silenced any lingering doubts I may have had as my body gave in to his assured touch. Quick. Slow. With a burning anticipation running through my veins, either way was absolutely fine with me. To be alone again with Max in the strong hold of his arms was wonderful. He was right, it had been far too long and now he was clearly in a hurry. His hands slipped beneath my top and he lifted off my sweatshirt up over my head, unclasping my bra with an expert one-handed manoeuvre and allowing it to slip off my shoulders. Quickly he took off his own shirt and pulled my naked chest to his, the sensation of my skin upon his sending ripples of delight along the entire length of my body. I never felt self-conscious in front of Max; his adoring gaze always took me to another place, somewhere where I was the most gorgeous, beautiful and enticing woman in existence, and his adoration only fuelled my own desire further.

Under his watchful gaze, I undid the button to my jeans and wriggled out of them while Max dealt with his own trousers, discarding them with a flourish to one side, which made me giggle. In nothing but his boxer shorts, Max's strong and powerful physique was clear to see. My toes curled in almost unbearable anticipation.

'Come here,' he said, grabbing me by the hand and pulling me towards him again. Laughing, we fell back on to the sumptuous queen-sized bed, our limbs entangling, our hands greedily exploring each other's bodies. My breasts immediately responded to Max's gentle, yet tantalising touch, my entire being wanting more of him. No man had ever made me feel the way Max did. Our physical attraction couldn't be denied, but it was much more than that. A connection, something that touched me at the very core of my being. A strength of feeling that scared me with its intensity.

Our lovemaking was tender and urgent and needy, and in the heat of the moment, I didn't want it to end, I wanted to be lost in that place forever. Just me and Max. Afterwards, totally spent and satisfied, we lay together, legs and arms flung haphazardly over each other, before Max rolled onto his back pulling me into his side, his breathing heavy and steady and reassuring in my ear.

'I wish it could always be like this. You, here with me.'

I twisted round, lifting myself up on to my elbows to see his thoughtful expression. 'Yes,' I sighed, 'it's so good when we're together.' And then my toes curled again, this time with embarrassment, realising how awkward I'd sounded. I found it hard to articulate exactly how I felt to Max, as if saying the words aloud might damage what we had in some way. Not that Max seemed bothered. He was observing me closely, a warm and knowing smile on his lips as his fingers played with my hair. It wasn't that I had any doubts about my feelings for him. They grew deeper with every moment I spent in his company. Just that the very core of me felt vulnerable and exposed, as though Max held the power to tear at my insides and rip them apart.

'I meant what I said about us seeing each other more. We should do that. Make time for each other. I get withdrawal symptoms if I don't get to see you for a few days, Ellie.' Those words in conjunction with his fingertips running down the length of my arm made me shiver inside. 'Is that what you want too?'

'Yes, I do, Max. Really I do.'

'Good, let's make it happen then. I've realised recently that I don't need to keep putting in the same ridiculous hours I've always done. I've got a great team of people around me. People I can rely on. I've always pooh-poohed the idea of a work/life balance, but I can actually see it makes a lot of sense now. I need to take a step backwards from the business. And I suppose with Katy here, now might be the ideal opportunity to start on that, and of course that means I get to spend more time with you.'

'Well, it sounds like a great idea, Max, but I'm having trouble imagining this new relaxed and laid-back Max Golding,' I said, laughing.

'You have such little faith in me, Ellie Browne.'

'Well you have to admit you're a bit of a control freak. I

give you about two weeks at the most before you're back in the thick of it.'

'You reckon, huh? We'll see,' he said, tapping me gently on the nose. 'Really though, I've enjoyed being part of the community here in Little Leyton and getting involved in village life. I've never had that before, that sense of responsibility and duty to my neighbours and friends. Being part of something beyond myself and my work, it's given me an appreciation of what's important in life.'

'Or maybe you're just becoming a boring old fart, Max. Have you considered that?' I teased.

'Oi!' he said, pinning my wrists above my head and tickling me under my arms. 'Less of the old and boring please.'

'Stop it,' I said, giggling and wriggling beneath him. 'Some of us have work to do today. We can't all decide to take such a relaxed attitude towards our businesses. I do have a pub to run you know.'

Laughing, Max jumped up and offered me a hand, pulling me up on my feet. 'Come on.'

A few moments later, down in the kitchen, we were saying our goodbyes, wrapped in an embrace, when the back door opened and Katy wandered in. Judging by the disapproving look on her face, I wasn't convinced that the Little Leyton air had done much to improve her mood.

Her gaze ran up and down our bodies, and I took a step sidewards, feeling as though I was the teenager, caught out by my mother.

'How long have you two being going out then?'

'Um…' Max was doing some mental maths, but clearly not getting anywhere. He looked at me and shrugged helplessly.

'Since Christmas, properly,' I said, helping him out.

'Oh not long then? You were with Sasha ages, weren't you?'

'Yes, although I'm not sure what that has to do with anything,' said Max, putting a proprietary arm around my shoulder.

Katy shrugged, her gaze flickering over in my direction. I suspected she might be the new membership secretary of the Sasha Fan Club, but I wasn't going to rise to the bait. As Max had intimated, Sasha was history and I was very much of the here and now. *Rise above it, Ellie. Just rise above it.*

'I'm going into town later, Katy,' I said. 'Do you want me to pick up some things for you. Or you could come with me if you fancied a trip out.'

Her brow furrowed as though she might actually be considering my offer, before shaking her head. 'No, you're all right,' she said, turning to walk out the kitchen. Clearly, I had some way to go until Katy joined my fan club too.

Seven

'Hello you...'

I'd just dashed upstairs to my bedroom to get changed when my mobile bleeped. Already today I'd popped into town to do some banking, opened up the pub, given a briefing to Dan and Josie who were covering the lunchtime shift and now I had three persistent dogs, Digby, Amber and Rosie waiting for me downstairs, bothering me for a walk. Now, definitely wasn't the time to be distracted by Max, not when he was using *that* tone of voice, I knew exactly what it meant...

A few days had passed since meeting Katy for the first time at the manor house and I'd been desperate to know how she and Max were getting on, although I'd shown exceptional restraint by not asking. I'd wanted to give them some time alone together so they could get to know each other better and build on their relationship. The self-control it had taken not to send Max a dozen text messages asking for hourly updates had been pretty amazing and the self-control it had taken not to go round and see him had been even greater. So my heart lifted on hearing his warm voice now. His low, smooth tones filtered down the line, caressing my ear and everything else too. Even from a distance he was able to do funny things to my insides.

'Hi,' I said, giving my misbehaving body a very stern talking-to. 'How are you?'

'I'm good, thank you. Much better now I'm talking to you. I have a big Ellie-shaped hole in my heart right now.'

'Oh Max,' I suppressed a smile, while cringing inwardly at the same time. Thank goodness, he couldn't see me blushing. 'Do stop with the soppy stuff, you know how much I hate it.' Although actually I was enjoying it much more than I was letting on.

'It's true though. What am I supposed to say? I'm missing you, Ellie. Everything about you. The sight of you, the feel of you, the taste of... '

'Where are you then?' I interrupted, putting a stop to that particular train of thought.

'In Dublin. I called into the pub on my way to the airport but you weren't around. It's just a flying visit. Back home tomorrow.'

'Right, so much for you cutting down on the business trips then?' I teased him.

'Yes, well I couldn't really get out of this one. It's a favour for a friend. I'm looking at a hotel development for him, and he's got a meeting with the bank tomorrow. You know, I really used to enjoy all the travelling I did for business, but it just doesn't hold the same appeal anymore. Your fault, Ellie Browne. All I want these days is to be in Little Leyton with you and the dogs and a good bottle of claret.' I could hear the longing in his voice. I recognised it because I was feeling the same way too, but I didn't want to say anything, not wanting him to feel any worse than he already did. Instead, I tried changing the subject.

'And Katy?' I offered.

'Hmm, well, that's another matter entirely.'

'How's it been going?' I asked, unable to hold back my curiosity any longer.

'Not great,' said Max. 'It's difficult to get anything out of her. She seems lost in her own head most of the time. Anything I suggest, like going out for a walk or getting the bus into town, is met with a roll of her eyes. To be honest with you, I'm at a loss as to what to do with her.'

'Right. And you think jumping on a plane and disappearing to another country is going to help. Honestly Max!' I said, chiding him gently.

'Hey Ellie, don't have a go at me. It's an overnight stay, that's all. She'll be fine. She might appreciate some time to herself. And she's got the dogs to look after. Besides, she keeps telling me how grown up she is.'

'Well perhaps I'll pop down to see her. Check everything's okay. I was about to take the dogs out, so we can always go that way.'

'Sorry, Ells, I should have mentioned it, but it was all a bit last minute. Katy will be fine.' There was a discernible pause where I heard his mind working. 'She will, won't she?'

'Of course she will,' I said, more to placate Max. I hated the idea of Katy being alone in that big house, especially in the frame of mind she was in. 'She's a sensible girl. And as you say it's not for long.' I wasn't sure if I was trying to convince Max or myself.

'Exactly. She can't get in to too much trouble in twenty-four hours, can she?' He paused, sighing. 'Christ, another twenty-four hours until I see you again. Have you any idea what that does to me?'

Good job we weren't Skyping or else Max would have seen me squirming on the spot, my face flushing a fetching shade of pink, and generally coming over all unnecessary. I fanned my face with my hands and picked up the mug of coffee I'd made myself earlier, taking a sip. 'Well I'm very pleased to hear it's not a case of out of sight, out of mind.'

'Never. How could it be? Although...' There it was again, the low and seductive drawl. 'It might help if you were to remind me exactly what it is I'm missing.'

I looked at my watch again. If I didn't get a move on soon...

'Lovely as it is chatting with you, Max,' I laughed, 'I really need to get on.'

'Oh, you're not going to leave me like this. You heartless woman. Go on, Ellie, make me happy, tell me... what are you wearing?' His voice was full of delicious mischief.

'Ha ha, absolutely not, Max. You're terrible, do you know that. I have to go.'

'A little black dress, stockings, high heels? Feel free to fill in the details for me, Ellie.'

'Sorry to disappoint, but I'm actually wearing jeans and a sweatshirt.'

'Your trouble is you have no imagination, but that doesn't matter, because I have enough for both of us. And in my mind's eye right now, you're looking pretty damn sexy.'

Looking at myself in the mirror of the wardrobe, I surveyed my reflection searching for the woman who might fit that description. Nope. I stood sideways on, my rounded tummy popping over the fabric of my waistline. I breathed in. Perfect. Ha, well not even close, but still I was happy enough with my curves and so it seemed was Max. Reaching up, I pulled my hair tight behind my ears and secured it tightly into a scrunchie.

'And I bet,' continued Max, who was clearly warming to his theme, 'underneath those jeans you have on some of that lovely, lacy, barely there underwear that I've had the pleasure of meeting before. Tell me it's true, Ellie?'

''Fraid not,' I said, my body reacting to Max's words despite what my head was telling me. 'Today is very much a big knickers and heavy-duty sports bra day, both in a fetching shade of beige. Sad, but true.'

'Hmm, well you know me. I'm not a difficult man to please. The beige two-piece on you, I suspect, would be a very tempting proposition.'

'Well I'm afraid you're not going to get a chance to find out, not with you being in Dublin and me being in Little Leyton. What a shame! Now, Max, I really have to go.' I said, pulling open a drawer in search of the hoodie I'd come looking for.

'I hate not being able to see you or to reach out and feel you, Ellie.' His voice, low and full of longing, lingered over my name. 'If I was there I'd want to run my hands over your body, to kiss your sweet mouth, to savour the taste of you and...'

'Max!'

'Wouldn't you like that too, Ellie?'

'Yes, yes, I would. But, it's going to have to wait,' I said, finding a resolve from somewhere.

'Oh no! Really, Ellie Browne, you are no fun whatsoever.'

I laughed, almost revelling in the frustration of his words.

Oh, the power I held over him could definitely go to my head.

'What about tomorrow then,' he pressed, 'when I get home, because we definitely have unfinished business? Don't you think?

'Goodbye Max.'

'Oh, Ellie. Just one thing before you go.' Now his tone was more serious.

'Yes Max?'

'Have I told you lately that I love you?'

'Oh Max!' His words took me by surprise, a warmth spreading through my body. 'Please tell me, you're not going to burst into song?' I said, aware of the distance between us and trying to lighten the tone again.

'I could do if you wanted me to. But I mean it, Ellie.' A pause, and then, 'I love you.'

Those three little words. I'd heard them uttered from Max's lips before. The first time he'd had far too much to drink for me to take him seriously. The second time I wasn't sure I'd heard him properly. And this time the words were caught in an echo down the telephone line, playing over in my head. *I love you.*

'I love you too, Max.' I said the words aloud for the first time, as though trying them out for size. *I love you.* Yes, they were definitely the ones I'd been searching for.

*

Downstairs, still on Cloud Nine from my call with Max, I jangled the leads and three dogs came running. I fastened on their leashes and, giving a cursory glance around the bar, I slipped out the back door, a satisfied smile on my face. One of my favourite parts of the day was my walk in the Little Leyton countryside. It gave me the opportunity to completely switch off from everything else going on in my life and to simply appreciate the beauty of the surroundings around me; the vibrancy of the leaves on the trees, the buds unfurling on the shrubs and the patterns cast by the sun filtering through the canopy of branches over the lane.

Today, with three dogs, all wanting to go in different directions, there wasn't much opportunity for quiet reflection. Although Digby could be trusted off the lead and would walk obediently to heel, Rosie wasn't the most sociable of dogs and, despite her small stature, was likely to bark fiercely at any approaching dog or person, and Amber, the long-legged gun dog, would do a runner across the fields and far far away at the first sniff of freedom, so it was safer to keep them all on their leashes.

The plan was to walk down the lane and around the woods before calling in at Braithwaite Manor on our way home, but no sooner had we reached the back path than I noticed someone walking up the lane towards me.

The person had their head cast to the ground, the hood of their zipped fleece jacket tied tight around their neck, but the strands of auburn hair peeking out from beneath made them instantly recognisable.

'Katy?'

She looked up at me, her brown eyes flickering in recognition. 'Oh hi.' She leant down to greet the dogs circling at her feet eagerly, their noses raised for a crumb of affection, so she had no choice but to stop and talk.

'What a coincidence. I was going to call in on you this

morning. How's it going?' I asked. 'Are you settling well into Little Leyton?'

She brushed the hood of her jacket down with her hands. Her skin bereft of any make-up was pale and wan, and there was a tangible sadness about her. She leant down and scooped Rosie up in her arms and looked into the little dog's face, making Katy smile.

'There's not a lot to do around here.'

'No, but that's just how I like it,' I said, suppressing a smile, imagining how tame it must seem to Katy. 'Well, like I mentioned, there are buses in the village, and a train station in town. We're not a million miles away from civilisation, you know. I think Max might even have a couple of bikes in the garage, if you fancied doing a bit of exploring.'

Her big round eyes widened further, not looking at all impressed by my suggestions.

'It must be very different from Spain,' I ventured. 'I guess you're missing home?'

'Nope. Not at all. Anywhere has to better than there. I'm not going back.'

This was presumably just in case I hadn't got the message the first time around. She took a sharp breath before fixing her gaze on me defiantly. 'Don't worry, I won't be hanging around here either, if that's what's bothering you.'

'It wouldn't worry me at all, Katy. Why should it?' I said, deliberately keeping my voice even. 'I think it's great for Max to have you staying with him. Look, where are you off to now?'

She shrugged. 'Nowhere.'

'Well, why don't you come with us on our walk. I can

show you all the delights of Little Leyton. It won't take long,' I said, with a wry smile.

To my surprise she nodded her agreement and we found ourselves walking side by side down the lane, Digby running ahead happily, me holding Amber on the lead, and Katy taking control of Rosie.

'So…' I said, tentatively, breaking into the silence, hardly daring to question her on her plans, but wanting to give her the opportunity to talk if she wanted to. 'If you're not planning on staying around here, where will you go? Have you got friends you could go and stay with?'

'No. I don't know anyone here apart from Max. We lived in Sussex before we went to Spain but that was years ago now and we didn't keep in touch with anybody. I've got some cousins up north, but we haven't met before. Doesn't matter,' she said, jutting her chin forward. 'I could always go to London, get myself a job and then find somewhere to live.'

I shuddered inwardly. She made it sound so easy, but really she had no idea what a cold and unwelcoming place the city could be at. An inexperienced seventeen-year-old girl alone in London, it didn't bear thinking about. I'd worked there for several years, but with a first-class honours degree and an accountancy qualification, I was able to pay the rent, albeit an extortionate amount, on a decent place to live. It hadn't shielded me from seeing the other side of life though, the poverty and the squalor.

'Right.' I nodded, glad Katy was unable to see my startled expression. She wasn't my sister. I barely knew her, so I couldn't go in all guns blazing, telling her what a rotten idea I thought it was. Knowing how prickly she was, she was likely to tell me to shut the hell up, before storming

74

off again. No, best keep her onside, if I could. Provide a listening ear and a shoulder to cry on for when she needed it, because I suspected she might. 'Well, there's no hurry. Take some time to think what it is you really want to do. Do you know, Katy, I'm really pleased you've come to Little Leyton because ever since you've arrived the weather's been so much better. I think you've brought some of the Spanish sunshine with you.'

'You reckon,' she said, raising her face to the sky. 'It is quite warm now, isn't it?'

'Lovely,' I agreed. 'I just love being out here in these lanes, seeing the countryside changing month on month. Everything seems to take on a pace at this time of year, the plants start growing and the hedgerows turn a lush vibrant green.' I sneaked a sideways glance at Katy, hoping I wasn't boring her to tears. 'Have you seen the bluebell wood yet?'

Katy shook her head.

'No? Well, come on then, I'll show you. It's really a breath-taking sight down in the woods right now.' We made a detour through a gap in the hedge picking up the path that led to Bluebell Wood. A few minutes later we came to a kissing gate and weaved our way through, before continuing on our route. 'See,' I exclaimed, when we reached the entrance to the woods, 'look how beautiful it is!'

A sea of bluebells swept all around us and into the distance ahead, carpeting the ground with their vibrancy, a faint sweet smell just about discernible in the air.

'That's pretty cool,' said Katy.

'What did I tell you?'

There was an otherworldy stillness in the woods, the trees offering a calming protective atmosphere. With the dogs mooching ahead, their tails held high in the air, it really was a magical sight, one even a surly teenager could appreciate. We stood for a while in silence just appreciating the beauty of the scene.

I turned to Katy. 'Fancy coming back to the pub? Or do you need to get back for Holly and Bella?'

'Not really, I've left them crashed out by the Aga. They've been charging about in the grounds for most of the morning.'

'Well then, I could make you a hot chocolate if you like?'

'You don't have to, you know.'

'I know, but I'd like to show you the pub and I'm not sure about you but I could do with a drink.'

Back in the bar at The Dog and Duck, Katy made herself at home, looking all around, examining the pictures on the walls, craning her head up at the hundreds of brightly coloured beer mats glued to the ceiling of the snug bar and studying in depth the blackboards showing the special ales available.

'Can I try one of these?' she said, pointing to a six per cent proof Belgian beer.

'Nice try, but no you can't.'

'What about a Malibu and Coke then?'

'Absolutely not,' I said laughing. 'The choices are tea, coffee, Diet Coke or any soft drink or one of my special hot chocolates with all the trimmings, marshmallows and whipped cream?'

'Well, I suppose that sounds all right.'

I detected the faintest of smiles hovering on her lips. Maybe, we were beginning to make some progress in our relationship after all.

Suppressing a smile, I left her in the bar while I headed to the kitchen to make the drinks.

'Here you go,' I said, when I handed her a steaming tall glass of hot chocolate topped with multi-coloured soft marshmallows a couple of minutes later. If anything could make you feel better it had to be chocolate, of any variety. 'Look, I know Max is away tonight, so if you need anything then come and see me. You can just hang out here for a while if you want to. I'll be popping out later to see some friends, but I won't be back late.'

'Thanks, but I'll probably just stay in with the dogs and watch a film or something.'

'Well, the offer's there. Ooh, come with me. There's something I want to show you.'

Katy followed me over to the open fireplace. The recent warm weather had put a stop to our daily fires crackling in the hearth, but filled with logs, pine cones and a vase of fresh flowers, supplied by Polly, it was still a warm and welcoming focal point.

'This chair here is what is affectionately known as Noel's chair. Your grandad came in here every day, at lunchtime and then again in the evening, for his pint and a chat with all his friends. He was much-loved in the village.'

'Really?'

Katy sat down in the old rocking chair, readjusting the cushions behind her to make herself comfortable, and pulled down the plaid blanket that had been folded over the arm of the chair. She tucked her legs beneath her and snuggled under the blanket, pushing herself backwards gently in a soft rocking motion.

'Oh this is cosy,' she sighed. 'I didn't really know Grandpa Noel very well. I remember him vaguely and have seen lots of photos of him, but...' Her words trailed away along with her thoughts. Best leave her to those, I figured. Max had come to the village to care for his grandpa in the last few weeks of his life, deciding to stay in Little Leyton after Noel sadly passed away, but Katy was much younger than Max and probably didn't have the same association or memories.

Josie and Dan were serving behind the bar and the pub was beginning to fill up with lunchtime customers. I needed to go and give a hand.

'There're loads of books on the shelves in the back and some magazines too, if you want a read. I should get on and do a bit of work, if that's okay.'

Katy nodded and I left her curled up in the chair, sipping on her hot chocolate.

'Who's that?' Josie whispered in my ear as she brushed past me behind the bar.

'Max's little sister, Katy.'

'Ah right, yes of course. She's a pretty little thing.'

'Ha ha, don't be fooled by that sweet and fragile appearance. She's feisty, opinionated and full of attitude, but saying all that, she seems like a great kid. By the way, Gemma's coming in shortly just to watch what's going on. She'll be working a couple of lunchtimes and evenings, and her first proper stint is tonight. Perhaps you can keep an eye on her until she gets the hang of things.'

'Yeah, sure thing,' said Josie with a smile.

Since Gemma's husband had lost his job last year, things had been difficult for the family. Not only had they had to give Digby up and move out of their modern detached house into smaller rented accommodation, but Gemma had needed to look for work too. I hadn't hesitated in offering her some shifts at the pub. It wasn't the most glamorous or best-paid job, I knew, but I hoped it might help Gemma get back on to her feet again.

When she turned up for her shift, she was looking very apprehensive.

'Come on through,' I told her. 'There's no need to look so worried.'

She grimaced 'I'm sorry, it's just that I'm a bit nervous. I've not worked since before the children. I don't want to let you down.'

'Don't be daft,' I said, giving her a hug. 'You won't let me down. It might seem there's a lot to learn, but you'll soon pick it up and everyone here is so lovely. Don't be afraid to ask. Digby will keep a watchful eye on you too,' I said, with an encouraging wink.

'Oh, hello boy,' she said, bending down to give him a hug. 'Goodness, do I miss you,' she sighed, ruffling his fur, 'but it's been so much easier knowing he's found his forever home here with you, Ellie.'

After showing Gemma around, running through the stock with her and introducing her to the foibles of the till, I left her in the capable hands of Josie, whilst I meandered through the pub, picking up the odd empty glass and passing the time of day with my customers.

I glanced over at the rocking chair where I'd left Katy. She wasn't there anymore. I thought she must have left without saying goodbye until I spotted her sitting in the bay window alongside George Williamson, chatting away animatedly.

'Hello George,' I waved as they both looked up at me

briefly before returning to something that was much more interesting on George's laptop.

Wonders would never cease. George, who barely said a word to anyone, and Katy, whose preferred method of communication was grunting, were deep in conversation. It was only as I went through into the kitchen and flicked on the kettle that I wondered what on earth it was they could have been talking about.

Eight

'Flowers!' I said, thrusting a bouquet into Josie's arms when we turned up at her house later that night.

'Prosecco and chocolates,' said Polly, handing over her offerings.

'Crikey, you two know how to spoil a girl. You can definitely come again. Come on through.'

Polly and I had been discussing Josie earlier in the week, and had both remarked how she hadn't been her usual happy self recently. We were certain that a girly night in might go some way to making her feel a little better.

'Drink,' said Josie, handing me a glass of Prosecco. It wasn't a question, more a directive and I was more than happy to oblige, taking a sip and following her through to the cosy living room.

'Oh, is Stella already asleep?' I asked, noticing the calm of the living room. 'I was hoping there might be time for a cuddle with my gorgeous girl before bedtime.'

'I've just put her down and with any luck that's how she'll stay for the rest of the night. Ethan's got football training so we have the evening to ourselves. A bit of me time with my two besties, I can't tell you what a treat that is.' Josie looked genuinely delighted.

'I'll drink to that,' I said, raising my glass in the air.

I sank down on to Josie's sofa next to Polly and she turned her head to look at me, peering closer into my eyes.

'What? What are you doing? Would you stop looking at me like that. It's unnerving,' I said.

'You! You look different somehow. Doesn't she, Josie? Not smug exactly, but there's a glow about you. A Chaka Kahn "I'm every woman" glow.'

Polly gave a hearty rendition, and Josie quickly joined in, just in case I was in any doubt as to what she was talking about. In unison, they screeched to a wobbly-noted end.

'Well that is one of my favourite songs, or at least it was until you two completely murdered it!'

'You definitely look like a woman who's having too much of a good time,' Polly continued. 'Too much loving, too much champagne or too much sex. Probably all three. Whatever it is, it simply isn't fair!'

Maybe Polly had a point. My mind couldn't help drifting back to my telephone call with Max and my spontaneous declaration of love. Where had that come from? I don't know if it had surprised Max, I didn't stay on the phone long enough to find out, but it had certainly surprised me. Still I didn't regret it for a moment. I'd felt liberated to say the words out loud. No wonder I had a glow about me. Wasn't that what love did to you?

'Well, whatever it is you're getting I'd like some of it too, please,' said Polly. 'I think it must all be down to ahem,' she coughed, 'the lord of the manor tickling your fancy, don't you reckon, Josie?'

Josie lifted her eyebrows, a knowing smile on her lips.

'Oh stop it please. I'm just at a good place in my life right now, that's all. Enjoying my role at the pub, having my friends around me, a faithful hound at my side.' My two friends looked at me expectantly, obviously expecting me to say more. 'And yeah, I suppose a certain local landowner might be throwing a frisson into the mix too.'

'Yes, see, I knew it!' Polly gloated.

'Well I'd say good for you, Ellie. Enjoy it while you can because from my experience it doesn't last. There's not a lot of romance in dirty nappies, I'll tell you that,' said Josie, sounding downbeat.

'Are things not great between you and Ethan then at the moment?' Polly asked, serious for a moment.

'Oh, I don't know. I suppose it's fine. It's just that we don't get to spend a lot of time together. He's busy at work, putting in lots of extra hours at the weekends, and then he's out a couple of nights a week with his different activities, and when he's not out, I'm working, so when we do get to see each other, we're both completely knackered. Honestly, I don't know how people ever get round to having a second child. Sex? I'd rather have a good night's sleep.'

'Well, at least you have the option,' said Polly, ruefully. 'The choice for me would be a fine thing!'

'Maybe you need some time alone with Ethan?' I suggested. 'A long weekend away. I'd always have Stella for you. She could come and stay at the pub. Polly would help out, wouldn't you?'

'Of course, I would. It's not as if I have anything better to do,' said Polly, sounding more depressed by the minute.

'Ah, thanks you two, you're the best. I honestly don't

know what I'd do without my friends. And at least I've got Dad coming home to look forward to. I think Ethan and I are just going through a tricky phase at the moment.' She reached forward to the coffee table and helped herself to a chocolate from the box Polly had given her. 'Blimey, a weekend away together? I'm not sure we'd know what to say to each other, or what to do!'

'Oh, a couple of hours away in a posh hotel and I'm sure it would all come flooding back to you.'

'Yeah, maybe,' she said looking thoughtful.

Josie was making light of the situation, but I sensed a discontent within her. Was it true what she said? That romance didn't last? In the past few weeks my feelings for Max had grown stronger and deeper but we were still in the early days of our relationship. Was it destined to turn into something more serious and long-term or would the glow peter out like a used sparkler?

'Well, you'll never guess who I heard from today?' said Polly, unable to resist the open box of chocolates, and wafting them under my nose. I deliberated, before taking a strawberry creme

'Who?'

'Johnny Tay.'

'Nooo!'

'Yes. What a bloody idiot! The man breaks my heart, tells me he needs to go and find himself, then sends me a postcard from some far-flung desert, saying what a great time he's having. Honestly, what's that all about?'

'Maybe he's missing you,' said Josie.

'Or has a guilty conscience,' I added.

'Well, so he should, but I really don't need to know what

he's doing right now. He's made his decision. Let him get on with it.'

'What you need is a new man,' said Josie. 'Someone to make you forget Johnny once and for all.'

'I know. And if you know of any please send them my way!'

'Talking of postcards,' said Josie, 'I had one from Dad today. I can't keep up with that man. He's travelling through northern Europe by train, stopping off at all the capitals and major towns. He's become a proper David Bailey, taking so many photos and uploading them all over the place. Who would have thought it? Dad didn't have a proper holiday in years, he's certainly making up for it now.'

'Good for him,' I said, 'if anyone deserves a bit of fun, then it's Eric. But I do miss him. The pub just doesn't feel the same without him. Quite often I'll be doing something and turn round to ask for his advice, and then I realise he's not there.' Sometimes I felt a complete imposter standing in his shoes. 'Don't you think it's funny,' I went on, 'that my parents are off in Dubai living the high life and your dad is trekking across Europe with a backpack slung over his shoulder and we're the ones stuck here. There's something not quite right there.'

'Yes, but it does mean we'll have something to look forward to when we're older,' said Josie, 'when our kids are grown up and off our hands.'

'Woah! Hang on a minute,' said Polly, 'I haven't even got to the lovely man and babies bit yet.'

'Oh, but you will,' said Josie, as though it was just a mere formality.

To be honest, I was having as much trouble getting past

the baby thing as Polly was. Anything beyond that was totally outside the realms of imagination.

'Sometimes I wonder if I'll ever have children,' said Polly in a reflective mood. 'I mean it would be great if it happened, but I'm not getting my hopes up. I'd want the engagement party, big wedding and cottage in the country first, and none of those are looking very likely at the moment.'

'Aw, you're such a traditionalist at heart, Polly,' said Josie.

'That's what comes from working in a florists!'

'What about you, Ellie?' Josie asked. 'Is your biological clock ticking in your ear?'

'Not really. I mean it's something I would definitely want for the future, but not now. Like Polly, I'd want a settled relationship first and, besides, there's so much I have to do at the pub. To be honest, a baby now would be a bit of disaster. That's why being a godmother is the next best thing – I get to experience all the good bits, without having to go through the messy, scary parts.'

'Yeah,' said Polly, pulling a face at my words. 'We've both got plenty of time ahead for the whole babies thing.'

'Well you two need to get a wiggle on because I want our children to go to the same school in the village and become friends, and when they do finally leave home, we'll be able to have our own grand adventure, just the three of us, going off touring the world.'

Polly shrugged. 'Well, count me in, even if I bypass the husband and babies bit.'

'Ellie?'

'Sounds good to me,' I said, joining in with the spirit of things.

'Let's make a pact that we'll do it then,' said Josie. She picked up the bottle of Prosecco and topped up all our glasses, raising her glass in the air. 'To the Leyton Girls' Grand World Tour of 2050.'

I raised my glass to meet Polly's and Josie's, signing up for our future adventure. Well, there was nothing like planning ahead.

*

We'd demolished another bottle of Josie's distinctly quaffable Prosecco, munched our way through all the bread and cheese and laughed till we'd made our tummies ache.

'Why don't we do this more often?' asked Polly.

'We should,' said Josie, 'you're always welcome here, you know that.'

I glanced at my watch. 'I could sit here all night long, but I really ought to get back to the pub.' I stood up and stretched my arms wide, shaking out my aching legs that had been scrunched up beneath me all night. I always liked to put in an appearance at the pub at the end of the day just to check everything was okay.

'I'll walk with you,' said Polly, standing up before falling back down again and giggling. She tried it again, at a slower pace this time, wobbling slightly before steadying herself on me, her arms waving comically in the air. 'I think I may have had one glass too many,' she said. That was the understatement of the year!

After we'd said our goodbyes to Josie, I linked my arm through Polly's in an attempt to keep us both upright and we lumbered our way back through the streets of Little Leyton towards the twinkling lights of The Dog and Duck in the distance.

'Let's have a nightcap,' I said as I pushed open the big oak door of the pub, the low lighting and warmth beckoning us in. There were a few people in the front bar but they were making moves to go. 'I'll go and make us a milky coffee,' I told Polly. 'Grab a seat. I won't be long.' Polly tottered away unsteadily and I made my way towards the bar.

'Hi Gemma,' I said, greeting my new barmaid, who was busy clearing glasses from the counter, 'how it's been?'

'Good, I think,' she said, looking relieved. 'It's been incredibly busy. We've not stopped all night, and my legs, I didn't think they'd be aching so much, but it's been great fun. I'm feeling much more confident now than I was at the beginning of the evening.'

'Great, that's what I like to hear. And you'll get used to being on your feet all the time. You can get off home now, if you like.' I was so pleased that Gemma seemed to have taken to it so well.

She went off to collect her coat and bag from the back and I wandered through the pub rounding up the stragglers. I poked my head round the entrance to the snug bar to see who we still had in. I stopped abruptly, my brain not making sense of what my eyes were seeing. *Oh god!* Nothing could have prepared me for this particular straggler.

'What on earth is going on here?'

A group of young lads were laughing and bantering, obviously in high spirits, but it wasn't them I was bothered about. My gaze landed on the young girl who was perched on one of the lad's laps, her arms draped around his neck and her head resting on his chest, all doe-eyed and red pouting lips. There was no keeping the disbelief from my voice.

'Katy?'

Nine

'Oh hiya.' As brazen as you like, Katy looked me up and down before returning her attentions to the unsuspecting young man she was currently entangled with.

'Please don't tell me you've been drinking, Katy?'

The furtive glances between the lads gave me the answer I needed to know.

'Oh for goodness sake! What are you playing at?' As far as I knew Katy had gone off home before I'd left for Josie's and I'd presumed she was staying in all night watching a film as she'd mentioned. Obviously not! If I'd been squiffy a moment ago, finding Katy in this condition had sobered me up straight away.

'I've just had a couple that's all. It's no big deal.'

'No big deal? You do know she's underage,' I accused the boys. 'She's seventeen. You could all get into big trouble buying her alcohol. Not to mention the trouble you'll get me into as well. I could lose my licence over something like this.'

'Nothing to do with us,' said one of the lads. 'We're just hanging out. Katy's bought her own drinks.'

'Is that true, Katy? Who served you?'

'Oh god, I am so sorry.' Gemma came in behind me,

looking sheepish. 'I did ask for I.D. and I thought everything looked fine.'

'Look, will you all stop talking about me as if I'm not here.' Katy swung her legs off the lad and edged away from him on the wooden bench. 'It's only a few sodding drinks. What's the problem? Who's even going to find out or be bothered in this dump?'

'I'm bothered, Katy,' I snapped, feeling affronted by her insult. 'This is my pub and I spend a lot of time and effort to ensure I run a respectable business here. I don't appreciate you taking advantage. Show me that I.D.'

Katy reached inside the back pocket of her jeans and handed it over reluctantly. I turned it over in my hands.

'Where did you get this?'

'Off the internet. It's dead easy when you know how.'

I bent the card in two and put the pieces of the offending item in my back pocket.

'Hey!' Katy scrambled over the table at me, her arms flailing. 'That cost me a tenner.'

'Tough luck. Come on, lads, it's going home time. I want you all out of here.'

'I am so sorry,' said Gemma again, looking as though she might burst into tears. 'All of this is my fault.'

'Not at all, Gemma. You did everything right. The only person at fault here is Katy and I'll deal with her later. You get off home now.'

Fury simmered inside my veins. Looking at Katy now it would be hard for anyone to believe she was only seventeen. The fresh-faced teen I'd met before had been replaced by a heavily made up young woman, with jet black eye liner sweeping up at the sides of her eyes, false eyelashes, powdered skin, and deep red lipstick. She would pass for twenty-one any day of the week.

The boys made moves to leave, muttering amongst themselves, and picked up their jackets and slunk out of the bar, giving me a nod of their heads on their way out.

'Hey wait for me, I'll come with you,' Katy called, stumbling over a low stool.

'No you won't, young lady,' I barked, surprised to hear my mother's voice tripping off my tongue. 'I need to talk to you. What do you think Max would say if he knew about this?'

'Max doesn't give a shit about me,' she said vehemently, the teen Katy definitely back in force now.

'You know that's not true.'

'It is! And besides he's away tonight so I can do exactly what I like.'

She flung her arms wide and attempted a twirling manoeuvre but only toppled over again, this time over a stool on the other side of the table. She landed on her bottom on the floor.

'How much did you have to drink exactly?'

'Can't remember. One or two. I'm fine. Really fine,' she said, grabbing onto the table and hauling herself up. 'Absolutely fine.'

'What were you doing with those lads? I'm sure they're all decent boys, but you can hardly know them, Katy. You don't want to be putting yourself into difficult situations that you can't easily get out of.'

Oh good grief. I really was turning into my mother, but I knew my reaction was nothing compared to what Max's would be if he was here.

'I can look after myself you know.'

'Sit down there and don't move. I'll make you a coffee.' I poked my head round the corner and called to Polly, beckoning her from the other bar. I explained the situation and asked her to sit with Katy while I made the drinks.

'There you go,' I said, a few minutes later, handing Katy a strong coffee, ignoring the fact she was turning her nose up at my offering. 'Drink it.' I went back into the kitchen to collect the drinks for Polly and me, putting a splash of brandy into our coffees. I didn't know about Polly, but I was in need of something. 'What do you think you're playing at, Katy?' I asked, sitting down to join her at the table.

'I don't know why you're making such a big thing about this. It's only a few drinks. And I am almost eighteen.'

'Almost being the pertinent word. You're underage and I would have thought with Max away you would have wanted to show him that you can act responsibly and that he can trust you to leave you on your own. Not go out and get completely wasted.'

'Ugh, I don't know why you keep going on about Max. He doesn't care what I do. I'm just a pain in the arse to him like I am to Mum and Alan. He's just looking for an excuse to send me back to Spain. '

'That's not the case at all. You're his family and that means a lot to Max. He only wants what's best for you.'

'Ha! Family? Are you joking? We don't know how to do that. Well not the good bits. We can do the bad bits, the lies and rows, the disappointments and secrets. Dysfunctional, I think you'd call it. No wonder Max got out as soon as he could.'

From across the table, Polly flashed me a questioning look. 'All families are a bit that way,' she said. 'Trouble is you can't do much about them. You're stuck with them. That's why I love my friends so much!'

'Well, I haven't got many of those either,' she said, with a dejected sigh. 'You won't tell Max about this, will you? He'll just have a massive go at me.'

'Oh Katy!' What the hell was I going to say to Max? He'd be absolutely furious, that much I knew, and I wouldn't fancy being in Katy's shoes when he did find out. 'The thing is, you're putting me in a difficult position. Max should know what's happened here tonight. He is your guardian while you're here, after all. If he finds out that I've been keeping something from him, especially something about his little sister, he'll go absolutely spare.'

'Well, he doesn't have to find out, does he? Not if we don't tell him. Please.' Katy's deep brown eyes travelled from me to Polly pleadingly. 'I'm really sorry. Honestly I promise you it won't happen again. No more drinking until I'm legal. If that's what it takes.'

'I don't know, Katy.'

'Pleeaaaase!'

I made the mistake of glancing at Polly, who was giving me the same imploring look as Katy.

'Okay, okay, but just this once, Katy. Don't let me down again.' I shuddered, trying to rid myself of the image of Max's angry face bearing down on me. 'I hate doing this, Max is my boyfriend and I shouldn't have to keep secrets from him but...' I sighed. 'Maybe it's best if we keep this one quiet'

'Oooh, thanks, Ellie,' she said, looking genuinely relieved. 'You're a babe.'

I dared to look across at Polly again, and she shrugged her assent as though there hadn't been any other option.

Katy sighed and slumped forward onto the table resting her head in her arms. 'Ugh... That coffee is disgusting, it's making me feel really ill.'

'Ha! Right. It's the coffee that's making you ill not the vodkas you've been tipping down your throat tonight?' Polly said dismissively.

Katy's eyes rolled as she lifted her head gingerly from the table. 'Look, can I stay here tonight? I don't really want to go back to the manor now. It'll be pitch black walking home and being alone in the house will be really creepy.' She wriggled her shoulders, shivering. 'There are all sorts of funny noises there, it wouldn't surprise me if the place was haunted.'

'Don't be daft. There're no ghosts there. Anyway, you can't stay here. You've got the dogs to think about and they can't be left overnight. Don't worry though, Polly and I will take you home and get you tucked into bed. You'll be absolutely fine.'

'I bloody well hope so. But I just want everyone to know that if I do get murdered in my bed tonight then that's down to you.'

'The only person you've got to worry about murdering you is Max, if he finds out what's happened tonight,' I said, gesturing for her to get up.

'Fine. Let's hope you're right. I'd hate for my unnecessary death to be on your conscience for the rest of your life.'

Polly shook her head and rolled her eyes. 'Blimey she's a bit of a drama queen this one, isn't she?'

But that wasn't the end of the drama. As soon as Katy stood up, she swayed on her feet, her skin taking on a grey cast; any colour, and there wasn't very much of it in the first place, completely absent from her cheeks.

'Oh god, I might just need... I feel... I really... I think I'm going to be...'

Too late! Katy lurched forward and all the excesses of her night were promptly sprayed over the floor of my lovely snug bar.

'Don't worry,' I said, dashing off in search of the mop and bucket thankful that it was a stone floor and would be easily cleanable. Even more grateful that Max was several hundred miles away and not around to witness to this pretty little episode.

'Everything okay?' asked Andy, wandering in, probably wondering what all the commotion was about. He'd been down in the cellar trying to fix our temperamental ice machine.

'Fine, just a little accident here. I'll get it cleaned up and then we'll take Katy home.'

'No worries,' said Andy, slipping his jacket off again, 'I'll see to it. You get off. Looks as though you've got enough on your hands as it is.'

'That's why I have the best bar staff in the country,' I said, giving Andy a kiss on the cheek.

'Come on, Digby,' I called, his ears pricking up at the prospect of an unexpected late night walk.

Somehow, Polly and I managed to manoeuvre Katy outside. We must have looked a proper sight, the three of us, propping each other up as we wandered down the High Street and then through the back alley into the lanes. Polly was clutching a torch, I had Digby on the lead who was providing a bit of extra light with his pink dayglo collar and Katy was in the middle, just about managing to put one foot in front of the other. Not that Polly and I were entirely sober either, but we were in a much better condition than Katy. Probably something to do with the years of experience we'd had.

I huddled into my jacket against the cold night air. Katy was right. It was dark and a bit spooky too. The wind rustled through the bushes and the local wildlife were obviously busy in the hedgerows as there was a constant rustle of activity from all around us. Ollie Owl was hooting away in the distance adding his own unnecessary frisson to our midnight walk.

'What was that?' Katy startled suddenly and looked over her shoulder.

'Nothing,' I said lightly, 'just an animal, I expect.' Katy's skittishness was rubbing off on me and making me feel a bit jumpy too, although I was doing my best not to show it.

'Oh god, what sort of animal? Not a rat I hope. I bloody hate rats.'

'No, not rats,' said Polly, not entirely convincingly. 'You're more likely to find them in the city, scavenging in the dustbins. Probably a fox, or a badger, or a mouse. Lots of field mice in the country.'

'I tell you something. If I come face to face with a mouse or a badger or a fox right now, I will literally scream and scream and probably die. Just warning you. The thought of something running over my feet. Eugh. I really don't know how can you actually like living in the countryside.'

'You get used to it,' said Polly, laughing.

'Don't worry, we've got Digby to protect us so we're perfectly safe. He'll see off any critters, won't you boy?'

Amazingly, avoiding the creatures of the dark and the potholes in the lane, and being scared witless by Katy jumping out of her skin and grabbing hold of our arms tighter every time she heard a noise, we finally made it safely to Braithwaite Manor. The floodlights highlighting the gorgeous Georgian building against the night sky were a welcome sight and we crunched our way along the drive, going round to the back door. Katy pulled out her key and fumbled with the door, before we all fell inside to be greeted by Holly and Bella who were overexcited to see us.

'Do you want me to take the dogs in the garden,' said Polly, 'while you get Katy settled?'

I nodded gratefully and handed Digby's lead over to Polly then led Katy through the kitchen by the hand and up the stairs where she took me into her bedroom, the biggest of the guest rooms. With cream floral linen, silk cushions, extravagant drapes and a walk-in wardrobe, it was a lovely feminine room, but I could understand why Katy might feel vulnerable staying alone in this big country mansion out in the middle of nowhere.

'You get ready while I go downstairs and check everything's off. Is there anything you need?'

Katy shook her head, looking tiny, and weary now. She padded over to the tall bay window and pulled closed the heavy linen gold-flecked curtains. The room and the plump king-sized bed looked so inviting I almost felt like curling up there myself.

'She will be all right, won't she?' I asked Polly a little later when she'd come in from the garden with the dogs, feeling guilty now at the prospect of leaving Katy here alone.

'Of course she will. She's got the dogs for company and the place is alarmed. Besides, the state she's in, I bet she'll be fast asleep as soon as her head hits the pillow.'

Back upstairs, Katy had climbed into bed. In her bunny-covered fleece pyjamas and with the make-up cleaned off her face, she looked almost childlike propped against the pillows. I felt a surge of affection for this girl, who I barely knew, yet who had stirred a whole host of reactions within me in such a short space of time; anger, annoyance and disbelief. And laughter too. Beneath her feisty and arrogant front, there was a warm, likeable and funny girl. I smiled at her, wondering what was going on in that head of hers to cause so much unhappiness, appreciating how lonely it must be for her, away from her mum, and everything she was familiar with.

'Are you okay?' I asked.

'Yep, I'm fine.' She pulled up her knees beneath the duvet and clasped her arms around the pretty cover. 'Sorry about tonight, Ellie, and thanks for getting me home in one piece.'

'Don't worry about it. I was seventeen once, believe it or not? You know you can always come and talk to me if you want to. I know you've got Max, but men don't always understand and sometimes only some good old-fashioned girly advice will do.' An awkward silence fell between us. 'Just putting it out there.'

'Yeah,' she said, dropping her gaze, and sucking on her lip. 'Thanks. Actually there is something you can do for me, Ellie, before you go.'

'Yes, sure. What is it?'

'I know this is going to sound really crazy but... could you just check the wardrobe for me and under the bed. You know, make sure no one's there.'

'Right.' I paused only a nanosecond, not long enough

for her to notice my surprise. I went over to the wardrobe and flung open the doors with a flourish, running my hand between the hangers and through the clothes to check there was no one lurking inside and then I went over to the bed and got down on my hands and knees and peered beneath. 'All clear,' I said brightly, as though it was a perfectly normal request.

Katy's relief was palpable and she gave me the sweetest smile before sinking down beneath the covers and closing her eyes tight.

Phew, job done. One teenage girl delivered safely to her bed. And Max wouldn't need to know a thing.

Ten

'Hey, what a lovely surprise! My two favourite girls in the world and they're here together. Oh okay,' said Max, leaning down to fuss Holly and Bella who were madly wagging their tails and circling his feet, 'you're two of my favourite girls too. So...' Max looked from me to Katy, his eyes narrowed, that cute little line forming between his eyebrows. 'You two are dog-walking buddies now?'

Max slipped his arm around my waist and pulled me into his chest, ruffling my hair with his hands. He smelt so good, his natural masculine scent playing with my senses.

'I was walking Digby so just popped in to see how Katy was doing and as it was such a gorgeous morning, I managed to persuade her to come along with me.'

'Really? Has my sister had a complete personality transplant in my absence? Fresh air, exercise, up and dressed and out of the house before midday? What on earth is going on? It's a miracle.'

Not a miracle at all. It had been bloody hard work and determination from me that had got Katy out of her bed this morning. I'd wanted to check that she hadn't suffered any ill effects from all the alcohol she'd drunk the previous night and see for myself that she hadn't been murdered in her bed.

Just a throwaway comment, I know, but it had come back to torment me at regular intervals during the night, waking me up with a start and an awful worried feeling at the pit of my stomach. More practically, I wanted to make sure Katy was presentable for when Max got home so he didn't pick up on anything being amiss.

Using the back door key Max had given me, I'd let myself into the house, turned the dogs out into the garden, and filled the kettle. Five minutes later with a mug of steaming hot tea, I was upstairs rat-a-tat-tatting on Katy's bedroom door.

'Hello, it's only me.'

Thankfully, she wasn't dead, just reassuringly grumpy. From beneath the covers she'd groaned and stirred before a flash of auburn hair poked above the duvet.

'Ugh, what are you doing here?' she'd asked, rubbing at her eyes, her brow wrinkled in confusion.

'Just checking up on you. How you feeling? How's the head?'

'Aargh, my head!' She'd clasped her hands to her brow as though she'd only just remembered. 'It hurts.'

'Hardly surprising. You were definitely on the wrong side of merry last night. Anyway,' I'd said wandering over to the window and drawing the curtains, 'it's a beautiful day out there. Some fresh air will do wonders for clearing any cobwebs.'

'Are you kidding? What time is it?'

'Just after nine.'

'No way! Are you mad? It's far too early and I'm not feeling very well. In fact, I think I could be dying.' She'd disappeared beneath the covers again.

'Oh no, you don't,' I'd said, whipping off the duvet and

throwing it aside on the floor to much leg flailing and screeching from Katy. 'Not dying, just hungover. Great feeling, isn't it?' I said, with barely disguised glee, hoping it was that great it might put her off drinking ever again.

I'd left her to come round with instructions that she needed to get downstairs as soon as, just in case Max decided to return home early.

Five minutes later, she slunk into the kitchen dressed in tracksuit bottoms, hoodie and with a killer scowl on her face, which I'd promptly ignored.

'You should have something to eat before we go, might make you feel better.'

'Eugh, no I couldn't.' She shook her head grimly. 'Although I might just have some water,' she said, running the tap and filling a glass, taking the smallest of sips. 'Right, let's go and do this, if we have to,' she'd said with a sigh.

'Great,' I'd said, grinning. 'It's lovely out there.'

The dogs were much more excited by the prospect than Katy, but it was good to be outside in the cool morning air, and I felt certain it wouldn't be long before Katy was feeling it too. As we walked, I savoured the beauty of our surroundings. I could never imagine tiring of this countryside, the rolling fields, the winding lanes and the changing landscape through the seasons. If I was ever feeling low or had something on my mind then I would always head outside with the dogs and walk. And walk and walk. There was something rejuvenating about breathing in the fresh air, focussing your mind on the here and now. It was as if the trees and the hedgerows and the swooping birds and scampering squirrels gathered you up in to their wholesomeness, offering a healing and protective back-to-nature hug. Invariably, after being outside for a couple of hours, I would have a different perspective on any troublesome situation and, if not a solution, then definitely a way forward. Last year when I'd been weighing up whether to stay in the village or return to London, my daily walks had offered me the clarity to come to the right decision. A decision I hadn't regretted for one moment.

Walking along the lanes in companionable silence with Katy I'd wondered if the charms of Little Leyton wouldn't work their magic on her too.

'Have you heard from your mum?' I'd ventured when we stopped by the river and the dogs had launched themselves into the water, their paws clawing through the water as their heads bobbed up and down happily.

'Yep, she texts all the time. Says I've got to go home, so that we can talk, "resolve our differences".'

'Ah right, and I'm guessing you're no closer to wanting to do that?'

'No. I'm not.' She'd shook her head vigorously. 'She's just feeling guilty, but that's her problem.'

'I see. And what does she have to feel guilty about?'

Katy had turned her head sharply to look at me and I wondered if I'd overstepped the mark, if my question hadn't been too intrusive.

'Oh just stuff.' For a moment I'd thought she was about to open up to me, but then she batted the question away. 'Stuff I don't want to think about now. I'm almost eighteen. I don't have to go home. Spain isn't my home anyway. I was born here in the UK, it was Mum's decision to move away when I was small. Now I'm old enough to make my own decisions and I've decided I want to be here.'

'Right.' I picked up the ball that Digby had just deposited at my feet and threw it in the water, watching him scamper down the bank to retrieve it. 'And have you had any more thoughts about what you'll do?' I really hoped she'd gone off the idea of going to London.

'Don't know yet. I haven't thought that far ahead. I'll have to do something. Maybe take the summer off and get something lined up for the autumn?' She fell silent into her thoughts again. 'Max wouldn't mind me staying here for a while, would he?'

'I wouldn't have thought so, but you'd have to ask him to be sure. You should talk to him, Katy. I'm sure he'd want to help you if he can.'

'Yeah, maybe,' she'd replied, pulling a doubtful face.

I could understand her reluctance. Max sometimes came across as being cold and unsentimental, but that was just because most of the time he was preoccupied with work and often forgot to take his business head off. Underneath his brusque exterior, he was the kindest and most thoughtful person ever. If Katy asked him for his help, I knew that he would do whatever he could to support her.

'You won't mention anything about last night, will you?' she asked me again, on the way back from our walk.

'Don't worry,' I told her. 'It'll be our little secret.'

Now, with Max in the kitchen, so obviously pleased to be home, making a fuss of me and Katy, and the dogs, it occurred to me just how bad it was going to make me feel, knowing I wasn't being totally honest with him. I had to remind myself that this was for Katy's benefit, and absolutely no good would come of Max finding out the truth. It wasn't as if any real damage had been done and Katy had promised me that there would be no repeat performance of her drunken antics last night. What harm was there in one little white lie?

I looked across at Max and smiled, guiltily. He was shaking his head as though he couldn't quite believe what he was seeing.

'Well, I'm amazed, but thrilled that you've decided to become acquainted with the early mornings. Best part of the day, I reckon, and honestly, I didn't think you had it in you,' he said, his tone playful.

'That's charming,' said Katy, laughing. 'I'm perfectly capable of looking after myself you know.' Her gaze flittered over to me and I had to turn away, for fear of giving the game away.

'Yes, of course, I know that,' said Max, 'it's just good to see you looking happier in yourself, that's all. I'll have to go away more often if I come back to this happy domestic scenario.'

'You need to have more faith in your little sister,' she said breezily, and I smiled weakly, fearful that she was overplaying it now. When she said she was going up to have a shower, I almost let out an audible sigh of relief.

'Katy,' I called after her. 'Are you up for a shopping trip into town soon? I need to find a christening present for Stella, and to buy some new clothes too. I'm such a rubbish shopper, can never find anything that I like. You could help me choose. We could make a day of it, if you like. Shop till we drop and then lunch, and then more shopping. How does that sound?'

'Great.' Katy's face lit up. 'I'd love to come. I could do with picking some bits up myself.'

Max turned to look at me when Katy left, complete astonishment in his expression. 'Well I don't know what you've done, but she seems in much better spirits than when I left. I do appreciate it you know, you spending time with her.'

'Well, she's a great kid. I just want her to feel welcome.'

'Come here.' Max pulled me close, pressing his lips against mine. My body immediately responded to his proximity, his touch alighting something deep down in my core. 'I missed you,' he told me, while massaging my back with his hand. 'I know we can go for days and not see each other in the village, but when I'm away from home that distance between us seems magnified somehow. I like knowing that you're round the corner, that I can pop in and see you whenever I want to. Yesterday, after I spoke to you on the phone, I had to go off to some boring business meeting and the only thing that kept me going was the thought of seeing you, hearing your voice, touching you.' He nuzzled his face into my neck, depositing a kiss there, his mouth on my skin making me squirm with delight at the delicious sensation.

'Well, I'm sorry if I was distracting you from your work?' I said, teasingly.

'Those sorts of distractions I don't mind at all.' He pulled back to look at me, his gaze unwavering on mine. 'The thing was I kept going over our conversation in my head. Wondering if you'd really said what you said?'

'What I said?' I repeated, my stomach performing a loop-the-loop, knowing exactly what he meant.

'Yeah,' he whispered in my face. 'What you said. Because you hadn't said it before, so I noticed. Did you mean it?'

Admitting my true feelings on the phone was one thing

but saying it to his face was something else entirely, but there was no going back now.

'I meant it,' I said, smiling, and then without any hesitation at all. 'I love you, Max.'

Max's eyes were filled with longing.

'Good. Because I love you too, Ellie.' He paused, the faintest of smiles forming on his lips. 'Just tell me again, in case I didn't hear you properly.'

'I love you, Max.'

'I should bloody well think so too,' he said, turning into a vampire and making loud slurping noises as he sucked on my neck.

'Stop it! Get off,' I said giggling. 'I have to get back to the pub.'

He made a low grumbling noise in my ear.

'Oh, what it is to be in love with a woman in demand.' His lips curled in that sexy way of his that did funny things to my insides. I would never tire of hearing him say he loved me, although there was a small part of me that still needed to pinch myself to believe this was actually happening to us. 'Okay, okay. I can take a hint' He glanced at his watch. 'Shit! I should be somewhere else too. I have a meeting and should have been there ten minutes ago. I need to go.' He paused, and I noticed something unfathomable flash across his features. Our playful romantic mood shattered in an instant as real-life intruded once again.

'Oh?'

'Yeah. I should have mentioned it, but it's Sasha I'm seeing actually.' His mouth formed into a half grimace.

'Sasha?' Just the mention of her name made my heart

plummet to the depths of my stomach. 'What, are you two working together again?'

'No, not exactly. She's thinking of moving back here.'

'Really?' That made no sense at all. Sasha wasn't a local girl, what possible reason could she have for moving to Little Leyton?

Max shrugged, looking apologetic. 'She's after a place to rent and asked me if I could help. As it happens one of the farm cottages at the bottom of Bluebell Lane became empty a couple of weeks ago so she's having a look at that today.'

'Oh…' A hundred questions flooded my head, but I managed only one. 'I wonder why she wants to move here?'

'Well you've said yourself that Little Leyton holds a special magic. Perhaps she wants a quieter pace of life. I know she always loved living in the village. Maybe she's after a bit of the good life that we're experiencing.'

'Yes, but…' I really couldn't put a voice to all the thoughts currently flooding my mind. Why here, though? Why now? 'But what about her work?' I managed.

'Honestly, Ellie, I don't know.' I heard the exasperation in his voice. 'It's not a problem is it?'

At this precise moment it seemed like a huge problem to me. Life was complicated enough without glamorous ex-girlfriends moving in just down the road. Why the hell couldn't Max have told her that he didn't have any properties to rent, like any normal man?

'No. I just wondered… that was all.'

I was left wondering. Of course it wasn't strange that Sasha wanted to move back into the village. Just down the road from her ex. There wasn't anything suspect about that behaviour at all. Well, if Max's reaction was anything to go by, there wasn't.

'Look, I'll have to go, darling.' He kissed me on the cheek. 'We can catch up later, yeah?'

'Yeah,' I said. The sensation of his kiss on my face wasn't the only thing Max left me with. Now I had a rising sense of panic in my chest too.

Eleven

Back at the pub, I walked through the front door to find a gaggle of my regulars gathered around the bar. They all turned to look at me, smiles on their faces.

'Well, it's all right for some, rocking up to work at this time.' Jake made a big show of tapping his finger on his watch, much to the amusement of his band of cronies.

On Saturdays the customers would come in early and stay late and it looked as though this motley crew might be in for the duration. The group currently propping up the bar were a bunch of lads – well I say lads, some of them were well into their fifties – who were well known at The Dog and Duck. This lot were noisy, mouthy and cheeky and some days the high jinks and banter flowed freely and on other days, like today, I really wasn't feeling it.

'You all right, lads?'

'Yeah. What about you? Been off to see the Master again?' Jim adopted his best country yokel accent which, judging from the reaction of the others, was absolutely hysterical.

Ordinarily I would have laughed it off, but my sense of humour, as far as Max was concerned, had deserted me today.

'You landed on your feet all right, didn't you, love? When

Max bought this place. I bet you couldn't believe your luck. You gained a boss, a pub and a lover all in one fell swoop.' Cue more guffawing from Jim and his mates.

'What?' I couldn't believe what I'd just heard. All I could see around me were smiling faces, or were they faces laughing at me instead? A fire burned through my veins. A fiery rampaging heat. I dug my nails into my fists at my sides. Under my breath I counted slowly to ten and plastered on my best landlady's smile. 'For your information, Max isn't my boss. He owns the freehold on the property, that's all. He has nothing to do with the running of this pub. We're in a relationship, not that that's any business of yours, but our professional and personal lives are totally separate. In case you were wondering.'

'Oooooooh! Someone's a bit touchy,' laughed Keith.

'All right, love. I didn't mean anything by it.' Jim added.

'You'd better watch what you say, Jim. We don't want to go upsetting the landlady do we?' Rob said.

'No, you really don't,' I said, sweeping out into the other bar where Josie and Andy were manning the fort.

'Hey, you all right?' asked Josie, immediately sensing something was up. She steered me to the back of the bar, where we couldn't be overheard.

'Oh, it's just Jim and his mates winding me up.'

'Well that doesn't normally bother you. What's so different today?'

I took a deep breath, and wrapped my arms around my chest, annoyed that I'd allowed their stupid remarks to get to me. If I took offence at every derogatory comment made from across the bar, I'd be in a constant state of the hump.

Deep down though, I knew this wasn't about my rowdy customers at all.

'Oh, it's Max. I've just seen him and it was absolutely great, and then just as I was leaving he announces that he's going to meet Sasha. That he's going to show her one of his houses and that she could be moving back into the village.'

'What!? Why would she want to move back here?'

'Exactly. I have no idea. She has a flat in London; it just doesn't make any sense.'

'And what, you're thinking there must be something more to it than Max is letting on?'

'I don't know. I thought things were really good between us and now this. Why the hell is he so friendly with his ex, anyway?'

'Well perhaps it just means he's a nice person.'

'Hmm, well I wish his niceness didn't extend to entertaining his exes.' I paused, thinking for a moment about me and Johnny. That was different. He was more of a teen fling than a proper serious ex-boyfriend. 'Oh god! Do you think I'm being unreasonable?'

'No, not at all. I'd be exactly the same. I'd want to know what was going on. You'll just have to hope she hates the house, and decides to move somewhere else.'

'Hmmm right. But Bluebell Cottage though? It's hardly likely she's going to hate it.'

Spotting a customer waiting at the bar, I jumped in to serve them, glad of the distraction. It was only when I was standing with Josie again that I tuned into the conversation going on in the other room. It was a trick I'd developed since taking over the pub. The ability to pick out certain conversations across a crowded room. Considering this conversation involved me, I was all ears.

'You see, we never had these problems when Eric was in charge, did we?' This comment came from Jake.

'No, I wonder how the old boy's doing. I miss his friendly face around this place. I mean, she's all right, this one, but the trouble with having a woman running the pub is that they haven't got a sense of humour.'

The bloody cheek of it!

'I know,' said Jim, chuckling. 'If I want some grief from a moody woman I can stay at home for that!'

I poked my head round the old oak upright beam that separated the two bars, earwigging a bit more.

'I suppose she does her best,' said Keith, peering into his glass as though it held a thousand answers, 'she keeps a good pint of beer, but it's not the same as having a bloke run the place. You felt you were in a safe pair of hands when Eric was behind the bar.'

I couldn't stand it anymore. I walked back into the bar where the guys were discussing the merits of me and the pub, their faces a picture of awkwardness as it dawned on them that I'd heard every word they'd been saying. This wasn't just about me personally. This was about my ability to run a good pub.

'I couldn't help overhearing, lads. I'm sorry you're not happy with things the way they are here. Obviously, as landlady, I like to keep all my customers satisfied, so if there's anything specific you would like to see changed then do tell me. I'm always open to suggestions.' I was amazed I managed to keep my voice even. 'Obviously I can't do anything about the fact that I'm not Eric or that I'm a woman, but anything else I'm prepared to listen to.'

'Now look, Ellie,' said Jim, conciliatory now. 'Don't take any notice of us. You know we talk out of our arses most of the time. It was just a bit of friendly banter that was all.'

'Of course! Friendly banter about how I'm not cut out to run the pub.'

'Nah, we all think you're doing a great job, don't we?' Jim looked around wildly at the others for some moral support, and they all nodded fervently, their earlier bolshiness now nowhere to be seen. 'We were just saying how we missed Eric that was all.'

'And what you think about a woman running the Dog and Duck. Honestly, guys, I thought better of you. I'm bound to do things differently to Eric, but actually I'm more than qualified to run this place. I pretty much grew up in the pub, it's in my blood. I might not have Eric's experience, but I do have a business management degree and an accountancy qualification, and a bloody good cellar manager in Dan. What would be really nice would be to have your support.'

'Honestly, Ellie, take no notice of us. We all love you and the pub, you know that.'

I took a deep breath, aware now that our little contretemps had gained the attention of most of the other people in the pub. It was only then that I noticed the customer sitting in Noel's chair, next to the fireplace, watching me closely. As I looked across at him, he dropped his gaze, but not before I recognised him. Typical, the man I suspected was from the pub guide had witnessed my whole little outburst. He certainly knew how to pick his moments. Still, I wouldn't have cared if it was Prince Philip sitting there, I was determined to have my say.

'Next time, guys, just tell me to my face if there's something you're unhappy with, rather than talk behind my back. At least then I can attempt to do something about it. Alternatively, if you're really unhappy, then you always have the option to go and drink somewhere else. I've heard The Red Lion at Upper Leyton serves a good pint.'

'But...'

From behind the bar, Josie winked at me and held her hands up to the side of face, clapping lightly. At least she had my back.

I waltzed out of the bar into the living quarters, feeling strangely empowered, an emotion that was quickly replaced by crushing guilt. What had I been thinking? Why couldn't I have just kept my mouth zipped instead of telling some of my most regular customers to go and take a hike and drink in another pub? I mean, what if they went? What if other customers followed? And what if that man, the one I suspected was from the Good Pub Guide, went and put all of this in his damn report? I groaned inwardly.

'Nice one, Ells,' said Josie, wandering through into the kitchen.

'Oh Josie, what have I done? I know, I shouldn't have, but I just couldn't help myself.'

'Don't worry about it. I think everyone was in total awe. Respect, sister.' She fist bumped me. 'Doesn't hurt to give the customers a few home truths occasionally.'

'Yes, but I think I may have just proved to those guys exactly what they'd been saying about me; that I'm a temperamental unreliable woman. Eric would never have behaved in that way.'

'Yeah, but then again, Dad would never have been subject

to that sort of criticism from his regulars. Or if he was, he would have thrown them out on to the pavement.'

'True.' I suppose it was a fact of life. Some situations I would never be able to handle in the same way as Eric.

Josie flicked on the kettle, pulled two mugs from the cupboards and heaped a teaspoon of coffee into each. 'They're all out there now, saying how much they love the pub and how they would never drink at the Red Lion because the landlady there is a frosty old so-and-so, and nowhere near as lovely as you.'

'Ha, well give me a few more years and I may be just like her too.'

'No, never,' said Josie, handing me my favourite striped mug. I took a sip of the coffee feeling better for having talked it through with Josie. Digby had slumped against my leg, his weight warm and comforting up against me.

'Did you see that guy out there? The one who was sitting by the fireplace?' I asked. Josie nodded. 'I think he's the guy from the pub guide.'

'Ah well, he's just ordered another pint, so he must be enjoying himself. It will give him something to write about, at least.'

'Yeah, I guess,' I said, dejectedly, wondering if I was on a one-woman mission to completely destroy the goodwill of my business.

Josie laughed. 'Really don't worry about it. You've just shown to everyone how passionate you are about your business. And that's a good thing. If people don't like that, they can always go and drink down the Red Lion,' she said, a mischievous glint in her eye.

Twelve

A few days later I turned my car into the entrance of Braith-waite Manor, and tootled along the driveway, imagining myself to be in a period drama, arriving for the start of a country weekend. Instead, maybe not quite as excitingly, I was on my way to collect Katy for our shopping trip into town. I hadn't seen Max since he'd had to dash off to see Sasha that day, but I'd had time enough to realise it wasn't an issue. How could it be after that delicious conversation we had about our feelings for each other? What I had to remember was that Sasha was in the past and I was very much here in the present. Well, that's what I hoped, anyway. Pulling up outside the pillared front doorway, I beeped on the horn and Max's dogs came running out to greet me, barking noisily. When there was no sign of Katy emerging, I climbed out of the car and wandered around to the back door.

'Katy, all I'm asking is that you talk to her,' I heard Max say in an imploring voice. 'You'll have to do it sometime. Mum wants to make things right, but she can't do that if you won't even speak to her.'

'I don't want to, Max. Don't you understand. I haven't got anything to say to her. She wants me to go back to Spain and it's not going to happen. However much you get on at me.'

I hovered there for a moment, trapped on the outside of their impassioned conversation, wondering if it wouldn't be better if I just turned round and went home. Tentatively, I stepped forward and knocked on the glass pane of the open door.

'Is this a bad time?'

'No,' said Katy quickly, 'I've been waiting for you.' Her relief at getting out of her conversation with her brother was palpable. 'I won't be a moment. I'll just pop to the loo, and grab my bag, then I'll be ready to go.'

'Oh dear,' I said to Max when she'd left. 'I'm guessing by the sound of that conversation that things aren't any better as far as Katy and her mum are concerned.'

'I've tried everything. I just can't get through to her. Mum is calling every two minutes wanting to talk to her, and Katy just refuses. If she would only open up to me and tell me what the problem is, I might be able to help, but she just won't have it. I can't seem to please either of them at the moment.'

'Give her a bit more time and I'll bet she'll come round.'

'Well I bloody well hope so, because I'm at a loss as to what to do next. She's clearly miserable and unhappy, but I can't see how that's ever going to change if she won't even help herself.'

'I'll see if I can talk to her when we're out. It might take her mind off things, a bit of retail therapy.'

Max shrugged. I wasn't sure if his irritability was down solely to Katy or if he had other things on his mind.

'I meant to ask, what happened with Sasha the other day?'

Max hadn't said a word about it, and not knowing what was happening was slowly turning me crazy.

He lifted his brow and I detected a flicker of emotion in his eyes. I wondered if her reappearance in the village had unsettled him in the same way as it had me. If seeing her again, he hadn't realised that he'd missed her and still held feelings for her. I steadied my breathing. *No. Stop it, Ellie, with the wild realms of fantasy.* I was being ridiculous.

'Yeah, she's good. The cottage was just what she was looking for so I think she was very relieved to find somewhere. She's moved in some of her stuff already.'

So Sasha wasn't as firmly placed in the past as I hoped. Now she was here again, in the present, and in the future too, I had to wonder, sadly.

'Already? That was quick.' Too damn quick for my liking. Why the hurry? And couldn't Max have just run it by me first? Had he not considered how I might feel knowing his glamorous ex had moved into a house just a stone's throw away from the manor.

I took a step backwards, my gaze scanning his face for an answer.

'Yeah, well the thing is…' Just then we heard footsteps padding through the kitchen and turned to see Katy approaching. What was it he had been about to tell me? 'It doesn't matter,' he said, as if hearing my silent question. 'We can catch up on the news later.' He pulled me to him, his hands on my shoulders, and kissed me tenderly on the lips, although I couldn't concentrate on his kiss when I was still trying to digest the news about Sasha.

'Oh pur... lease! Stop with all the lovely-dovey stuff. It's gross,' said Katy, her disgust entirely genuine.

Max and I exchanged a look and we giggled, and for that moment I could forget about my concerns over Sasha.

'You know, you're very welcome to come with us,' I told Max.

'Er, thanks, but no. My idea of hell is traipsing around the shops, I'm afraid. But I know you two will have the best time ever.'

I laughed, mainly at Katy's horrified expression that I'd even invited Max along in the first place. What she didn't know was that I'd only asked because I'd known there wasn't the remotest chance that he would have accepted.

Max reached inside his jeans pocket and pulled out a wad of cash, handing it over to Katy. Wide-eyed, she looked at the money and then back up at Max.

'What's this?'

'Well you can't go shopping without money, can you? Why don't you buy some new clothes.'

'Really? You are brilliant. The best brother ever.' She stood on tiptoes, throwing her arms around his neck and reached up to kiss him. 'Thank you!'

Max looked at me, bemusement on his face, but I could tell by the glint in his eye and the smile on his lips that he was touched by Katy's unexpected show of affection.

*

'Oh my god, my feet!'

In the bustling Italian restaurant the waiter showed us to a corner table – I'd never been so pleased to sit down. We dumped our numerous bags on the floor and received the menus gratefully, immediately putting in an order of a white wine spritzer for me and a Diet Coke for Katy, as we were both gasping for a drink. I swear we'd been in every clothes shop in the arcade, possibly twice, but Katy clearly had tons more stamina than me for shopping. Still, I couldn't complain because it had been a wholly successful trip. First off, we'd managed to find an adorable silver bracelet for Stella's christening, one that I'd be able to buy charms for on each of her birthdays, and a complete set of Beatrix Potter's books in a presentation case. Then we started on the search for something for me to wear to the inaugural Little Leyton summer ball. In my mind I knew exactly how I wanted to look, elegant and sophisticated, yet understated too, so I was thinking something long and classic, in a neutral colour, that made me look two sizes smaller. It should have been an easy task, but it wasn't. Spending most of my time in jeans and sweatshirts, I hated trying on clothes at the best of times, but today everything I picked up seemed too fancy, too expensive and just not me. The couple of dresses I did try on made me look like a small girl dressing up in her mum's clothes. Thank goodness Katy was there. She convinced me, when my enthusiasm was waning and I was about to give up and go home, that we couldn't even think about leaving until I'd found the perfect dress. Going back to the very first shop we'd visited, Katy's eyes had alighted on a pale turquoise bias-cut dress.

'Try this,' she'd said. 'It's in your size.'

I felt my lip curl involuntarily in disbelief. Not only was it in a bright colour that I would never have chosen for myself, it was far too fussy with lots of layers at the top falling like a soft waterfall, and a long sweeping skirt.

'I'm not sure...'

'Just try it. You never know it might suit you.' She'd almost manhandled me into the changing rooms.

Now, sitting in the restaurant, my feet throbbing as though I'd just run a marathon, I was so pleased that Katy had pressed me to try it on. Left to my own devices I would never have picked it up but as soon as I put it on, I knew it was the one. Cinderella would go to the ball after all! It was less formal than I'd been looking for, much more floaty and summery, but the colour suited me and the sensation of the fabric swishing against my skin had given me a delightful thrill of anticipation at the thought of wearing it on the night of the ball. With some silver strappy sandals we found, I knew I had the perfect outfit. Hitting the shops with Katy had definitely been a good idea, helping us to bond on so many levels.

The waiter delivered our drinks and I took a much longed for sip.

'So are you pleased with what you've bought?'

Katy nodded, surveying the bags at her feet. After we'd picked up my bits, she'd headed for a sprawling mega-store where she'd swept around like a woman on a mission, filling her huge basket with T-shirts, shorts, jeans and underwear and a small piece of black fabric which was supposedly a body-con dress. When she'd showed it to me, my eyes had widened and I'd had to bite my tongue to stop myself from commenting on just how revealing it was. Honestly, I felt a hundred years old!

'Yes. I'm so happy.' She grinned. 'I didn't think I'd be able to buy anything and now I've got a whole new wardrobe. Maybe Max isn't so bad after all.'

'Oh, he's lovely,' I said, jumping in with my agreement. Did I detect a thawing in her attitude towards her brother? 'I know he can be grouchy at times, but he's a real softy at heart.'

'Yes, I'm getting used to him. Slowly,' she said laughing, raising her eyes. 'To be honest though, I find it much easier talking to you. He can be a bit...' Her gaze drifted around the restaurant, in search of the right word.

'Intense?' I offered.

'Yep, that's it. He's a bit full-on, isn't he? He has this sort of wild energy that fills all the air in a room, and then when he leaves, it's like you can breathe again.'

I couldn't help smiling at Katy's description of her brother. He was a bit of a whirlwind, admittedly, his presence demanding your full attention, but in many ways, Katy was just like him.

'Max just wants to help. If there's a problem he wants to solve it. He thrives on that kind of thing. Admittedly his problems usually involve late deliveries and dodgy building practises which he knows exactly how to handle. I think teenage girls and mothers might be a little out of his comfort zone.' I managed to raise a smile from Katy. 'Really though, he'll be there for you. If you do want to talk.'

'Yeah.' Her gaze dropped to her fingernails. 'It's hard though, it's like I don't know what to say.'

My hand reached across the table for hers. 'What happened Katy? With your mum? It must have been something bad for you to fall out with her?'

She looked at me warily, as if weighing up whether she should tell me or not. In the background, the sound of a tray full of crockery shattering on the floor reverberated around the room and everyone turned to look at the embarrassed waitress who was staring at the ground in disbelief. I turned my attention back to Katy, hoping the moment wasn't lost.

'Katy?'

She took a deep breath.

'Oh, I guess it's been building for a while. I always thought Alan was okay, we got on really well when I was small, but things changed as I got older and became a teenager. He's always having a go at me, telling me what I can and can't do. He just doesn't stop, always criticising what I wear, the way I have my hair, the friends I hang out with. Mum never takes my side. It's always about keeping Alan happy.'

'Perhaps your mum was just trying to keep the peace.'

'No, I think they'll both be relieved to have me out of the way.' She sighed heavily and I wondered, seeing her sadness, if I'd done the right thing in bringing up the subject. We'd had such a lovely time this morning, mooching around the shops, chatting about make-up and clothes. Katy was the happiest I'd seen her and then I had to go and ruin things by bringing up the one subject she was trying to escape from. 'I think he's always been jealous of me. Of the relationship me and Mum had. Well, they've no need to worry anymore, have they?'

'Don't say that,' I urged. 'She's your mum, and she's going to worry about you. I know you've not been getting on with Alan, but that's perfectly normal. Show me a teenager that hasn't had huge rows with their dad.'

'That's the point though, he isn't my dad. He's nothing to me. Mum might want to share her life with him and that's up to her, but I don't have to now.'

Katy's jaw was set firm, the look in her eye telling me firmly not to even try and convince her otherwise.

'I remember when I was about fifteen,' I said, eager now to take the conversation in a different direction, 'I met this guy who I really liked. He was nineteen and was studying at the local college, but he was unlike anyone I'd ever met before. He drove a 400cc motorbike and wore these red and black leathers, and he used to take me round town on the back of his bike. I still remember that feeling of hanging on tight to his waist and feeling the air rush past me as we whizzed around the streets. Of course, I never told my mum and dad because they would never have allowed me to see him. One night he invited me to go to a gig so I told my parents I was staying round a friend's house, which would have been fine, but Dad bless him, decided I would need my medication because I'd been suffering from a cold, so he turned up at my friend's house. Oh my god! Dad went completely spare when he found out I wasn't there but at a nightclub instead. He waited for me outside the club and when I came out, he didn't say anything, he just literally dragged me away by the arm. It was so embarrassing. I was grounded for weeks and I never did get to see that guy again.'

'Oh no!'

'Yeah. I was devastated at the time.' I gave a passing thought to that young guy, wondering what he might be up to. 'Just think we could be married now with three kids. Ha, probably a blessing in disguise though or else I would never have got together with Max.'

Katy smiled. 'It's funny how life pans out, isn't it?' she said, her face betraying a thousand emotions.

'Yes, and it will work out for you too, Katy. I know

it might not seem that way at the moment, but it will, I promise you.'

Katy looked up as she took a bite into her oozing croque monsieur, a long strand of cheese, hanging from her mouth and sticking to her chin. She grinned and wiped it away. We'd both opted for the same thing, served with chips and salad, and it was going down a treat. She took another bite, her warm intelligent eyes, the same intense shade as her brother's, flickering over me.

'Thanks for all this,' she said, 'it's been really great.'

'I've really enjoyed it too,' I said, meaning it, and feeling relief that there wasn't any awkwardness between us after the conversation about her mum. 'We'll have to do it again.'

When we'd finished, I settled the bill and we picked up our belongings and started on the walk back to the car park, laden down with all our carrier bags. We were just leaving the main doors to the centre when I heard someone call out my name.

'Ellie? Oh, and Katy too. How lovely to see you both.'

I swung round to look, my whole being struck rigid to the spot at the realisation of who was standing in front of me. I felt sure my heart stopped beating too. No, it couldn't be. Yes, it definitely was. No, she couldn't be… Oh god, it looked as though she definitely was. And if my expression was anything like Katy's, who was open-mouthed and wide-eyed, then I knew there could be no hiding my complete and utter shock and amazement.

Thirteen

'Sasha?' It was Katy who spoke first, which was just as well because I'd been struck completely dumb.

'Hi, gosh look at you! Haven't you grown up? Mind you, it must be a couple of years since I last saw you. Max told me you were here for the summer. How lovely! And Ellie? It's lovely to see you again too.'

She swooped in to kiss me on the cheek and then did the same to Katy, who had managed to close her mouth and was doing a much better job at covering up her surprise than I was. I'd dropped my bags to the floor and had adopted the expression of a startled goldfish. With supreme effort, I managed to rearrange my facial features into something approaching normal and smiled.

'Well, it looks like you two have been having fun?' she said, eyeing up our bags.

'Oh yes, just a little retail therapy,' I stuttered.

'Me too,' she said holding out a solitary bag. And then I saw the logo which only confirmed to me what had been staring me right in the face these last few minutes. I looked at Sasha and then back at the bag. When was it I'd last seen her properly. That was it, Christmas Eve...

Max and I had just come from a busy evening in the pub

when the whole community had been celebrating the fact that The Dog and Duck would be remaining open. We'd walked arm-in-arm to the church to join in the midnight mass service, and with the snow falling on our faces, I could remember how happy and joyous I'd felt. When we reached the lychgate I'd spotted Sasha, looking glamorous as ever, emerging from a car. I'd thought it strange at the time that she was back in the village, but I hadn't dwelt on it, my mind was full of so many other happy events at the time. I can remember thinking how happy Sasha looked too. Happy and radiant and blossoming and… Now, I just about managed to find my voice.

'You're…?'

'Pregnant?' asked Katy, filling in the blank and failing spectacularly to keep the surprise from her voice. Katy and I looked to each other for guidance, as though one of us might come up with an explanation that would confirm Sasha wasn't pregnant at all, just that she had a huge cushion stuffed up her jumper.

Sasha laughed, brushing her chestnut coloured hair away from her face. Her skin was clear and glowing. Her eyes bright. She reminded me of an advertisement for vitamin supplements. I could just imagine her running through a meadow, her hair flying behind her.

'Yes!' Sasha paused, her face clouding as she noticed our reactions. 'You must have known?'

We both shook our heads, slightly manically. No this little snippet of information must have passed us by. Even when I'd seen her the other day in her car in the High Street, I could never have imagined what she'd been hiding beneath that steering wheel.

'Oh I would have thought Max would have told you.' *Me too*, I thought sadly. 'Typical man, huh?' She chuckled. 'You do know I've moved back into the village though?'

'Oh yes,' I said, desperately trying to recover a bit of ground. *Think. Head. Straight.* Thankfully Sasha was only too willing to fill me in on all the details.

'Yes, Max has been a complete rock. I don't know what I would have done without him these last couple of weeks. He really has come to my rescue. Obviously this wasn't planned at all.' She cradled her arms around her bump, a dreamy expression on her face. 'It was such a huge shock when I first found out, and to be honest with you, I was in a bad place for a while, but I've got my head around it now and being back in Little Leyton feels like a new start. London is no place to bring up a baby, so it made sense to come back here.'

Did it? None of this was making any sense to me at the moment. All I could thing about was why Max hasn't said anything to me and why he was even involved in the first place.

'Do you have family in this area then?' I managed.

'No, I barely know anyone around here, apart from Max, and you, of course, and a couple of others… But Little Leyton has always struck me as a really friendly place and I'd love to become a part of the community here. It's where I want to make our home and the cottage is such a beautiful space.'

Of all the beautiful villages in the country and she had to choose this one.

Katy flashed me a look, which I didn't want to acknowledge.

'It sounds great. And you look really well,' I said, re-locating my manners from somewhere. 'Doesn't she look well?' I elbowed Katy in the ribs.

'Yeah.'

Funny how Katy was singing Sasha's praises only a short while ago. Now, with a distrustful expression on her face, there wasn't much evidence of that love.

'Well, we should be getting on,' I told Sasha. My head was spinning, I really needed to sit down again. Maybe if we just got away, things would become clearer in my head. It would all make absolute sense just as soon as we got down the road. Or not. 'No doubt we'll bump into you again soon then.' *Oh no*, I had bumps on the brain now.

'Yes, I expect so. I'm definitely going to have to pop in the pub soon. Max tells me you're doing a grand job there, Ellie.'

'Oh yes, drop in anytime,' I said, really hoping she wouldn't take me up on that offer. 'Anyway, must dash, so nice to see you again Sasha.' I smiled and waved, desperate to get away. Katy followed me, muttering something in my ear, but I wasn't hearing her. How come Max had filled Sasha in on me and the pub, but had failed to tell me about the small matter of Sasha being pregnant? Anger fizzled up within me. My hand reached up to my neck, a heat throbbing beneath my skin. Didn't I deserve to know that his ex-girlfriend was back on the scene, very much pregnant and intending on making her home just a stone's throw away from my boyfriend?

It was only when we were back at the car and we'd loaded all our bags in the boot and climbed into our seats that I tuned back in to what Katy was saying.

'Crikey!'

'Did you really not know?'

'We didn't ask her when the baby was due. Although she looks quite far gone. Must be any day now.'

'How long do you think Max has known?'

'Why didn't Max mention it?'

Katy's questions came out in a chaotic tumble, putting all my thoughts into words. I don't think she was really expecting sensible answers, which was just as well because I had no answers to give her. Just questions of my own. So many questions.

Everything had been going perfectly. I'd been so happy looking forward to my first summer at the pub, spending time with Max in the beer garden and at his beautiful house, walking the dogs, long lazy days enjoying the sunshine, preparing for the summer fair. Then seeing Sasha like that, so suddenly and unexpectedly, so obviously with child, had shaken me to the core. My gaze drifted across to Katy, I wasn't the only one. I could sense the disbelief radiating from her beside me.

Somehow I managed to gather myself enough to start the car and begin the journey home. We were both lost in our own thoughts, until Katy couldn't contain herself any longer, blurting out the one thing that had clearly been at the forefront of both our minds ever since we'd run into Sasha.

'Do you think it's Max's baby?'

'What? NO!' I think I may have shouted. I certainly turned and glared at Katy for her audacity at mentioning the unmentionable.

'Ellie, keep your eyes on the road,' she admonished me.

I gripped the steering wheel tighter feeling a knot of fear deep in my stomach.

'How can you be sure?' she continued.

'What?'

'How can you know it's not Max's baby?'

'Because… well because it wouldn't be possible.' My heart was flapping away in my chest about to explode. 'Besides, Max would have told me,' I said, sounding a lot more confident than I felt.

'You think?' she said, damning her brother in that split second. 'When did he and Sasha split up?'

We pulled to a stop at a junction, the traffic streaming past me in a blur in both directions. I really needed to concentrate.

'Oh, I don't know!' I said, growing exasperated. 'I don't keep a log of these things. Last year sometime. Late summer, perhaps?'

'Right. And when did you two start going out together then?'

'Properly? Not until Christmas.'

I'd fallen in love with him long before that. Hook, line and sinker. I first realised I had feelings for him when we went away together on the charity run to France. Of course I hadn't known then he had a glamorous girlfriend back at home. It wasn't until after he and Sasha split that the flame between us began to grow. We'd had a few false starts, a few reckless nights of passion, some misunderstandings, but we'd come together in the end. At Christmas. Like a festive romantic comedy film with the perfect happy ending. Only now it wasn't looking so perfect.

'Right. Exactly. So it could be Max's baby then?'

'No!' *Yes.* 'Of course it isn't.' If I just kept telling myself that then maybe I could make it be true. Katy gave me a doubtful look. 'Look Katy, I know about as much as you do. It's Max we need to talk to.'

'Well what I don't understand is why else would Sasha come back to the village?'

All I wanted was for Katy to stop talking. Her constant questioning was making my head throb, her questions only giving voice to the very concerns and fears I had. I really liked this girl, but honestly, I was on the verge of throttling her.

'I have no idea. She said she liked it here. That it would be a great place to bring up a baby.' Even to my own ears, I was sounding reasonable, level-headed and calm. The complete opposite to what was going on inside of me.

'I mean, Sasha does know that you and Max are an item now?'

'Yes, of course she does.' I paused, pondering on that. 'Well, I think she does.' Truth was, I wasn't sure about anything anymore.

'Oh my god, the bastard!'

'Katy. Please! There's no need for that.'

'If Max is messing you about then I'll bloody murder him!'

Glancing across at her, I didn't doubt her intention for a minute.

'You're jumping to conclusions,' I told her. The very same conclusions I'd been jumping to myself, admittedly.

Maybe Max had only just found out himself. Maybe this had been what he was going to tell me. That Sasha was pregnant. The only remaining question was who exactly was the father?

'Are you not coming in?'

We'd driven up the long and imposing drive of Braithwaite Manor and I'd pulled the car up beside the water fountain in the turning circle.

'No, I won't. I have to get back to the pub. There's a meeting tonight of the summer fair committee and I've said I'd be there.' I was glad of the excuse even if it was the last thing I wanted to do right now.

'But what about Max? You need to speak to him. Find out what's going on. Aren't you desperate to know all the details?'

'Yep,' I nodded. 'But not now. I really can't face Max yet. It will have to wait.'

'What am I supposed to say to him then?' asked Katy. 'Just pretend that we didn't bump into Sasha today?'

'Do what you think is best?' I said, pulling her towards me for a hug, feeling a surge of affection for this young girl. In just a short space of time I'd grown to love her feisty, opinionated, and funny ways. I loved her directness and her honesty. At her age I hadn't been nearly as gutsy. I certainly wasn't about to tell her what she should or shouldn't say to Max. I didn't want her feeling caught in the middle of us. And even if I asked her not to mention bumping into Sasha, I wouldn't have the slightest hope she'd be able to keep to that promise.

I shared Katy's impatience, but I knew for the sake of a couple of days, I was better off biding my time and seeing what transpired. If I spoke to Max now I couldn't trust myself to say the right thing, not to fly off the handle, or worse still, dissolve into a snivelling heap of tears.

I suppressed a sigh. It would have to come though and my heart sank at the prospect of that conversation, but at the moment I was too much of a hot mess of emotion. My head was a complete muddle, tangled thoughts vying for attention. I needed to get myself under control, to present a calm exterior to Max when he told me the truth of the situation with Sasha. Why were we even needing to have this conversation though? Part of me still couldn't believe it. Up until today the only thing we needed to worry about was when we were going to next see each other, if we could find the time to snatch some precious moments together. Now, there was something hanging over us, that could change our relationship forever. There was no way I was going to stand back and watch Max and Sasha play happy families right under my nose, if that was what he wanted. And if it wasn't his baby, then, as Katy had quite rightly asked, what exactly was Sasha doing back in the village? If she didn't want to bring up her baby in London, she could have chosen to go anywhere else in the country, so why exactly had she picked Little Leyton?

After dropping off Katy and her bags at the manor, I headed back to the pub in the car, relieved to be on my own at last. A bit of distance and some time alone was just what was needed.

Outside, the weather was warm and the windows to the pub were opened when I pulled up. It looked so inviting, taking centre stage in the High Street. A few hardy types were sitting on the wooden benches, enjoying an afternoon drink. Polly had put up the hanging baskets and they lined the front and sides of the old building in a riot of bright colours. Pinks and mauves and reds, heralding the arrival of summer. Any other time and I would have been buoyed by the sight, but right now it was as if I was immune to their charms.

'Hi Ellie,' said Dan, greeting me as I walked through the main door. 'Oh, is everything okay? You look a bit peaky?'

'Yes, fine. Just a bit tired that's all.' Exhausted more like. The events of the afternoon had depleted all my energy. A tiredness, like nothing I'd experienced before swept me up and wrapped me tightly in its hold. 'Everything okay here?' I asked, looking around.

'Yes. Busy,' said Dan with a smile. 'I think the sunshine has brought everyone out. You look as though you're in need of a cuppa and a sit down. Do you want me to put the kettle on?'

'No, don't worry, I might just pop upstairs, but just give me a shout if you need anything. I...' Well, I didn't get to finish my sentence. A sudden surge of nausea overtook me and I rushed out of the room, dashing to the loo and promptly throwing up everywhere, cursing Max Golding as I did. Damn that man. As much as I loved him, if he had the ability to make me physically ill then I really needed to consider if he was good for my well-being.

Hot, sweaty and exhausted, I stayed curled over the toilet bowl feeling wretched. Later, after cleaning myself up, I climbed into bed, and closed my eyes for a moment, determined to shut out all thoughts of Max and Sasha. A ten-minute power nap would do me the world of good.

Fourteen

'Oh shit!' Two hours later I woke with a start. For the briefest, most blissful moment, just as I was coming to, the earlier events of the day escaped me, until the bombshell came crashing back into my world again.

Then something else dawned on me as I looked at the clock, I should have been downstairs five minutes ago for the meeting about the summer fair. To be honest, it was the last thing I needed, but duty called. I dashed into the bathroom, splashed my face with cold water, ran the brush through my hair and, looking at my reflection in the mirror, decided it would have to do.

'Oh there you are, Ellie. We were just about to start without you. We do have rather a lot to get through this evening.' I heard the admonishment in Josh's words, but chose to ignore it. I was still too caught up in thoughts of Sasha and Max.

A group of villagers had gathered around the long table in the back bar for the final planning meeting of the Little Leyton Summer Fair Committee. Josh Reynolds from the antiques shop, our Chairman, was presiding over the proceedings and I intended to hover in the background, eager to hear about this year's plans but also keeping an eye on the goings-on in the pub. We had a full house in tonight. The knitting group were in the front bar, their needles clicking in tune with their lively conversation. A bunch of my lovely regulars – not the same ones who I'd had my falling out with the other day – were propping up the bar discussing last night's European football cup tie, and my parents' neighbours from Ivy Lane Cottages, Paul and Caroline, were huddled together in the bay window peering over a laptop deciding on their next holiday destination. George Williamson was in as well, I noticed, occupied by a book and with a pint of beer at his side, giving out clear 'please do not disturb me' signals.

'Right, well following on from our previous meeting,' said Josh, addressing the table. 'All the stallholders from last year have been contacted and all, without exception, have signed up to be part of this year's festivities, which is good news. We've also got some first-timers coming along too, they're all shown on the bottom of the list in front of you. New events include the fun dog show, do you want to say a bit about that, Ellie?'

I grabbed a copy of the list Josh was referring to from the centre of the table and forced myself to focus on the summer fair.

'Oh, right, yes, er well it's going to take place in the main arena, and all dogs are welcome. It will be a £1.00 entry for every class and we're thinking of having six classes, most handsome boy, the prettiest dame, waggiest tail, best OAP for the over eight's, best newcomer for the under two's, something like that anyway, and then an overall best in show.'

'Hmm, I haven't got a dog, but I'm thinking I could

enter my Steve in the best OAP class,' said Betty Masters, chuckling.

'That's a bit unfair,' said Tim Weston, editor of The Leyton Post and golfing buddy to Steve. 'Don't you think he'd be better suited to Most Handsome Boy?'

Betty grimaced exaggeratedly before saying, 'Well that's a matter of opinion. One thing I can tell you, he's never going to qualify for waggiest tail, that's for sure!'

'Right, well, moving on,' said Josh, trying to bring back some order to the proceedings, as the table erupted into floods of laughter. 'The other new event is the children's fancy dress competition. I think there's going to be a theme of some sort, but Ann Jones from the Mother and Toddler group can provide all the details,' he said, gesturing in her direction. I sighed inwardly. I'd been trying to push all thoughts of Sasha and Max to the back of my head, but just the mention of a mother and toddler group could bring it to the forefront of my mind again.

Ann handed round some posters she'd prepared for the 'Beneath the Sea' competition which would go up around the village and in the local schools.

'Good. Well, this looks splendid. The produce competitions will take place as usual in the village hall with plenty of different categories. Refreshments will be served there and on the Green. And I'm sure, as in previous years the pub will be doing its own brand of special hospitality throughout the day.' Josh cast me a glance.

'Oh yes, hopefully, and weather permitting, we'll be out in the garden serving a selection of exotic summer cocktails, fruit punches and some special summer ales and ciders too, alongside our normal drinks obviously.'

'Right, a reminder that the date of the fair has been brought forward this year and is now confirmed as the 21st of June. We will need to make sure that everyone is aware of the change.'

'Well,' grumbled Bill West, who hadn't said a word up until now. 'I don't know what this nonsense is all about. It's part of the Little Leyton tradition to have the fair over the bank holiday weekend in August. We've done it that way for years, so why change it now?'

'I can understand your reservations, Bill,' said Josh, 'but as you know it's something we've been considering for a while now. It was felt that it was too late on in the year and a lot of people were missing out because they choose to go away that particular weekend just before the schools go back in September. Bringing it forward we're hoping more people will be able to attend. I have to say we've been very unlucky with the weather over that particular weekend too. Who knows, maybe June will be kinder to us.'

'Pah!' Bill was clearly not impressed. 'We can't rely on good weather anytime of the year and a bit of light rain never hurt anyone.'

That was true, I thought smiling, but in recent years we'd seen more than a bit of light rain. It was uncanny. Last year there'd been thunder, lightning and torrential rain, and the previous year had been a complete washout too with the grass becoming water-logged and swampy and a lot of stallholders throwing in the towel early to escape the miserable conditions. Then there was the year there'd been a terrible gale and the wind had ripped through the tents on the Green, sending plastic tables and chairs flying through the air. There'd been a lot of cursing then and a lot of laughter too as people chased across the grass attempting to retrieve their possessions. Ah, the joys of an English summer! Still, it had only proved to me one thing that I'd always known, that Little Leyton villagers were nothing if not hardy and stoical. A bit of bad weather couldn't mar our enjoyment of what was one of the highlights on the Little Leyton social calendar. Still I was keeping my fingers crossed that this year the sun would actually shine on us for once.

With Josh working his way down the agenda at a steady pace, I slipped out of the room and popped behind the bar to check that Dan and Andy were coping okay, and with their reassurance that they were, I went through to the kitchen. Earlier in the day, before our fateful shopping trip, I'd prepared some trays of sandwiches and put them away in the fridge for later. Now I peeled off the cling film and carried the silver platters through to the back room, laying them down in the middle of the tables.

'Oh, Ellie, you always look after us so well,' said Mary, her eyes lighting up at the arrival of the food.

'Has everyone got drinks?' I asked. 'I can make some teas and coffees if anyone would like one.'

'No, come and sit down, Ellie,' directed Josh, helping himself to an egg and cress on brown bread. 'We're just coming on to the evening celebrations. I think you probably know more about this than I do. First off, where is this shindig going to be taking place?'

'Well, there's good news on that front,' I said, pulling out a chair and sitting down next to Mary. 'Max Golding has said we can use the grounds of Braithwaite Manor for the event. Becks' Farm Shop have offered to provide a marquee and Max will take care of all the services to the tent, like power and electricity.'

'Really? Well that's splendid news.'

'Yes.' I nodded, agreeing, but I couldn't help acknowledge the pang of sadness I felt inside. I'd been so excited when Max had agreed to my idea to hold the do at Braithwaite Manor, he hadn't needed any persuading at all. Now, I wasn't even sure we'd still be a couple by the time the summer fair rolled round.

'Did someone mention it would be a barn dance with a hog roast?' asked Mary.

'Well that was one suggestion, but having asked around, the most popular idea seems to be a masked summer ball,' I said, crossing my fingers behind my back. Now I had the perfect dress for the night I really didn't want to have to change it, even if the very idea of the ball had lost some of its appeal now. 'That's if everyone here is in agreement, of course?'

'Oh, I like that idea,' said Mary.

'Yes, I think Max's place would lend itself wonderfully to a summer ball.' I still had a job to do convincing the others that the ball was the right event for the occasion. 'Imagine...' I said, taking the opportunity to give my sales spiel, '... a sultry summer evening, fairy lights lining the pathway down to a billowing tent, everyone dressed up in their best clothes, sparkling wine flowing, music playing in the air and love and goodwill all around.' I looked across at the faces of Bill, Tim and Josh, who were obviously not feeling it yet, and I wondered if my low mood was rubbing off on them. 'No really, think about it!' I said, rallying. 'It would be great fun.'

'Yes, absolutely,' said Ann, who was doing a great job as my wingman.

'Well it sounds okay to me,' said Betty. 'A good excuse to get my posh frock out and I don't get many of those opportunities these days.'

Bill shrugged noncommittally, which to be fair wasn't a bad sign coming from him. 'I've got a balaclava I could wear, would that do?' he asked wryly. 'To be honest, as long as I can get myself a few beers, then I don't really mind what's going on around me.'

'Right, well are we all agreed on this idea of the ball then?' Josh asked, his gaze casting around the table to be met by a muted, if resolute acceptance. 'Okay splendid! A midsummer's night ball, it is then.'

Strictly speaking, I shouldn't be party to these conversations as I wasn't actually a committee member, but ever since they'd been holding their meetings in the pub I'd become an honorary member, providing advice and suggestions when required, not to mention a lovely selection of sandwiches. Besides, I liked being in the thick of the action and knowing what was going on ahead of time.

Now, the discussion moved on to the catering – a three-course sit-down meal was the preferred option – and music – a live band playing a selection of old classics and some current pop favourites. Someone mentioned that Ryan Lockwood who worked at Becks' Farm Shop played in a jazz funk band whose growing reputation was spreading around the county, so Ann was given the task of asking Ryan to see if they'd be available to play at the ball.

We were very lucky in Little Leyton to have a great number of talented and creative people to call on for support in providing both financial and practical help. The local butchers would supply the meat at cost price, the caterers were offering their services for free, and Polly had already agreed to provide some table flower arrangements at a knock-down price too.

After a bit of toing and froing, the ticket price for the summer ball was agreed upon and Mary jotted it down in the minutes.

'I think that's a very reasonable price,' I piped up. 'When you think that people will be getting a three-course meal and live entertainment, and a brilliant time to boot. And there's still enough room in that price for us to hopefully raise some funds for our chosen charities. Because, after all, that's one of the main aims for this event.'

'Good point,' said Josh. 'Which leads us on quite nicely to the thorny topic of where we want the proceeds from our summer extravaganza to go. Last year, our two charities were the Calais refugee fund and the local children's hospice. Two very worthwhile causes.'

'I don't doubt that's true, them being worthwhile and everything,' said Bill, 'but so is every other charity out there. And there're so many of them. The village and the pub, in particular, have done a lot of fundraising for the refugee fund, but I wonder if we shouldn't look at charities a bit closer to home now.'

'Oh, I do agree,' said Betty. 'The summer fair is very much a village affair. It would be nice for the proceeds to go to organisations within the village. We want to keep supporting the hospice because they do such vital work, but there are plenty of other groups locally that could do with a bit of help too.'

'Yes, you're right, Betty. I think we should support those local charities, but I also think there's room for us to give to an international charity too. You only need to turn on the news or look in the newspapers to see all the terrible things going on in the world today. It would be nice to think we could do something small to help. You never know, our money could go to help out people living in a village just like ours, on the other side of the world. How about we come up with a list of the charities we think we might want to support and then go from there?'

In the end, and with less arm-wrangling than I'd expected, we agreed that proceeds from this year's Little Leyton summer fair would go toward four charities. Three local charities – the children's hospice, the scout hut new roof fund and the local dog and cats rescue centre – and an overseas aid fund too.

'Right, well I think we've covered everything,' said Josh, looking relieved to have got through the agenda without any major fallings-out. 'Unless there's anything else anyone would like to mention?'

'I was thinking,' said Mary, 'as we're going all out this year, if we might be able to rope in a local celebrity to do the grand opening of the fair. It would be good publicity and might bring in some more people from outside the area.'

'That's a great idea,' said Tim Weston. 'It would definitely generate some interest and make for good copy in the paper.'

'Yes, depending on who it is, we could ask them to donate something to the charity auction too. A signed football from a footballer or a dinner for two cooked by a celebrity chef,' said Josh.

With a lot of head nodding, everyone was in agreement that it was a fantastic idea.

'Only trouble is, do we know any local celebrities we could ask?' said Ann.

'Hmm, well Sylvia Robbins used to live in Upper Leyton,' said Tim.

'Who?' Ann and I asked in unison.

'She's an actress,' explained Tim. 'Appeared in those old Ealing comedy films. She was a real beauty in her day.'

'Didn't she die a few years ago?' asked Betty.

'Oooh.' Tim grimaced. 'You might be right there. Alive and kicking celebrities need only apply then.'

We all fell silent for a moment, obviously going through our address books in our heads to see if we could find any famous people lurking there. Going by the blank expressions it wasn't looking hopeful, but our thoughts were soon interrupted by someone appearing in the doorway.

'Oi, oi,' said Tim, jocularly. 'Here's the Lord of the Manor. Perhaps he should be our celebrity for the day. What do you reckon?'

Everyone laughed, amused by the interruption, but not me.

'Max?' I said, my heartbeat immediately going into overdrive.

'I need to speak to you, Ellie. Now please.'

Was he really expecting me to jump up from my seat and go running to him. Er no, especially not when he had that pompous voice on and a disapproving look in his eye. I raised the palms of my hands in the air, gesturing to the people around me. Had he failed to notice that I was in the middle of something here?

'I'm busy at the moment, Max.'

He'd had plenty of occasions to talk to me about Sasha, but he'd decided now was the time that suited him. Well tough luck, I wasn't about to drop everything just to fit in with him.

'This is rather important,' he insisted.

'Yes, and so is this.'

A nervous giggle came from Betty which cut through the tension currently radiating between Max and me. She leant across the table and picked up the piece of paper with the agenda on.

'Let's have a look here,' she said. 'Ah yes, as I thought, under Any Other Business – Max to talk to Ellie.'

I glared at her, really not appreciating the comment, and she gave an apologetic shrug.

'Well actually, I think we're all pretty much done here.' Josh picked up his pile of papers and tapped each side of them on the table, indicating that he was bringing the meeting to a close.

'No, no we're not. We were just discussing our local celebrity. Go away, Max,' I said, pointing to the door, unable now to hide my irritation. 'Whatever it is will have to wait until we're finished.'

'Right,' he said brusquely. 'I'll be in the other bar.'

I breathed a sigh of relief when he went. How dare he waltz in here and expect me to drop everything for him. Causing an unnecessary scene in front of my friends.

'Soooooooo...' Josh attempted to pick up where we'd ignominiously left off, while Betty took a sip of water, Bill smiled, and everyone tried to act as though that whole embarrassing episode had never happened. 'I think we're all agreed that having a celebrity to open the fair is a good idea. It's just a case of finding one. Perhaps I can leave that with you, Ellie? You have a lot of contacts locally. Maybe you can find us someone?'

'Sure, leave it with me,' I said resignedly. Alongside running the pub, and sorting out all the other hassle going on in my life right now, I was certain finding a local celebrity would be an absolute breeze.

Fifteen

After the members of the committee had left, I took a moment to compose myself, hoping that Max would have given up waiting and gone home. I really didn't want to face him now. Tomorrow, after a good night's sleep, I could go down to the manor and we could talk everything through in a calm and reasonable manner. Although obviously I would need to practise calm and reasonable thoughts in my bed tonight.

No such luck. As soon as I ventured out of the back bar, Max jumped up from his stool and came over to my side.

'Look Max, can we do this tomorrow?' I asked. 'I'm tired. It's been a long day and I really don't think I can face this right now.'

'Don't you? Well, it won't take long.'

Why was he being so arsey towards me when I hadn't done anything wrong? What had Katy told him? That I'd been upset and angry after we'd bumped into Sasha? What else would he have expected?

I led him into the kitchen away from prying eyes, annoyance prickling the length of my skin. 'Right.' I turned to look at him, caught by the intensity of his gaze. 'What is it, Max? What's so important?'

I braced myself for his reply.

'You really need to ask me that?' His shook his head, his jaw held rigid with tension. 'Is there anything you want to tell me, Ellie?'

'What?'

No. He wasn't going to turn this on me and make me feel guilty somehow. He was the one who wanted to talk, so he could go right ahead and start talking. Only he didn't. He just stood there, filling my kitchen with his imposing presence, staring at me accusingly.

A knot of unease grew in my stomach.

'About my sister, perhaps?' he said, finally.

'Katy?' I said, tentatively. What had Sasha being pregnant got to do with Katy? And why was he angry at me?

'Yes, that's right. Katy! That sister. Remember? The one who's seventeen years old and was apparently in here the other night paralytically drunk, making out with a load of guys. What would you know about that?'

'Oh Max!'

I turned away from the intensity of his gaze, trying to get my head straight. Max wanted to talk about Katy? But what about Sasha, I wanted to scream. Didn't I deserve some kind of explanation? Emotion flared in my chest, but throwing his ex-girlfriend's name into the mix right now would only make matters much worse. I took a deep breath.

'Look, I know how it must seem, but it wasn't like that. She was just a bit tipsy that's all.'

'Right. So you were aware that my sister was drunk, tipsy, call it what you will, and yet you decided not to mention it? I came back from Ireland and both of you looked me in the eye and told me everything had been fine in my absence. I had to find out from someone I barely know while out in the village this afternoon. What the hell is wrong with you, Ellie?'

My whole body bristled as Max looked at me, contempt in his eyes. 'Don't you dare blame me!' I brushed past him and pulled the door closed so that our voices wouldn't reach into the bar. Half my clientele thought I was a temperamental woman as it was, I didn't want the other half jumping on the bandwagon too.

'What were you doing serving her in the first place? She's just a kid!'

'I wasn't even here. I'd been out with Polly, round at Josie's, and when I came home I found her in the back bar with a group of lads.'

'That's no excuse. This is your pub and you have responsibility for who gets served. Don't you train your staff to look out for underage drinkers?'

'Please do not presume to tell me how to run my own pub.' I could have cried I was so annoyed at him, but I wasn't about to give him that satisfaction. I steadied my voice. 'I know that it's my responsibility and I take that very seriously, but Katy had managed to get a fake ID from somewhere – it was very convincing.'

'Oh come on! You only need look at her to tell she's underage. God, Ellie, I wouldn't have expected this from you. I go away for one night and this is what happens!' He lifted his hands in the air, shaking his head.

'Max,' I said, trying desperately to keep my bubbling frustration and anger under control. 'You're acting as if this is my fault. It isn't. Yes, it was unfortunate that she got drunk, but it certainly won't be happening here again.'

'*Unfortunate*! It was more than bloody unfortunate.

Anything could have happened to her. It doesn't bear thinking about.'

'Yes, well it didn't. And she seems none the worse for the experience. Come on, Max, you were seventeen once. You must know what it's like. She's probably learned a valuable lesson from what happened the other night.'

'Oh believe you me, she's learnt a lesson, all right. She's grounded. Until further notice. If she's going to act like an irresponsible teenager then that's how I'll treat her.'

'For goodness sake, Max!' His indignant self-righteousness was seriously winding me up. ' She's struggling with enough as it is. You laying down the law will only make matters worse.'

He turned to glare at me. How could such dark and beautiful eyes that held the power to seduce me with their intensity now appraise me so dispassionately.

'I really don't need your advice on how to look after my sister. Not when you think condoning her behaviour and keeping secrets from me is a responsible way to behave.'

'And *I* really don't need to listen to this. You're completely out of order. If you want to question anyone's behaviour then you'd do better looking at yourself than blaming me. If you hadn't gone swanning off on yet another business meeting then all this would never have happened. You left a seventeen-year-old girl alone, what did you expect to happen? Katy admitted she doesn't like being stuck in the manor on her own and I don't blame her. How much time have you spent talking to her? Really talking to her. Finding out what's troubling her? Finding out what she does and doesn't like? When I took her home, she was really scared about being left alone. Thankfully she was so tired, she fell straight to sleep, but she shouldn't have been put into that position.'

'You took her home?'

'Yes, and Polly. You don't think I'd leave her to make her own way home in the state she was in, do you?'

'Right.' His mouth was set in a firm, hard line. 'Well thanks for that anyway,' he said, begrudgingly.

'I don't want your thanks, Max.' I turned away from him, biting on my lip, not trusting myself to come out with something much worse, clutching my arms around my chest. I was furious at his attitude, that somehow this whole situation was down to me. Only a few days ago he'd been whispering sweet nothings in my ear and now he was spitting venom at me.

'What I don't understand is why the hell you didn't tell me about it. You had the perfect opportunity at the house. Instead you keep me in the dark and let me find out from some guy I just happened to bump into in the High Street. That's what pisses me off the most, Ellie. She's my sister. You don't have the right to keep those sorts of things from me.'

'Oh get over yourself, Max. I didn't tell you because she asked me not to. She got drunk, it's not the biggest crime in the world. She knew what your reaction would be and swore me to secrecy. What was I supposed to do? She put her trust in me and I didn't want to abuse that trust. I get the distinct impression that Katy could do with some friends around here. There wasn't some great conspiracy to keep you out of the picture. It just seemed like the easiest way to deal with the situation.'

'Why does that not surprise me. That you'd take the easiest option rather than doing the right thing.'

'What! Don't twist my words.' I span round to look at him again. Our eyes locked in mutual loathing. 'You know that's not what I meant. I can't believe you would even say that. I went out of my way to help Katy and all you can do is have a go at me.' Suddenly I wanted him out. Out of my pub and out of my way. I didn't want to look at him anymore. To hear his voice, sharp and unforgiving. 'Just go, Max.'

'I really didn't need this, not today. Not from you, Ellie.' He stormed towards the door, flinging it open and strode out.

Unthinking, fury filling my veins, I ran after him.

'There you go again! Blaming me! This wasn't my fault and you are being totally unreasonable. You're an idiot, Max Golding,' I called after him. 'Do you know that?'

'Thank you. I'm glad you hold me in such high esteem, Ellie.'

I could have said so much more. It took all my self control not to confront him over Sasha, to demand to know what secrets he'd been keeping from me. It was only knowing that there were still some customers drinking in the bar that stopped me. But although there were plenty of people around, I realised, with a pang of sadness, I had never felt more alone in my life.

Sixteen

It had been a less than peaceful night as I'd lay tossing and turning, mulling over the argument I'd had with Max, and now it was a less than peaceful morning. A loud banging on the front door accompanied by the chorus of a rabble of barking dogs roused me from my bed. I dashed along the landing to the front bedroom and peered out of the window overlooking the High Street to see Katy standing below with Holly and Bella at her side. 'Hang on a minute,' I said, relieved to see her. 'I'm coming down.'

I pulled open the door. 'Crikey, you're an early bird,' I said, checking my watch. 'And anyway, I thought you were grounded?'

'I was, but I offered to walk the dogs and Max agreed. You don't mind, do you? Me just turning up like this. I wanted to see how you were.' We wandered through into the kitchen and Digby gave a friendly welcome to the other two dogs before they all scooted outside into the beer garden. I popped the kettle on and Katy sat down at the kitchen table. 'I know Max came down to see you last night and I was worried. He was in such a filthy mood when he left and then an even worse one when he came home again. I really hope I didn't get you into too much trouble. It's not fair that he had a go at you about it though. It wasn't your fault. You were only trying to help me. I told him as much, but he wasn't really listening.'

'Well, he's your brother. He's bound to feel protective towards you. And I don't think he took too kindly to me not telling him what happened.'

'I'm so sorry, Ellie. You two are still good together though?' she asked, looking concerned.

To be honest, I had no idea. A couple of days ago and I'd thought my future with Max had been looking promising, but in the space of twenty-four hours we'd had our first humdinger of a row and I still didn't know why he was suddenly taking such a keen interest in the life of his pregnant ex-girlfriend.

'I'm sure it will all blow over,' I said noncommittally. *One way or the other.*

'And what about Sasha? Did you tell him we ran into her?'

'No.' So clearly Katy hadn't mentioned it either. Thankfully. After our row, I really couldn't face any more confrontation just yet. 'We never got round to it. I will have to talk to him some time though.'

She took the mug of tea I proffered and blew on it, before taking a tentative sip. She winced as the boiling hot liquid stung her mouth, but it didn't deter her, as she immediately took several more lip-burning sips. Her gaze drifted around my kitchen, searching out the worktops, lingering over the bread bin, and eyeing up the couple of boxes of cereal on the side.

'Are you hungry by any chance?' I said, laughing. 'Would you like some breakfast?'

'Oh well, I wouldn't want to put you to any trouble,' she said, smiling sweetly, as though the idea hadn't occurred to her.

'Bacon sandwich?' I asked, pulling out the frying pan from the cupboard, as she nodded her eager response.

'So how did the meeting go last night?'

'Yeah, it was good. Well it was until your brother showed up and made a scene, but I think we'll just gloss over that bit. Honestly, I think it's going to be our best summer fair ever this year, we've got so many events lined up, culminating in an amazing masked summer ball at the manor in the evening. You'll have to come, Katy, if you're still here by then.'

'Oh, I'll definitely be here, well unless Max carries out his threat to put me on the first plane back to Spain, if I should go drinking again.' She glanced across at me and gave a little giggle.

'You know he doesn't mean it?'

She shrugged. 'Well, I've told him, if he does, I'm getting the first plane straight back to England again.'

I smiled, those two were more than an equal match for each other. I buttered four slices of bread and loaded the sizzling bacon evenly between them, squirting a generous dollop of tomato ketchup on top. Wedging the two halves together, I handed one plate over to Katy and took mine over to join her at the table.

'I've been given the lovely job of finding a local celebrity to open the summer fair and to make an appearance as Guest of Honour at the ball. Trouble is we couldn't come up with any suggestions as to who might be able to do it.' Seduced by the smell of the frying bacon, the dogs had come flying in and were mooching beneath the table on the scrounge. 'At this rate, I might have to make Digby the Guest of Honour for the night.'

'Well you know who you should ask, don't you?'

'Who?'

'GG Williamson.'

Katy was looking at me as though I should know exactly who she was talking about, but despite a very faint bell ringing in the back of my head, I had no idea.

'You know, the writer!' she cried, growing impatient with me. 'I've read every single one of his books. I just love them and can't wait for his next one to be released. That's what he's working on now. It's coming out just before Christmas.'

'Ah right, yes.' It was coming to me now. Vaguely. 'The one who writes those funny detective stories?'

'Yes. There's going to be a TV series next year as well.'

Katy was clearly a super fan and if she had her choice of celebrity to open the summer fete then it would be this GG Williamson person. If it had been down to me it would have been George Clooney, but then we all have our dreams, don't we?

'Great,' I said, half-heartedly, distracted by the thought of George Clooney now and, more seductively, the second half of my oozing sandwich.

'So why don't we ask him then?'

'What? Oh, I think he lives in LA and has a villa on the Italian Lakes. Oh, and a beautiful wife too. I'm not sure the charms of Little Leyton are going to be enough to drag him away.'

Katy looked at me blankly, her head dropping to one side, her expression questioning.

'George Clooney? I was just thinking about...'

'*Nooooo*. Not George Clooney. Have you been listening to a word I've said? GG Williamson! I bet he'd say yes if we asked him.'

My mind snapped back to the moment. 'Do we even know where he lives or how would we contact him?'

Katy shook her head slowly. 'Honestly, Ellie! Do you really not know? GG Williamson. He comes into your pub most nights. Dark blond hair, stubble, sits on the front table with his laptop and notebooks, and a pint of beer.'

'Oh my god! You mean George! No. Surely not? George Williamson?'

'Yes.' Katy laughed. 'That's what I've been trying to tell you.'

'Oh my goodness. He lives in my house, well my parents' house. I had no idea what he was doing up there and I did wonder. I thought he was a bit of a loner. Someone who likes to keep himself to himself. I didn't think. I didn't know... He's...'

'Hot. Talented. Super cool.' Katy was only too willing to fill in the blanks. 'All of those things. The reason he's been so quiet is that he's been working to a deadline. That's why he came to the village. To finish his latest book. His series of books are bestsellers and if he doesn't produce his next book in time, then all his readers will be up in arms and he'll get into trouble with his publishers. I recognised him in the pub and went over to talk to him, to tell him how much I admired his work. He was so lovely, he offered to sign all my books for me and he's promised me a signed copy of his new one when it's released.'

'Crikey. Who would have thought it? Here we are

searching for a celebrity and all the time we've had one in the village right under our noses.'

'He said that's why he chose Little Leyton because he didn't know anyone here and he thought he'd be able to blend into the background without anyone recognising him.'

I cringed inwardly thinking about the first time I'd met him, turning up unexpectedly on his doorstep with my cake wanting to stop for a long getting-to-know-us chat, when he'd been clearly desperate to get rid of me. Now I knew why!

'Yes, but if he's come to the village specifically to keep a low profile, I don't suppose he'd be very keen on being our face of the summer fair, and being plastered all over the local newspaper.'

'Well we won't know until we ask him. I think his deadline should have passed now. He told me that once that was out of the way, he'd have a bit more time. He said he was going to be brainstorming ideas and planning out his next book.'

'Right, well we should definitely ask him then,' I said, grateful that my hunt for a celebrity might be solved as easily as that. If only all my other problems could be fixed quite so easily too. 'Next time he's in I'll go and have a word with him.'

At the back door, with Holly and Bella back on their leads, Katy leaned in to kiss me on the cheek, taking me by surprise. 'Thanks for breakfast, and sorry for all the trouble I'm causing you,' she said, looking genuinely contrite. 'You will make it up with Max, won't you?'

Her dark, and oh-so familiar eyes, were flecked with

concern, reaching me inside with their sincerity, but I wasn't about to make any promises I couldn't keep.

'I'll speak to him,' I said, nodding. It was the only thing I could tell her.

*

After the high drama of yesterday, it came as a huge relief to know that today was my day off. To be honest, I'd not been terribly good in making use of my free days and usually just stayed at home, before getting roped into whatever was going on at the pub. Today I was determined not to let that happen.

I knew my stress levels had been building, making me feel tired and out of sorts for the last few days now, and I couldn't blame that entirely on Max Golding. If Mum was here she would have told me to slow down, to get a few early nights in and to look after myself properly. It was easy to forget those simple things without your mum gently chiding you with her concern.

What advice would she be giving me now about Max?

'Don't let him mess you around.'

'If he's not being straight with you then walk away.'

'You don't deserve to feel second best.'

I could hear her voice in my head and would agree one hundred per cent with her sentiment, but I knew it wasn't as straightforward as that. The events of yesterday played on my mind and I mulled them over, trying to see if I could make more sense of them now. Maybe I'd overreacted to Sasha's news, feeling unnecessarily threatened by the unexpected discovery that she was pregnant, my shock only heightened by Katy's presence, who had whipped up my confusion with her constant questions. Maybe I was building this up into something much bigger than it actually was. I just needed to take a step back from it all today.

Upstairs, with my hair wrapped in a towel from my shower, I padded over towards the window and looked out over the beer garden. The sun filtered through the clouds casting a warm glow over the enclosed space. A few weeks ago, Dan, Rich, Andy and I had put in a mammoth cleaning up session. We'd pressure-washed the tables, chairs and benches, repainted the walls a warm cream colour, pulled up the weeds, trimmed the climbing bushes, installed some patio heaters and replaced all the cushions with new candy-striped ones. The blankets in the basket by the door to the garden, for those nights when there was a cold nip in the air, had been replaced with some new cosy ones too. A raised decking area had been installed at the back of the yard to provide more seating and with Polly's beautiful hanging baskets and the tall ferns in the patio containers providing bold and striking relief, it made for a warm and welcoming space. The barn at the back of the patio, where we held our open-mic nights, and private parties, looked so pretty with the wooden boxes of bright red geraniums outside. I felt so proud of the wonderful space we'd created and relished the thought of how busy it would be soon with all our visitors over the summer. With it being totally empty and peaceful now though, and the warmth of the sun beckoning me outside, it seemed like an opportunity too good to miss.

Quickly, I threw off my towel and gave my hair a quick blast with the hairdryer, before climbing into my clothes, and going downstairs. Making myself a mug of tea, I ventured outside with my book, surprised at how warm the sun was on my skin. I pulled out one of the big wooden chairs and sat down, stretching my legs out in front of me on to another chair, lifting my face to the sky, luxuriating in the warmth of the day. I delved into my book, and soon I was lost in another world, pleased to escape the realities of mine. It was only when a shadow fell over me and I looked up, squinting my eyes against the brightness of the sun, that I realised I'd been sitting there for over an hour.

'Oh hi Dan!'

'Feeling better today?'

'Oh yes, all fine now, thank you,' I said, brushing his concern away. 'I reckon we did a good job out here, don't you? It's such a beautiful space. You know, I might make it part of my daily routine to come out here for a quiet spell each morning.'

'You should. You won't get much chance when the punters start flooding in.'

'I'll be out today, Dan, but any problems and you can always call me on my mobile.'

'Don't worry. We'll deal with them. Just go out and have a good day, and forget about the place for once.'

'Thanks, Dan.'

Knowing the pub was in safe hands, I left and went straight round to Polly's shop. I found her behind her worktop surrounded by buckets of flowers, green foliage, cellophane and ribbons, a pencil behind her ear.

'You look busy!'

Her face lit up to see me.

'Oh I am. Two big corporate orders have come in, plus the usual daily arrangements and bouquets. Mind you, I'm pleased for the distraction. It keeps me from dwelling on a certain Johnny Tay.'

'I've told you, Polly, you need to put the man right out of your mind. That way lays madness.'

'I know and it would be much easier to forget about him if he'd only stop texting and emailing me. Part of me wants to tell him to go and take a running jump, but there's a part of me that loves seeing his name in my inbox.'

'Oh, Polly!' I sighed, rueing ever having encouraged the relationship in the first place.

Just then the bell on the door rang, signalling the arrival of a new customer.

'Look I'll leave you to it, I'm off to see Josie now. She said if you're free after work then to pop in for a glass of wine.'

'You bet! That idea's going to help me get through the rest of the day.'

I wandered off down the road with Digby trotting along happily at my side. In the past few weeks a new energy had been breathed into the High Street. With the arrival of the warmer weather, a lot of the shops had opened up their doors and were displaying their wares outside in brightly coloured baskets. Enjoying my stroll in the sunshine, I put all thoughts of Max and Sasha out of my head, determined not to let those worries spoil my day. I arrived at Josie's house a while later, and she opened the door to greet us, a big smile on her face and baby Stella in her arms.

'I know you weren't expecting me and Polly till later on, but I hope you don't mind me inviting myself around now, do you? It's just that my free days usually whiz past without me really doing anything and I thought this morning, now who would I most like to spend the day with, and of course there was only one possible answer to that question.' I took Stella out of Josie's arms and held her high up in the air, her little face gurgling happily at me.

'What? Are you kidding? It's never an inconvenient time as far you're concerned. Come in. To be honest, I've been going a bit stir-crazy. I could do with some company.'

'What's up?' I asked as we wandered through into the living room. Digby trotted ahead, sniffing all the way, on the lookout for any tidbits that Stella may have dropped, before I called him to my side and put him on his lead. I popped Stella down on her play mat and she immediately took off, on all fours, laughing at Digby, as she did.

'Oh, just the normal stuff. Stella's really grizzly, she's teething I think, so I'm not getting much sleep at the moment. I know she can't help it, bless her, but I turn into a mummy monster if I don't get my eight hours. You know, I sometimes wonder if I'm cut out for this motherhood lark.'

'Don't say that, Josie. You're a brilliant mum.'

She raised her eyebrows, and gave a wry smile. 'Oh, take no notice of me. I didn't know love like this until I had my little girl and I wouldn't swap her for the world, but I guess I just didn't realise how hard it can be at times.'

'Oh Josie, of course it's hard. Have you talked to Ethan about the way you're feeling?'

'Not really.'

'Well it might help. And you could always talk to your doctor too if you needed to. I hate to think of you being unhappy.'

'I'm fine. Really. And Dad will be back soon. That will make everything seem so much better.'

A wave of guilt washed over me. I saw Josie most days

when she came in for her shifts at the pub, and sometimes she popped in for a coffee and a chat, but mostly those meetings were only fleeting. With everything else I'd had going on, I wondered if I'd been guilty of neglecting my oldest friend, at a time when she needed me most.

'Do you fancy a walk?' I asked her. 'It's so beautiful out there.'

'Yes,' she said, jumping up. 'I could do with getting out. I'll just go and grab Stella's changing bag. I'll bring some bread too in case we go down by the pond.'

As we walked around the village, through the park and down the back lanes, with Digby leading the way and me pushing Stella's buggy, we spoke about the christening and the likely numbers for the catering. Josie had decided to have the reception in the back barn at the pub, which was a lovely space for a small gathering. She reckoned on about forty people coming along and I'd offered to lay on the catering.

'What do I need to bring?' she asked.

'Nothing,' I said. 'We'll provide everything. Just bring yourselves and the star of the show, of course.' I stopped for a moment to peer into the buggy. The star of the show was currently fast asleep and looking as cute as a button.

'You'll never guess who I bumped into yesterday?' I said, a little while later, once we'd finished making plans for the christening. I dropped it in casually, as though it was just a small, inconsequential piece of news.

'Who?'

'Sasha.'

'Oh really? I meant to ask how she got on with Max and the cottage?'

'Yep, she loved it apparently; she's already moved in.'

'Oh dear,' said Josie, recognising my less than genuine response to this news. 'So what, is she working with him again then?'

'No. This is a personal move. She wants to make her home here.' I paused, preparing myself to say the words aloud. 'Now that she's pregnant.'

'What the...?' Josie actually stopped dead in her tracks, reached one hand out for the buggy as if to steady herself and turned to look at me, her face a picture of utter disbelief. 'You are kidding me?'

'No.' I shook my head, slowly, purposefully. 'I wish I was.'

'Oh god! Is it Max's baby then?'

I'd been sounding Josie out, wanting to gauge her reaction. To see if I was being totally unreasonable in thinking the worst of Max. But instead my worst fears were being confirmed right here and now. I wasn't being unreasonable after all. Or hormonal or overreacting. Max's ex-girlfriend was pregnant and the natural assumption to make was that it was his baby.

I shrugged my answer and made the mistake of glancing in Josie's eyes, seeing the shock there.

'What? I don't believe it. What's he said about it?'

'That's the thing. Absolutely nothing. I only found out when Katy and I were out shopping yesterday and we bumped into Sasha. There was no way she could have hidden the news. Max hasn't mentioned anything to me. And in a way I wonder if that tells me everything.' I sighed. 'Sasha even said what a rock Max had been.'

'Really? What's that all about then?'

'I honestly don't know.'

'Oh darling!' Josie stopped and threw her arms around me, hugging me tight. 'This is awful. You can't have this hanging over you. You need to speak to him, find out exactly what's going on.'

Feeling the support and affection in Josie's arms around me made me buckle. A huge swell of emotion lodged in my throat and tears filled my eyes. I blinked them away, cross with myself that I was reacting like this. I knew I'd have to have that conversation with Max, but I was scared. Scared of what I'd find out.

A pain ripped through my stomach. What if it was his baby? Knowing Max, he'd want to be fully involved in his child's life. Any decent man would, but would he want to rekindle his relationship with Sasha too to create a proper family environment? There'd be no place for me in that happy little scenario. How would I cope seeing Sasha and Max building a life together in the village? This was where I felt happy, secure and protected, but that peace would be shattered if I knew Max was starting a brand new life with someone else.

'Well do it soon. You have a right to know what's going on. It's not fair on you to be kept in the dark when it affects your life. He is your boyfriend after all.'

That was true, but we'd been going out for less than six months. He and Sasha had over five years in the bank. We didn't even live together. He was occupied by work and I was immersed in the running of the pub. Our relationship was important to both of us, but it hadn't been our main priority. And now it seemed it might never be. Max might have more important things to worry about now.

'God it's all such a mess. I know I'll have to talk to him, but I'm frightened. I just have this feeling, Josie, that I'm going to lose him.'

'You can't know that. Not until you talk to him. Do it soon. Do it now. Go and find him, have it out with him?'

'No,' I shook my head vigorously. 'I can't!'

Normally I didn't stop to think. Normally, I'd go straight ahead and act. Not this time. Something was stopping me from getting in the car and racing round to the manor, knowing that once we'd had that conversation it was likely to change our lives forever. I really wasn't sure I was ready for that yet.

'Let's not talk about it now,' I said. 'Let's just enjoy the sunshine today.' Although that would be easier said than done when my head was full of thoughts of Max, Sasha and an image of their beautiful little baby.

*

Much later, back at Josie's, I fed Stella her tea, a bright orange concoction of sweet potato and carrot that was gobbled up enthusiastically, and then spent a fun time playing with her wooden farm set on the floor, before I happily volunteered to do the bath and bed routine.

'Oh, you should come round every evening,' said Josie, still slumped on the sofa as I carried Stella up the stairs. 'I could get used to this.'

It was no hardship for me. I loved spending time with my goddaughter, even if it was far less often than I would have liked.

With the same red hair as her mum and bright blue

eyes, her little face lit up as we sang songs in the bathroom and later when I placed her in the cot, her little eyelashes fluttered closed as I read a bedtime story. Before Stella came into our lives I hadn't felt in the least bit broody – babies had never featured in any of my plans – but her arrival had stirred all sorts of emotions within me. Love and longing and pride, and she wasn't even mine! Now as I stroked her fine hair over her head, I knew the special bond I had with my best friend's daughter was one that would last us a lifetime. A baby was life-changing in so many ways, a change I could now imagine and hope for myself one day. With Stella drifting off to sleep, I pottered around her bedroom, folding up her clothes, enjoying the moment of peace and quiet.

I bent down and planted a kiss on Stella's head, inhaling her delicious scent. Creeping out of the bedroom, giving one last glance to the now sleeping Stella, my heart swelling at the sight of her tucked up beneath the covers, I made my way back downstairs to find Polly had arrived and was chatting with Josie in the kitchen. Thank goodness for the wonderful women in my life, young and old. They were always there to support me and I was determined not to let whatever was going on with Max spoil my time tonight with my friends. That could wait until tomorrow.

'Hi Ellie,' said Polly, turning to greet me, and pulling me in towards her with a hug. 'How's things?'

'Well...' Best get it over and done with as quickly as possible. I gave her a very rapid-fire run-down of recent events, her mouth dropping open in amazement as I mentioned the pertinent facts.

Sasha, Max's Ex.

Pregnant.

Baby.

When I finished recounting the sorry tale, Polly yelped. 'Noooo! And is it Max's baby?'

The case against Max was growing by the hour.

'I don't know and I really don't want to think about it now. It's been tying me up in knots all day. I'll have to see him tomorrow. Talk to him. I'm not looking forward to it one bit but at least then I'll know for sure one way or the other.'

Both girls pulled a sympathetic face, before Polly said, 'You don't know. We're jumping to conclusions. It's just as likely to be someone else's baby as it is Max's.'

Now it was my turn to look doubtful.

'Anyway, enough about my sorry love life,' I said, desperate to get off the subject. We had moved outside into Josie's small garden and were sitting on the patio, the sweet smell of the blossoming honeysuckle wafting in the air. It was cooler now and I'd wrapped my cardigan around my shoulders. 'You'll never guess what I found out today?'

'There's something else?' said Polly, looking alarmed.

'Yeah, but this isn't bad. This is a bit of juicy gossip. You know that guy who comes in to the pub? The good-looking one who we thought might be from the pub guide?'

'George, you mean?'

'Yes, you'll never believe who he is.' Both Polly and Josie nodded blankly. 'He's actually GG Williamson, the writer. I had no idea, Katy was the one to tell me. She's a real fan of his work and recognised him in the pub. Apparently he came to the village to finish off his next book, although I don't think we're supposed to know that, so keep it under your hats. He's trying to keep a low profile.'

'Really! I thought there was something familiar about him, but I would never have guessed,' said Josie.

'I don't know about familiar, I just think he's really lovely-looking. He's got nice brown eyes,' said Polly, her thoughts clearly taking her off to some faraway place. 'And he's very charming too. And a best-selling writer, you say? Hmmm, I wonder if we can convince him to stay? Little Leyton is in desperate need of some eligible men about the place.'

I laughed. 'I'm not sure about that, but Katy suggested we ask him if he would open the summer fete celebrations for us. It would be a bit of a coup. And would certainly add an extra element to the day.'

'Well if you need my help in persuading him,' said Polly, her throaty chuckle ringing out, 'then just let me know. I'm always willing to do my bit for the village and, to be honest, I could do with the distraction.'

'Oh?'

'Just Johnny,' she said sighing, her shoulders slumping. 'He texted me again. As bold as you like.' She pulled out her phone and read the message aloud:

'Hi Polly, how are you? Been thinking about you a lot recently, wondering how you're doing. Coming home soon. Maybe we can catch up?'

'Aw, it definitely sounds as though he's missing you, Polly,' said Josie.

'What? He has no right to miss me! And there's no

apology. No, "sorry I broke your heart and disappeared into the sunset without a word." Nothing like that. If it was up to me, I wouldn't let him back in the village. I still don't know what went so wrong between us. I thought we had something special together, it felt so exciting being with him and everything seemed full of possibilities. And then out of nowhere he decides he has to get as far away from me as possible. Was I really that awful to send him packing to the other side of the world?'

'You weren't awful at all, Polly. It was just Johnny being an arse,' I offered.

'Definitely. A prize arse,' said Josie, agreeing with me wholeheartedly.

'I suppose you're right. I just don't know how I'm going to cope with him being back on the scene.'

'You'll be fine, Polly. Do all your crying with us in private. And then when he shows up, put on a brave face and show him just what he's been missing all these months.'

'Yeah,' she said, nodding. 'You missed your chance, Johnny Tay!'

'What is it with the men in our lives, Polly?' I asked.

'I've got an idea,' she said, excitedly. 'You know that Grand Tour we talked about for our retirement. Any chance we could bring it forward by about thirty years and go this weekend instead?'

We laughed and raised our glasses to that. If Max was going to start playing happy families with Sasha in the village, then getting as far away as possible from Little Leyton might just turn out to be the best idea ever.

Seventeen

A couple of hours later, we said our goodbyes to Josie, and Polly and I made the short walk back to the pub.

'Think I'll come in,' she said, when we reached the front door. 'I don't fancy going home yet.' She linked her arm through mine, leaning into my side and led the way in, quickly disentangling herself when she spotted George Williamson sitting in his usual spot at the front window.

'Ooh look,' she whispered, a gleeful tone to her voice. 'There's our very favourite author. I won't be long,' she told me, going off to join him. I smiled to myself and slipped behind the bar to chat to Dan and Andy.

'Have you seen Max?' It was the first thing Dan said to me.

'No,' I said, squashing down the sense of alarm his name caused me. I really hoped the Little Leyton grapevine hadn't been working overtime. Did everyone already know the news that I was waiting to have confirmed?

'It's just that he's been in a couple of times looking for you. He went off to find you. Seemed as though it was quite important. He's just rung again actually to see if you were back.'

'Oh, my phone's been playing up,' I said by way of explanation. It was only a little white lie. I'd deliberately turned it off, not wanting to be a slave to it all day long, jumping every time it beeped, thinking it might be Max. Today I'd been trying to forget about the whole matter, although without much success admittedly. 'Do me a favour though. If he calls again can you tell him I'm not home. I'm very tired and I'm sure whatever it is can wait until tomorrow.'

I saw the flicker of surprise cross Dan's face. 'Sure thing.'

In the back bar a group of regulars had gathered and Arthur, one of my favourites, beckoned me over. He'd been a good pal to Noel, Max's grandfather, and the pair of them were always found together sat beside the inglenook fireplace having a chat and a chuckle.

'Hello lovely, how are you?' he asked. 'Come and sit with me awhile.' He patted the empty seat beside him. 'What are you having to drink?'

'No, you have one with me on the house, Arthur.' I called Andy over and asked for a pint of the special ale for Arthur and a long cool glass of elderflower cordial for me. A few days off the booze and I would be back feeling renewed and invigorated. An occupational hazard of the job, drinking too much. I could always tell when I needed to rein it in a little. I would start to feel sluggish and out of sorts, just as I had been these last few days.

'You're not looking your usual bright-eyed self,' said Arthur fondly, peering into my face. 'You're not working too hard, are you, love?'

'No more than usual,' I said with a smile.

There was a nice warm vibe in the back bar this evening.

People huddled together in conversation, the sound of laughter reaching up to the eaves. Those who'd been sitting in the garden had drifted indoors now that the air was that much cooler. A crowd had gathered around Owen Jennings, a local tree surgeon, who had brought his guitar in and was sat on a stool, strumming a few chords, the mellifluous sounds wafting around us in a warm inviting glow. Some people swayed to the gentle notes, others tapped their feet, the music soothing our souls.

'You know, I for one, am very grateful to you for keeping the Dog and Duck just as it has always been,' said Arthur, tapping me on the knee. 'Eric did a grand job, but you've brought something new to the pub, something fresh and special. You've given the place, and all of us, a new lease of life.'

'Aw, Arthur, that's such a lovely thing for you to say.' I leant into his side. 'I've had a few moments when I've wondered if I'm doing things the right way.'

'No, you're doing a brilliant job, love. Look at the crowd in here tonight. They're all having a great time. When you think how many communities have lost their village pub. We're lucky that ours is still thriving and that's all down to you, sweetheart.'

He laid his arm around my shoulder, and I rested my head there. For a moment I closed my eyes, lost in my thoughts, the music washing over me. Owen started singing, his hoarse soulful voice resounding with emotion and honesty. My eyes flickered open again and my gaze travelled around the room alighting on each of my customers. I knew every one of them by name, where they lived and who were the important people in their lives. Arthur telling me what a good job I was doing made me swell with pride. If my regulars were happy then that was all that mattered.

Digby came and joined us, slumping down at my feet. He'd been on walkabout around the pub, mooching around the tables in search of a crumb of affection or a crumb of anything else. He was such a chancer, that dog. I leant down, running my hand across his soft warm fur.

Now, Owen's seductive voice warbled out a familiar folk song and we all joined in, swaying in time to the music. It had been a long time since we'd had a good old sing-song in the pub. In Eric's day they'd been quite a regular occurrence. Impromptu get-togethers, where someone would start humming a tune, and someone else would join in, tapping their hands on the table or whistling in harmony, until the whole of the pub would be singing along. Joyous, life-affirming occasions that made you thankful for all the good things in your life. Right now, with everyone singing their hearts out, I was grateful to be here among my customers and friends.

Just then Dan popped his head across the bar holding the phone up to me and mouthed, 'Max?'

I shook my head. Why spoil the moment? Tonight I just wanted to live for the here and now, without a care or thought to the future. That, I knew, I'd have to face all too soon.

Our singing session went on late into the night. I didn't really see Polly again, apart from when she popped her head around the door to give me a wave goodbye, telling me she'd catch up with me tomorrow. I gave a thought to George and smiled, hoping he hadn't minded being monopolised by Polly when I suspected all he'd wanted was a quiet drink.

With Dan and Andy's help we'd just seen off the last

of our customers, with a lot of hugs and back-slapping, and a promise that we would have to do it all again very soon. Andy was giving a final wipe down of the tables, Dan emerged from the cellar and I was just straightening some chairs, when the front door was flung open and we all stopped what we were doing and turned to see who it might be. A punter returning to collect their belongings? Dan's girlfriend Silke perhaps? Someone trying it on, in the hope they might get a cheeky nightcap?

'Max?' I couldn't hide the surprise in my voice, even if he was beginning to make a habit of late-night visits to the pub.

'Ellie.' His mood always preceded him. Tonight his body was rigid, the set of his jaw and the coldness in his eyes told me he wasn't in the sunniest of moods. Oh... This was just what I needed.

'Have you been avoiding me?' he asked.

Andy discreetly moved out of the way, grabbed his jacket and quickly left. Dan, ignoring the laser death stare radiating from Max, came to my side and asked if I wanted him to stay.

'No, you get off, Dan. Everything's fine here,' I said brightly, following him to the main door, seeing him out and locking up after him. My stomach churned with anxiety, in anticipation of what was about to come. Taking a deep breath, I turned to face Max, who was still appraising me intently. He shook his head as though not even remotely interested in my answer.

'Have you seen Katy?'

'What?' His question took me completely by surprise. 'What do you mean? Is she not at the house?'

'Nope. She went out a few hours ago. I've been texting

and calling her, but she's not picking up. When you weren't taking my calls either I thought perhaps you were together.'

'No, I've not seen her since this morning. She popped in with the dogs for some breakfast. She seemed perfectly fine then.'

Max let out an audible sigh. 'I assumed she was with you. It's me she has the problem with. God, I couldn't have handled this any worse if I'd tried. When she came home from that shopping trip I confronted her about her drinking and she just went completely ballistic at me, saying how I wasn't in a position to judge her. She was totally wound up and then just turned everything back on me.'

My gaze drifted out of the mullioned windows onto the High Street. It was gone midnight and it looked especially dark out there tonight. I'd always felt totally safe and protected in the village, but the thought of Katy being out there alone, upset and emotional, made me nervous.

'I don't know where she could be,' Max went on, the concern in his voice evident. 'I've tried everywhere she might go but I can't find her. And she's still not answering her phone.'

Guilt washed over me. Max had tried to contact me to find out if I'd seen Katy and I'd stubbornly ignored his calls. What if something had happened to Katy? 'I'm sure she's fine, she probably just needed some time out and will already be back at the manor.' I hoped I was right.

'I'll have a drive around the village and see if I can spot her and then I'll get back to the house.'

'Do you want me to come and look for her with you?'

'Thanks, but no. Probably best if you stay here just in case she does turn up.' He glanced at his watch and sighed.

He came across to me, something indefinable in his eyes. I half expected him to pull me into his embrace as he had done so many times before, only he didn't. He held himself back as though an invisible boundary existed between us. I wanted my old Max back. The one who would welcome me into his arms, to rest my head against his chest, for him to tell me everything would be okay, but with Katy missing in the dead of the night, we couldn't know that for sure.

A shiver of fear ran down my body. All thoughts of Max and Sasha, our disagreements, vanished from my mind. Max could have triplets with Angelina Jolie, for all I cared, if it only meant Katy would come home safely now.

'Phone me if you hear anything, won't you?' he said, tersely.

'I will do. I'll have a ring round to see if anyone's seen her. Polly might have done on her way home. If not, I'll try George, he's my parents' tenant. Katy met him in here the other day and I know they've spent a bit of time together recently. Try not to worry, Max. She'll turn up soon enough, I bet.'

'She'd better do,' he said, his voice heavy with emotion. 'I'll never forgive myself if something should happen to her.'

Eighteen

Polly hadn't seen her. Neither had George. I thought of the lads she'd been with the other night – I knew a couple of their names, but not where they lived, although I could probably find out if I just made a few more phone calls. First, I rang the manor, thinking she may have gone home while Max was still here, but the number just rang out.

Oh Katy, where on earth are you?

Then I tried her mobile number and to my surprise and utter relief, she picked up straight away.

'Katy!'

'Oh hi, Ellie,' she said, her voice ringing out brightly, clearly having no idea that Max had been going frantic over her whereabouts.

'Where are you?'

'I'm down at the barns with Ryan and the rest of the band. You know, The Leyton Boys, the ones who are appearing at the ball. I've been watching them rehearse. Oh my god, they're amazing.' She lowered her voice and whispered down the line, 'And Ryan is just dreamy.'

'Right. Well, that's good to know. But do you have any idea what the time is? Max has been going out of his mind with worry.'

'Um… yeah.' Now she was beginning to sound contrite. 'I just needed to get away for a bit. He was really cross with me and I didn't want to have another row with him. So I thought it best if I just went out for a couple of hours.'

'What, when he'd grounded you?'

'Oh god…' She fell quiet, clearly contemplating the seriousness of the situation. 'Maybe I'd better not go home tonight. Should I come and stay with you instead?'

'No, you need to get straight home, Katy, right now. You can't just ignore Max. He only gets mad because he's worried about you. You could have texted him and told him what you were doing, it would have made all the difference.'

'I'm not sure it would. He'd still have been as mad as hell.'

'Oh, Katy!'

'I'm fine. Honestly, I don't know what all the fuss is about. I'm almost eighteen. I can look after myself, you know.' As she liked to keep on reminding me.

'I don't doubt it for a moment. But if you're as grown up as you say you are then you need to start showing a bit of respect to Max.' I could hear the exasperation in my own voice and half expected the phone to be slammed down in my ear. Instead, I got a begrudging apology.

'Sorry Ellie.'

'It's not me you should be apologising to. Look, you really need to be getting back home now. I'll come and get you.'

'No don't,' she said, quickly. 'Ryan said he will bring me home. There's no need to worry. Look, I've got to go, but I'll speak to you soon, yeah?'

'Katy…'

Too late. She'd already hung up. I glared at the phone in my hand accusingly. At least she was safe and that overrode any other emotion I might be feeling. Straight away I called Max to tell him the news, his obvious relief and gratitude filtering down the line.

'Thank goodness for that.' He let out an audible sigh. 'I might have known she'd answer her phone to you, but not to me, but anyway that doesn't matter, at least we've found her, that's the main thing. Thanks, Ellie, I appreciate you tracking her down.'

'It's fine.' A pause wafted down the line – I couldn't help thinking of it as a pregnant pause. Our conversations had never been punctuated by awkward silences. Why were we now struggling to find things to say to each other?

'Look, Ellie, I don't know what's happened to us these last couple of days, but we can't carry on like this.'

'You're right,' I said, on the defensive now. 'If there's something you want to say, tell me now.'

'No, Ellie, not like this. I need to see you.' I took a breath. Obviously the kind of news that needed delivering in person then. 'Shall we say tomorrow, early in the morning, 9.00 ish?'

He sounded as though he was arranging a business meeting, just managing to squeeze me into his busy schedule.

'Fine,' I said, as though consulting my own. 'See you then.'

*

I hardly slept. How could I when my mind was totally wired, thinking about Katy, and going over the events of the last couple of days. She texted when she got back to the manor, saying she was home, but had sprinted straight up the stairs to bed just to avoid having to face Max. Followed by a scary face emoji. I'd smiled knowing exactly how she felt. If I could put off my conversation with Max then I would, but barring broken limbs, natural disasters or raging food poisoning – all much more appealing propositions – then it was something I was just going to have to get over and done with.

Eventually, with daylight edging through my curtains, I gave up on the idea of sleep, and went downstairs to the kitchen. Even Digby, who usually leapt out of his basket to greet me, thought it was too early, as he curled up into an even tighter ball and gave a barely perceptible wag of his tail. With my freshly made cup of tea, I sat at the kitchen table, but couldn't bring myself to drink it. Instead it grew cold in front of me.

I felt sick just thinking about seeing Max again, anticipating what he might have to tell me. Now I knew how Polly felt at the thought of having Johnny back in the village. Living in the same community as your ex, the one who messed with your heart, was one thing, but the thought of having to watch Max bring up his baby, with another woman, was something I wasn't sure I'd be strong enough to cope with.

Stop it, *with the surmising*, I chided. It was turning my head in circles. Giving myself a stern talking-to, I reached across for the wicker basket on the table which doubled as my filing tray. It was overflowing with random bits of paper, but for once I was glad of the distraction and after a couple of hours concentrated effort I was done, with a warm glow of satisfaction at seeing the basket empty for the first time in months, and all before breakfast too.

After quickly showering and dressing, I looked down at Digby who'd been waiting patiently at the back door.

'Come on then boy, let's go and do this.'

Outside, the morning had its cheerful sunny face on and I tried to match my mood to the sense of hope in the air, but all I felt was a deep trepidation.

We'd just reached the front gates to Braithwaite Manor when I noticed a familiar figure wandering up the lane towards us. With his distinctive rolling gait and straw trilby perched on his head, I would have recognised him anywhere.

'Hello my lovely, well there's a thing. I was just on my way to see you.'

'Really? It's a bit too early for a pint, Arthur.'

'No,' he chuckled to himself. 'I was going to drop in this rhubarb to you. Fresh off the allotment this morning. My first decent crop of the year. You do like rhubarb, don't you?'

'Love it!' Although I wasn't about to admit that I had no idea how to cook the stuff. That was Mum's territory, and I was suddenly reminded of all the wonderful food she made in her kitchen, not only with rhubarb but with all the lovely fruits that were in such abundance in the village over the summer months. Fruit tarts, pies, jams, chutneys. What I wouldn't give for a big bowl of rhubarb and custard right now. Slightly weird, first thing in the morning, but at that moment I couldn't think of anything I'd rather eat. 'That's very kind of you.' I took the bundle of rhubarb from Arthur, gratefully. 'Next time you're in, there's a pint on the house for you.'

'Sounds like a good exchange. You know, when my Marge was alive, she'd make a smashing rhubarb crumble, that's one of my favourites, you know.' *Mmmm, fruit crumble.* 'Not that I've had it in a while now,' Arthur said wistfully. 'I could make you a crumble,' I said, with a confidence I had no right to possess. I had made one before – in Year 6 in Food Tech, although that had actually been an apple crumble. I couldn't remember it being that difficult. And surely you would just have to swap the apple for the rhubarb. I mean, how hard could it be?

'Well, I wouldn't want to put you to any trouble...'

'No trouble,' I said, feeling a sense of joy at having located my inner Mary Berry. 'I'll do that this afternoon.'

'Lovely,' said Arthur, smiling. He gestured to the big house at the end of the drive. 'Expect you're off to see your young man now.'

'Yes,' I said, happily, before my smiled faded, remembering the purpose of my visit.

'He's a lucky fella. If I was forty years younger, I'd give him a run for his money that's for sure.'

'Aw, thanks, Arthur.' I said, feeling buoyed by his words. *Take that, Max Golding, I am a desirable woman and have a whole queue of men lining up to woo me.* Well maybe not a queue, and what did it matter that my suitor was in his seventies, it was the sentiment that counted. I tried to keep that positive thought at the front of my mind when I reached the back door of the manor and banged on the door.

The door flew open much quicker than I was expecting, taking me by surprise, my heart speeding up at the sight of Max.

'Ellie, come in.'

I followed him through to the kitchen, thankful that Digby was with me, providing some much-needed moral support.

Max turned to look at me, his early morning stubble

lending him a gorgeously sexy air, that was entirely unnecessary today. 'Is that a peace offering?'

'What?' He was staring at my rhubarb in a covetous manner. 'Oh, no, no it's not,' I said, clutching it tighter to my chest. 'Arthur's just given me this.'

'Shame. I love rhubarb, especially a crumble. Haven't had one of those in years.'

It was funny the things you learnt about people, at the most unlikely times too. If I'd been feeling more well-disposed towards Max, I would have offered to make him one as well. But I didn't.

'Anyway, why would I be bringing you a peace offering?'

'Well, in fairness, you did call me an idiot the other night.' The faintest of smiles appeared at the corner of his lips, sending the sensuality factor soaring, but I was determined not to be distracted by his physical presence – his very distracting physical presence.

'In fairness, you were acting like one!'

He shrugged, as though it was, indeed, a fair point.

'Coffee?' he asked, gesturing for me to sit down.

I nodded, the aroma of roasted beans wafting over from the gurgling machine in the corner of the room enticing me with its promise. I pulled out a chair at the table, taking a measured breath, conscious of not wanting to bombard him with a barrage of questions.

'Look, I'm sorry,' he said, when he placed two full mugs on the table and came and sat down beside me. Max leant down to stroke Digby behind the ear, who immediately rolled over onto his back, asking for his tummy to be tickled. My trusty four-legged friend. The traitor.

'I know it's no excuse, but that day was a shocker. It was one thing after another, constant interruptions, demands from different quarters, and then finding out about Katy, what she'd been up to and you covering up for her, well it just kind of pressed all the wrong buttons. I overreacted, I admit it, but it upset me that you would keep something like that from me.'

'I did it for Katy. She asked me not to tell you and I wanted to keep her confidence. If I thought she'd been in any serious danger, then of course I would have told you.'

'I don't like the fact that you kept it a secret from me, Ellie. What else don't I know?'

'Huh? You really want to talk about secrets?'

Max lifted his brow, narrowing his eyes. 'How do you mean, Ellie?'

'Oh come on, Max. I'm talking about Sasha, your ex. The one who's pregnant. You've not been very forthcoming on that subject.'

'Ah right. This is all making sense now. That's what this is all about, the fact that I didn't tell you Sasha was pregnant?'

'Well how did you expect me to react?' I said, frustration tempering my words.

'Honestly, Ellie, I wouldn't have expected this from you?' He looked at me accusingly. 'Why didn't you just pick up the phone or come to the house and speak to me?'

'Well, I reckoned if you wanted to tell me about Sasha then you would have done. But you didn't. Admittedly it would have been nice to have been told your ex was pregnant, rather than coming face to face with that very obvious fact myself, but then I expect you have your reasons for not telling me. As you have for moving Sasha into a house just down the road from you.'

Hearing my words aloud made me realise how needy and possessive I sounded, but didn't Max owe me some kind of explanation?

'Look there was no big conspiracy not to tell you, and I tried to on a couple of occasions, but there was always some kind of interruption. I decided it would be better if we sat down when we had some time together, and discussed it then. Not that we can seem to manage much of that these days.'

He looked at me with reproach in his eyes, as a heavy, tension-filled silence fell over us.

'It's not my baby, if that's what you're worried about.'

I swear my heart stopped beating in that moment.

'Isn't it?'

'No!' he countered, incredulous.

'Are you sure?'

'Yes!'

'Right, I see,' I said, turning my face away, feeling a whole lot of pent-up emotion and relief seep from my body. But even then I couldn't leave it. There were so many more questions I needed answers to. 'How do you know?'

'What?'

'Well how do you know it's not your baby?'

'I asked her.'

'Oh! Right. So you thought it could be your baby then?'

I was trying to keep my emotions under control, but I could feel my face flaring a bright red and my heart pitter-pattering ever faster in my chest.

'I was as surprised as you were. I had no idea she was

pregnant until she turned up to view the cottage. And then, well, it seemed only polite to ask.' He gave a tentative smile, our eyes locking, and I couldn't help smiling too, probably from the relief washing over me. 'Sasha assured me it wasn't my baby and later when I thought about it I realised it couldn't have been. The dates didn't work out.'

'Okay.' *And breathe*. 'So what's she doing back in the village then, living in one of your houses?' It still didn't make any sense.

'I'm sorry about that. I should have run it past you first, but I didn't really think. She came to me and said she needed somewhere to live and could I help her out. I could hardly say no. She told me she wanted to make a new start for her and the baby,' he went on. 'And she thought Little Leyton was a good place to do that. Yes, it's one of my houses, but it's purely a business arrangement. She's paying the going rate for the rent. Honestly, Ellie, what do you think's going on here?'

I felt a prickle of shame tingle in my cheeks. 'Nothing.' Max really didn't want to know what had been going on inside my head. 'I just wondered that was all.'

'To be honest, I feel a kind of responsibility towards Sasha.' He raked a hand through his brown hair, sweeping it away from his face. 'She's on her own expecting a baby. Some might say that's down to me.'

'What?'

'Well...' He shook his head, resigned. 'In the final months of our relationship I pretty much neglected her. I'd moved on emotionally although we hadn't actually split up. She was spending a lot of time at the house while I was working away. She found solace in a colleague of mine, Peter Anderson. You know, the surveyor?'

'Really?'

'Yeah. They had a bit of a fling, but the trouble was Peter was still very much involved with his estranged wife so he was doing a bit of toing and froing. He and his wife are back together again now trying to make a go of their marriage which has left Sasha high and dry.'

'Oh goodness.' A mix of emotions flooded my body. Relief that it wasn't Max's baby after all, but a twist of concern too for Sasha, wondering how I would feel in the same situation. 'Where are Sasha's family then?'

'That's the thing, she doesn't really have close family around her. She has a sister who lives in Australia, and she's kind of estranged from her parents. Her dad was in the military, so they moved around a lot when she was growing up, and then her parents split up when she went away to university. I think relations have been a bit strained since then.'

'Oh dear.' Now I was feeling desperately sorry for Sasha.

'Yeah, I think that's why she decided on Little Leyton. She mentioned how much she'd enjoyed living here and how she appreciated the sense of community. Not something she'd really experienced before.'

I stood up and wandered across to the window, admiring the stunning view that was Max's garden. If I was in Sasha's shoes I'd probably want to do the same. Find a small and friendly village where I could settle down and make a new start for me and my baby. The sun bearing down on the lawns only caused to remind me that my problems were insignificant compared to Sasha's. I had no reason to feel threatened by her coming back into the village.

'Look, I'm sorry if I didn't think to talk to you first about offering Sasha the house. I didn't stop to consider that it might be a problem. It's not a problem, is it?' Max asked me now.

'No!' I said, desperately backtracking. 'It was just seeing Sasha so... so pregnant, it was a bit of a shock.'

'Yeah, well you can imagine how I felt.'

'Ha, must have given you a heart-stopping moment?'

'It did. I mean I've never been one to walk away from my responsibilities, but I must admit to feeling relieved when I found out the baby wasn't mine.'

He wiped the back of his hand against his brow, and shook out his hand. I smiled, relieved that he was telling me everything I'd wanted to hear.

'You didn't relish the idea of becoming a daddy then?' I joshed, relieved that the tension had lifted and I could speak openly again, with no fear of any of this being true.

'I can barely look after my teenage sister, can you imagine what I'd be like with a baby? I'd probably drop it, or forget to feed it. I'd definitely make it cry. I seem to have developed quite a knack for doing that, at least with Katy.'

I laughed. Funny thing was, I'd given a lot of consideration to what sort of father Max would make these last couple of days. Fierce, passionate and demanding, I suspected, but intensely loving and kind too.

I returned to my seat at the kitchen table. It felt so good to have cleared the air, to be able to talk easily again, finally back on track. 'So, dare I ask, how is Katy today?'

'No idea. She hasn't surfaced yet.' He shook his head ruefully. 'Well, you know, she got in at god knows what time last night. Turned up on the back of a motorbike.'

'Oh good grief...' No wonder she'd been so insistent

that I didn't collect her. She'd obviously made other more exciting travel plans.

'Yep. She came in the house and ran straight upstairs, slamming her door shut. I told her to come back down, that I needed to talk to her, but she wasn't listening to me. Honestly, Ellie, I really don't know how to get through to that girl.'

'Do you want me to talk to her?'

'No, I'll have another try. I'm wondering though if this is the right place for her. Mum is quite insistent now that she goes home and completes the last couple of weeks at school, and I tend to agree with her. I'm not sure she's gaining anything from being here. I think she needs to go back to Spain.'

In some ways, I had a lot of sympathy for Katy even when she was being stroppy and contrary. She'd fallen out with her parents, had come to a village where she didn't know anyone apart from her brother who, as I knew from personal experience, wasn't always the easiest person in the world to talk to, and had no idea what she was going to do next in her life. Being a teenage girl sucked at times. The extremes of emotion, one minute feeling on top of the world, the next in the depths of despair. So many worries that took up all your time: boys, friends, how you looked, were you funny and interesting enough, were you good enough?

Max was the sort of man who worked on logic, reason and practicality. He could have no idea or understanding what his little sister was going through.

'Hmm, Katy's not going to like that idea one little bit.'

Nineteen

'What am I not going to like?'

Katy appeared in the doorway to the kitchen, looking shiftily at Max and then smiling at me. Wearing short pyjamas in green and with her elfin-cut hairstyle and the smattering of freckles over her nose she looked like a very fetching Peter Pan.

'What time did you get home last night?' Max asked, immediately getting up from the table. You know, I sometimes wished Max would take a moment to think before coming straight out with whatever was on his mind. He shared that trait with his sister. Up against each other it was hard to call who would come off best.

Katy padded over to the fridge and pulled out the carton of orange juice and carefully poured herself a glass, studiously avoiding Max's question. She turned to me. 'How are you Ellie?'

'Good thanks.' The atmosphere was so charged that even the dogs slunk out into the utility room. I wished I could follow them, but instead wittered on cheerfully in the hope that I could build some bridges between this stubborn pair. 'Oh, did I mention, Max,' I said, blithely, 'the other day when we went shopping we must have visited every possible shop in the arcade and finally when I was giving up hope that I would ever find anything to suit me, Katy picked out the most beautiful dress for me. It was something I would never have chosen for myself, but do you know it fitted and suits me perfectly. I was so pleased and just can't wait to wear it at the ball.'

Max gave me a cursory glance, clearly not in the least bit interested in what I'd been telling him. 'Katy, I asked you a question,' he said, instead.

'What? Oh, I don't know,' she said, airily, still carefully avoiding his eye. 'I've forgotten now.'

'Well, I'll tell you, shall I? It was gone one o'clock.'

'Right, so why are you asking me then if you already know the answer?' Katy asked, quick as a flash.

'Because it's not acceptable, Katy. If you're living under my roof then you need to abide by my rules. I had no idea where you were or who you were with. You could have been lying dead in a ditch somewhere for all I knew.'

I cringed, realising I was very much in the way and wanting to be anywhere but here right now. Best leave these two alone to sort out their differences. 'Look, I should go,' I said decisively.

'No, don't!' Both Katy and Max said it at the same time, halting my imminent departure and I sat straight back down again.

Max turned to address Katy. 'And who brought you home? On a motorbike, Katy? Really?' He shook his head, dismayed. 'Do you know how dangerous those things are?'

'Oh, that was Ryan. From the band. He's lovely and...' Katy clocked Max's expression, '... and a very safe rider too.'

'I can vouch for Ryan. I've known him for years. He's a lovely lad and...'

I guessed from Max's withering glance that he didn't appreciate my glowing character reference. Best not to mention Ryan's bad-boy past then, although I was pretty sure that was all behind him now.

'I don't want you seeing him, Katy. He's obviously not a good influence if he's happy for a seventeen-year-old to stay out until the early hours of the morning. And you're certainly not to go on his motorbike again.'

'You can't tell me what to do.' She span round, throwing her hands in the air. 'You're always having a go at me. It's like being back in Spain.'

'Well, Katy, if I'm being honest with you, I think that's where you should be. Whatever problems you have with Mum they're not going to be sorted out if you're here. It's just making matters worse.'

Katy was staring at me imploringly, but I couldn't hold her gaze. This had nothing to do with me; it was something they had to sort out between themselves.

Max went on, his voice low and steely now. 'Why don't you go back to Spain, sort things out with Mum, and then you'll be in better position to move on in your life.'

'No! I know you just want me out of your way but you can't make me go. I'll run away and never come back.' Katy's deep brown eyes flared angrily, colour staining her cheeks, her small stature held tall and proud. Her chin jutted out defiantly and her gaze didn't leave Max's face. Only a fool would choose not to believe every word she was saying. 'Ellie, tell him.' Katy actually stamped her foot on the stone floor in frustration. 'He's being unreasonable, isn't he?'

I looked from Max to Ellie, seeing two siblings, both as stubborn and pig-headed as each other. Neither one of them about to back down. Max held all the power and Katy's exasperation filled every corner of the kitchen.

'Max does have a point,' I said, gently, choosing my words carefully so as not to inflame a tense situation even further. 'He's only saying these things because he worries about you and wants what's best for you.'

'What? Sending me back to Spain? More like what's best for him.'

Max let out an exasperated sigh.

'Well, I'm sure you can work something out between the pair of you. If you just sit down and talk about it. But all the time you're here, Katy, I do think you need to consider a bit more the consequences of your actions. Keep Max informed so he knows where you are and what you're doing and what time he can expect you home again. Max doesn't want to cramp your style, he just wants to make sure you're okay. That's all it is.'

Max shrugged noncommittally, although I took that as his agreement to what I was saying.

'Ugh. It's not fair. I have to tell everyone what I'm doing, and yet it's okay for everyone else to have secrets. Do you know how that feels? It's horrible, really horrible to be kept in the dark all the time.' I glanced across at Katy, but she'd dropped her gaze to the floor, avoiding eye contact. I had the distinct impression we'd been talking about one thing but suddenly the conversation had taken a turn, and now, well who knew what this was all about. Then, she came straight out with it. 'Did you ask him about Sasha?'

'What?' This from Max.

'Sasha. Did you ask him about her, and the baby?'

Max didn't give me a chance to respond. 'Oh for Christ's sake, Katy! What is your problem exactly? Why are you wanting to stir trouble up all the time? Sasha's my ex-girlfriend and she's pregnant. So what? And what the hell has it got to do with you anyway?'

'Yes, she was your girlfriend, and now she's pregnant and living in one of your houses down the road. It doesn't take a genius to work out what's going on, Max!'

My mouth opened involuntarily in complete and utter surprise at the venom dripping from Katy's words.

'Doesn't it?' said Max, sarcastically. 'Well forgive me, but you'll have to explain to this particular idiot,' he said, pointing to his chest, 'because I haven't got a clue.'

'Every child has the right to know who its real father is. It's really important.'

'Honestly, Katy, I think you've got hold of the wrong end of the stick,' I said, trying to find a way to reconnect these two. 'Max has explained. It isn't his baby. Sasha just asked if Max could help her out by providing her with a house to live in.'

'Oh god, Ellie. And you really believe that? Can't you see? It's all an elaborate charade to cover up what's really going on? Why else would she be living next door to Max? It's so that he can see the baby, his baby. He's not being honest with you, Ellie.'

'Get out!' Max pointed to the door in a dramatic movement. His brow furrowed and his eyes narrowed, a thunderous expression across his features. 'I'm not listening to this. Just get out, will you?'

'No,' I protested, chastising Max with a disapproving look. 'Oh, Katy.' I stood up, and grabbed her to my side, wrapping my arm around her shoulder. She was hurting, doing her best not to give into the tears gathering in her eyes. 'This is all just a terrible misunderstanding. Max is telling the truth. Sasha's having another man's baby. Really. Max isn't lying.'

Was I in some way to blame? Had I completely overreacted the other day and Katy had picked up on my insecurities? As soon as Max had sat me down and explained the situation with Sasha then I'd known with a hundred per cent certainty that he was telling the truth and I'd had to wonder why I'd ever doubted him in the first place. But I was puzzled as to why Katy was so agitated over the whole matter.

'Tell us, Katy, what is this really all about?' I still had hold of her and could feel the nervous energy radiating from her. 'This isn't about Sasha, is it?' I said, sensing a very distinct wobble in her bearing. 'What is it that's troubling you, lovely? You can talk to us about it, you know? You don't have to keep everything bottled up.'

That did it. Katy's chin wavered, her bottom lip wobbled and then the tears that she'd been valiantly hanging onto tumbled down her cheeks.

'Oh Katy,' I said, pulling her to my chest and wrapping my arms tightly around her. 'I hate to see you so upset. What's the matter, why don't you tell us?'

Max was looking increasingly more uncomfortable by the moment.

'It's… just… the… the…' It was hard to make out Katy's

words through the sobbing, but I heard the word baby and her distress was evident.

She turned away and plonked herself down at the kitchen table.

I looked across at Max who'd raised his eyebrows in concern, about to say something, before thinking better of it. We were both thinking along the same lines obviously.

'Oh, you're not pregnant, are you?' I said, unable to stop myself. I saw Max brace himself as though he didn't want to hear the answer to that question.

'Nooo!' she said, crossly, through her tears. I dashed across to the other side of the kitchen, pulling off some kitchen roll from the holder and handed it to her. The look I exchanged with Max was one that said we were both very relieved about that. She blew her nose noisily into the tissue and sank her head into her hands.

'Come on, Katy.' I sat down beside her and wrapped my arm around her shoulder again. The sobbing had subsided a little, but she was still gulping for air. She was on the brink of telling me. I didn't want to lose the moment. For her to close up and to retreat back inside her prickly shell. 'Whatever it is, it can't be that bad, can it?'

She nodded, as though it was.

I squeezed her hand, urging her on, willing her to confide in me.

'It's just when I heard about Sasha, I thought...' she shrugged, uncertain of how to go on. 'I thought... about the baby.' She shook her head as though she could barely make sense of her own thoughts. 'That little baby. Coming into the big scary world. Would it grow up with its proper dad in a real and loving home? Or would it be shunted around, never really feeling wanted, as though it never really belonged to anyone.'

'What on earth do you mean, Katy?' Max asked.

She shrugged again and I could sense the barriers coming back up.

'Come on,' I said gently, giving her hand a little shake. I was prepared to sit there all day, if necessary, until Katy felt comfortable enough to tell us what was troubling her.

'People are selfish. They do things because it's right for them. But they don't think about the consequences. They never think about the child in these circumstances.'

'You're not making any sense, Katy,' said Max, his puzzlement plain to see. 'What on earth are you going on about?'

'I know, Max. You don't have to pretend anymore. I know the truth about our family. Alan's told me everything.'

Twenty

'What? What on earth do you mean?'

Max was looking at his sister fiercely and I had the distinct impression I'd walked into the middle of a soap opera that I had no right to play a part in. Too late now to slip out the back door and pretend I hadn't heard any of this. Katy was crying again, Max was pacing up and down the kitchen and I was sat awkwardly in the middle of it all, wishing I could wave a magic wand and make everything better.

'Do you want me to go? I think this is something you two need to discuss alone.'

'No!' Still Katy and Max were insistent that I stay. Whether I liked it or not, I'd been sucked into this drama, and I wanted to support them both the best way I could. 'Let me make some more coffee then,' I said, jumping up, desperate now for something practical to do.

As I spooned coffee into mugs and went across to the fridge for the milk, I saw that Max had taken my place next to Katy at the table, and had taken hold of her hand. The concern in his expression melted my heart.

'Tell me, what did Alan say exactly?'

She looked up at him, all big brown eyes appraising him

carefully, wondering if she could trust him enough to open up her heart. 'We had a row. A big, big row. He told me that I couldn't go to a party. I'd been looking forward to that party for weeks. Everyone was going. All my friends. Everyone from school. How would it have looked if I'd had to tell my friends that I couldn't go, that my parents wouldn't let me? It would have been totally humiliating. Alan came down all heavy on me and said that there was no way I was going, that I needed to learn some respect.' Max looked across at me, smiling wryly at the recognisable scenario, no doubt.

I wandered across and put their coffees on the table, and then busied myself at the sink, wishing I could just blend into the background.

'Okay, and then what?' Max asked.

'Well, I told him. I said he couldn't tell me what to do because he wasn't even my father. And that if Dad was still around then he would have let me go to the party.'

'Oh dear,' said Max gravely. 'I can see why that might have upset Alan.'

'Yeah, well, he flew off the handle and said that I'd never shown him any respect at all. And he went on and on and on about how much he'd done for me over the years, and how I'd just thrown it all back in his face. That he'd tried to treat me like his own child, but all I'd given him was abuse. And then it came out. Suddenly. Out of nowhere. Alan told me Dad, or the man I thought was my dad, wasn't my real dad after all.'

Katy's words fell out in an emotional tumble, but she wasn't crying now. Her tears had dried and there was an urgency to her words. As though she needed to set the record straight, to get her side of the story out there. I span around to look at her, to check that I hadn't misheard, but I could see immediately that everything she was telling us was true.

'Oh Katy,' I said, my heart bleeding for her as Max drew her closer to his side, trying to comfort her as best he could. 'That must have been awful. Such a terrible shock.'

'It was. I couldn't believe it. I know I was only little when Dad died but he was the only dad I'd ever known. All those photos and memories. I had no reason to think he wasn't my real dad. Mum used to say I was daddy's little girl. After he died, I used to fall asleep thinking about him, crying into my pillow trying to conjure up his face. Sometimes I could manage it and I could see him as clearly as if he was standing in my bedroom and other times I couldn't do it at all. And that used to make me sad. And now I find out he wasn't really my father at all.'

'Oh, Katy.' Max kissed her lightly on the forehead, her hurt reflected in his own eyes.

'You knew, didn't you Max?'

'No! I promise you, this is the first I've heard about it. I never knew anything.' Max sighed. 'You have talked to Mum? What did she say?'

'Well, she couldn't deny it. We had a big bust up. She had a real go at Alan for telling me and then she started crying, saying how sorry she was and how she should never have kept it from me. I just couldn't believe it. Why would you keep something like that from someone you loved? I just don't get it.' Katy looked from me to Max as though we might be able to give her the answers she'd been desperately searching for.

'I expect Mum had good reasons for not telling you.' Katy's face flared with indignation. 'I'm not excusing her behaviour,' said Max quickly, holding up his hands defensively, 'all I'm saying is that I don't think she would have deliberately set out to hurt you or keep secrets from you. Sometimes things happen, people get into difficult situations and they don't know how to get out of them or what to do for the best.'

'She lied to me. I can never forgive her for that.'

'She kept the truth from you, and that's something slightly different,' Max said. 'Again, I'm not saying it's right, I'm just trying to see it from Mum's perspective. I don't suppose it could have been easy for her.'

More than ever now, I felt in the way. I tried to imagine myself in Katy's shoes, but couldn't. To find out that everything you held dear, that everything you thought was your reality, was in fact something else entirely, must be devastating at any age, but for Katy, a young and impressionable teenager, it was life-changing.

'I don't want to talk to her. It's as if she isn't my mum anymore. I've lost my mum and my dad. My whole life has been a lie.' Katy's voice quivered as she spoke, the sadness of her words filling the kitchen.

No wonder she'd fled her home to come to the UK. It was the reason she'd been so emotional and temperamental. She'd wanted to get away from everything she knew and start again, but something as important as that, who you are and where you came from, you could never run away from.

Max picked up Katy's hand and looked his sister directly in the eye. 'I know it must seem that way, but it isn't true. Mum loves you. She'll be devastated that this has happened and she'll want to do anything to make it up to you. You are her daughter, after all. You're still the same person, Katy, that hasn't changed. I know you've received shocking news, but it doesn't change who you are.'

'It seems that way to me. Honestly, I feel like I don't know who I am anymore.' She looked up at us both and shrugged. 'The man I thought was my dad isn't my dad. I've not even met my real dad, although Mum's told me who he is now. And you're only my half-brother, not even my proper brother,' she said, laughing ruefully.

'Listen, I don't want to hear anything like that again. This changes nothing, do you understand? You're still my sister. My pain-in the-arse little sister who winds me up and drives me mad with all the cheeky backchat and attitude, but, do you know, I wouldn't change one single thing about you. You're stuck with me, kiddo, whether you like it or not. I might not always show it, but I love you Katy, and nothing is ever going to change that.'

At Max's words Katy broke down in tears, sobbing into his arms, her body shuddering with the effort of it all and I had to turn away and concentrate on the view outside for fear of doing the same. Seeing Max acting so tenderly towards his sister touched me deep down inside, his discovery that she was only his half-sister only serving to make him more protective towards her. He held her head to his chest and soothed her tears by rubbing his hand up and down her back.

'I thought you might not want me here when you found out I wasn't your real sister.'

'Stop saying that. You're my sister, that's the beginning and end of it.'

'But when you kept saying you'd send me back to Spain, it got me really anxious. I know I haven't been easy to live with, but I really like it here. I didn't know what I would do if you sent me away. I can't bear the thought of it.'

'Look you're not going anywhere. You can stay here with me as long as you like.' He screwed up his face, a mischievous twinkle in his eye. 'I don't suppose I would have ever really sent you home anyway, despite what I was saying.'

'Nah,' I said, throwing Katy a complicit smile. 'I would never have let him.'

'I'll always be here for you, Katy,' Max said now. 'This must have come as a complete shock and I can see why you've been so upset. That's totally understandable. You must have so many questions that you need answers to. But in a way, it's a good thing, that this has all come out now. It's a new start, Katy. When you're ready, you can talk to Mum, I don't mind acting as go-between if that's the way you want to do it.'

'Thanks Max.' Katy let her head fall again onto his chest and I could sense the relief flooding from her body. All the anger and frustration of the past few weeks now seeping from her body as Max cradled her in his arms.

'So, what did Mum tell you about your dad then?' he asked gently.

'Only that his name's Andrew Wren and that he was a painter and decorator who worked on the house for a short while. Mum said she can give me the last address she has for him, but I'm not sure if I even want to meet him at this stage. Did you know him, Max?'

Max shook his head. 'No, I can't remember anyone of

that name. Mind you, Dad always was terrible at DIY.'

At least Katy could see the funny side, and when she sniggered, Max and I joined in too.

Digby, Holly and Bella came up to my side at the sink and started nudging me with their noses. They circled Katy, unsettled by her tears, and were now coming to me for reassurance that everything was all right.

'Look, I think I might take these hounds out for a walk.'

'Can I come?' said Katy, immediately brightening.

'Of course you can, I just thought you might want to stay here and talk to Max.'

'Nah, I love you and everything, Max, but to be honest with you I'm all talked out,' said Katy, with a smile, as she jumped up out of her chair.

As she disappeared upstairs to get changed, Max beckoned me over and pulled me into his arms.

'Well,' he said. 'I wasn't expecting that, although I guess it explains a lot now. That poor kid. I do feel for her.'

'What a shock. Did you really have no idea?'

He shook his head. 'None whatsoever, but you know, I'm not totally surprised. My mum and dad were the most unlikely couple you could ever meet. She's really bubbly and outgoing whereas Dad was very serious, an academic whose main focus was his work. Dad adored my mum, but he was never a very demonstrative man. She spent a lot of time on her own and well, I guess, she found solace in her gentlemen friends. I remember a few of them around.'

'I see.' Max rarely spoke about his upbringing, but when he did it helped me to understand better the man I'd fallen in love with. I'd seen a softer, more compassionate side to him today. 'As you say though, probably best it's all out in the open now. Families, eh?'

Max pulled a face. 'I know. It makes you think, doesn't it? If that happy family scenario we all strive for actually exists?'

'Yes, of course, it does,' I said defensively, thinking about my own family set-up. My mum and dad had met as students at university and had been together ever since, happily devoted to each other. Now, they were into their second adolescence and having the time of their lives, indulging in the good life on the other side of the world.

'Perhaps you're right,' he said, with a resigned smile.

My gaze flittered over Max's shoulder and out into the garden. The sun was waiting for me, calling me outside. I glanced at my watch. We needed to get going soon if I was to fit in a walk and get back for opening time.

'Thanks for everything today, Ellie. It made all the difference knowing you were here. That I had your support.' Max placed the gentlest of kisses on my forehead.

'No problem. I'm just pleased Katy could finally get everything off her chest. For a while I felt a bit awkward, as though I was in the way and that I shouldn't really be here. That I was intruding on family business.'

'Not at all. I'm sure if you hadn't been here Katy wouldn't have opened up in the same way. She trusts you, Ellie, and adores you too. I can tell that.'

His words warmed my insides with their sincerity.

'I love her too. She's a great kid.'

Max nodded. 'Yeah, she can be when she's not giving her big brother grief. So, we've sorted out Katy, hopefully. We've cleared the air over Sasha. Now,' he said, taking hold of my hand by the fingertips, 'It's just you and me that needs sorting.'

'I'm ready,' said Katy, bowling into the room.

I threw Max a questioning glance.

'Don't worry. That can wait for another time.'

Twenty-One

Later, when I was back at the pub, I unlocked the front door ready for any early customers and my mind cast back over the discoveries made today. Hopefully now that Max knew what had been going on with Katy, he would be more understanding of her moods and perhaps now she didn't have to keep that huge secret to herself she would act more thoughtfully towards her brother. And maybe, George Clooney would turn up at the summer fete after all.

My nerves were frazzled by the charged emotions of the last few days. I'd never been one for confrontation and I was just grateful that we'd been able to clear the air over Sasha and Katy. Mind you, I was still puzzled by Max's comment about needing to sort our relationship out. Weren't we good now? Couldn't we just get back to the way things were before all of this had blown up?

Mulling over that thought and with Digby shadowing my every move, I ventured over to the back door and opened it up, letting in the warm air. I peered outside into the beer garden, my mood lifting at the sight. The hanging baskets were growing more plentiful and colourful by the day and the climbing honeysuckle and clematis spread over the walls in a flush of delicate blooms. I walked outside and turned on the hose, giving the baskets and tubs a light drenching. Lifting my head to the sky, I savoured the sensation of the sun caressing my skin. We were so lucky to have this little oasis at the back of the pub. Enclosed by brick walls on each side, and with a wooden canopy covering the first part of the garden providing a sheltered area for when the weather turned bad, you could almost forget you were sitting outside when you were cocooned within the foliage and flowers of the blooming garden. Only today, I suspected there wouldn't be much time for sitting outside and enjoying the sunshine.

I heard the front door open and wandered back inside to find Gemma arriving for work.

'Hello lovely, how are you?'

'Good thanks, what do you want me to get started on?'

Gemma had been such an asset to our team. She'd been quick to learn and enthusiastic, and very popular with the customers too.

'Well, if you can just man the bars, that would be great. I've got to put in the order with the brewery, so I'll be out the back, but just holler if you need an extra pair of hands.'

On my way through I spotted my gift from Arthur sitting on top of the worktop, a reminder of that promise I'd made him. I quickly pulled out a saucepan from the cupboard, chopped up the rhubarb into chunks and tossed them into a saucepan with a little water and a sprinkling of sugar, ready for cooking.

Then I sat myself down and went through the order for the brewery, put together a list of the food and drinks required for Stella's upcoming christening and prepared another list to take to the cash and carry, feeling a sense of satisfaction at ticking off items on my to-do list. Then

I pottered around the kitchen seeing to some long over-due jobs.

'Sorry to disturb you, Ellie, but Max Golding is out in the bar, asking to see you.' Gemma was standing in the doorway.

What was Max doing here? I hadn't expected to see him so soon after this morning's heart-to-heart with Katy. I just hoped they hadn't had another big bust-up. I glanced at my watch. The day had run away with me. Gemma had manned the bar single-handedly over the lunchtime period and would be off soon in time for the school run. I'd cover until Andy turned up in a short while.

'Thanks, Gemma. I'll come through and see him. You can get off if you want to.'

Walking out into the bar, my gaze landed on Max, my heart immediately lifting at the sight of him. He stood in the snug, his arms spread wide resting on the top of the bar. Was it just me or did everyone else feel the same magnetic pull towards him? I felt sure they must. His tall, broad frame seemed to fill the bar, his dark eyes intelligent and compelling as usual, his mouth, such an eminently kissable mouth, set strong and inviting. It sent a frisson rippling down my backbone. Our eyes met and he acknowledged me with a smile.

'Hi Max, everything okay?'

'Fine, thanks. I've left Katy curled up on the sofa watching Netflix. I think the poor girl's exhausted.'

'Hardly surprising.' No worries on that front then. This was just a normal friendly visit. Or was it? 'Did you want a pint of our special ale, it's new in, it's a hoppy beer with a sweet, fruity nose to it.'

'Thanks, but I think a cup of tea would go down better actually. I thought we might have that chat, if this is a good time?'

The pub had emptied out, so I could hardly say it was a bad time, even if I'd wanted to. 'Sure, I'll go and make us a drink. I'll be back in a jiffy.'

For some reason I was full of trepidation trying to imagine what Max might want to discuss. Distractedly, I mooched around the kitchen waiting for the kettle to boil and then when it had and I'd made the tea I went and joined Max again, placing the drinks down on the table.

Resting his chin in his hands, Max turned to look at me, his gaze scanning mine as though looking for some sort of answer to the most unfathomable question. The awkward silence made a reappearance making the snug bar seem much more snug and much more claustrophobic. Unable to bear the quiet anymore, I turned to him.

'So, what was it you wanted to talk to me about then?'

'Ah, yes well...' He steepled his fingers and hesitated. Max's reticence made me nervous. What could he possibly want to say that was so difficult? 'Look, let me ask you,' he took hold of my hand, as though about to impart some very bad news, 'are you happy? You know, really happy?'

I had to stop and think about that for a moment. To define what that transient indefinable state meant to me. I loved living in the village, being amongst my family and friends, running the pub.

'I mean happy in our relationship,' said Max, as if following my thought process.

'Oh... well...' Where could this possibly be leading?

'You know how much you mean to me, Ellie.' Max's

gaze was imploring. 'The way I feel about you I've never felt about anybody else before, but…'

Oh god, there would just have to be a *but*, wouldn't there? My heart pounded dramatically in my chest and a prickly heat rose up my neck. This was Max's way of letting me down gently. Why hadn't I seen it coming? This was all my fault. I'd been so uptight over Sasha these last few days that I'd pushed Max away. Like ripping off a plaster, it would be best just to get this over and done with as quickly as possible.

'But what, Max?'

'Well, I don't know how you feel, Ellie, but for me, this… us… well, it's just not working, the way things are.'

'Oh.' It was all I could say, as a searing pain ripped through me.

'You must feel that way too? We rarely see each other. You're tied up with the pub, I've been preoccupied with my business, I know, and now with Katy here, it's almost as if we don't have time for each other anymore.'

'Right. I see. I'm sorry you feel like that.' A tumble of emotions flooded my body. Yes, we were both busy and had commitments elsewhere, but until these last couple of weeks, I'd thought we'd been getting on fine. It was still early on in our relationship, but my feelings for Max grew stronger with each passing day. I thought he felt the same too, but obviously not. I stood up and walked over to the bar, trying to make sense of what Max was trying to tell me, but none of it was making any sense at all. I turned to look at him. 'Is this about Sasha?'

'What?' He screwed up his face, perplexed. 'No, of course it isn't. I told you, Sasha's just a friend who's going through a rough patch at the moment. This has nothing to do with her. Why would you even say that?'

Funny how we'd been getting on fabulously until Sasha turned up pregnant and looking for somewhere to live and now suddenly everything felt uncertain between us.

'Well, I wondered if you might want to get back with her.' Only actually realising the truth of that statement as I said the words aloud.

'What?' Now, it was Max's turn to push the table aside and he threw his hands to the air. 'I've told you, it's not my baby, Ellie.' He was doing well to keep a lid on his evident frustration, but it was bubbling beneath the surface just waiting to spill over.

'I know, but you wouldn't be the first man to step up to the plate and take on another man's child. You said yourself you felt a responsibility to Sasha.'

'Yes, but not in that way. Jesus Ellie. Why are we even talking about Sasha anyway? This is about you and me.'

'Yes,' I said, hearing the sadness in my own voice. 'And I get what you're saying. You think we should split.'

'What?'

I'd wandered over to the window, turning my back on Max, not wanting him to see my distress. I peered outside, only thankful we had no customers in. Soon, he was behind me, his warm breath in my ear, his hands on my waist. He spun me round, his face a whisker away from mine. So close I felt my skin tingle in anticipation. He pulled me even closer, clasping my face in his hands, my body relinquishing control under the intensity of his gaze. He stepped back.

'I don't want us to split up. No way. That's not what I'm saying. It's not what you want, is it?' he asked, concerned.

'No! I just thought...' My words trailed away, relief flooding my body.

'God no. I've not been explaining myself properly, Ellie. That's the last thing I want. All I'm saying is that we need to make some changes in our relationship. Don't you think? This, us, is really important to me.' He stroked the hair away from my face, looking into my eyes imploringly. 'I'm just worried that if we don't give each other, our relationship, the time it deserves, then it will suffer as a result. It's happened before in my previous relationships. I was so wrapped up in my work that inevitably things fizzled out. I don't want that to happen to us, Ellie. I want us to spend much more time together. That's what I came to say. What do you think?'

'Yes, yes.' I was nodding my head in agreement, but feeling slightly dazed too. It was everything I wanted to hear. 'Well, we'll just have to make sure we make time for each other. Have date nights and see each other at the weekends, even if it's only for breakfast and a dog walk.'

'Yes, but we're supposed to be doing that now and it's not working, is it? The days slip by when we're both so busy and soon it's a whole week since I've seen you.' He hugged me to him tighter and the firmness of his body up against mine sent swirls of delight rippling through my body. 'Ellie, I need more than that. I want to go to sleep with you every night and wake up beside you in the morning. I don't want to have to keep calling you to find out where you are and what you're doing. Second-guessing what you're thinking. It's too stressful. Why don't you move in with me?'

'What? At the manor?'

'Yes,' he laughed, seeing my bewilderment. 'Why not? There's plenty of room.'

It was true, there was plenty of room at the manor. And I'd be lying if I said I had never entertained a fantasy about living in that big country house, swanning around amidst all that luxury, with Max making me breakfast every day. It would be the most magical place to live. A proper family home. But... Why did there always have to be a but?

'It's a lovely idea, Max, but I couldn't leave The Dog and Duck. I've committed myself to running this place and I want to do the best possible job I can. I need to be here, on-site, to keep an eye on things. This is my home and my business,' I said, wishing there could be a way around this.

'But think about it, Ellie. You could still run the pub living at the manor. It's only up the road. How long does it take to walk up there, about five minutes? And you could get someone else in the living quarters if you really felt you needed a presence here. What do you think?'

My heart was soaring, believing it to be the most amazing idea ever and part of me wanted to throw my arms around Max's neck and scream my agreement. Moving in with Max would be no hardship at all, living with the man I loved, wasn't that what it was all about? But what sort of message would it give out to my customers? They might take it as proof that I wasn't totally committed to my role as landlady of the pub.

'I think... well I'm very flattered that you've asked me. I really wasn't expecting that. It's just a bit of a shock, that's all.'

Max chuckled and kissed me firmly on the lips. It was hard to think straight when I was locked in his arms, his breath warm against my cheek. 'Just tell me you'll think about it. I know we could make it work.' He pulled back holding me at arm's length, the intense appraisal of his dark eyes not leaving my face for a moment. 'I want to be with you, Ellie. Properly. If we really want to make a go of our relationship and build a future together, I think we have to do this. If that's what you want too, then I can see no reason to wait, can you?'

The trouble was Max could be totally convincing when he was enthused about an idea and it would be so easy to be swept away by his conviction, but already in my head I was mentally preparing a list of reasons why it couldn't happen:

- I had the pub to consider – it was my home and my livelihood and I wouldn't want to do anything to jeopardise that.

- Max and I had only been properly going out together for six months – perhaps it was too soon for such a big commitment.

- Digby would hate it! Scrap that, Digby would love it. With two canine friends to lark around with and extensive grounds to run around in, he would be absolutely in his element.

I sighed inwardly. Max was right, whatever obstacles were in our way, we would be able to overcome them and find a way to make it work. But there was one huge scary thought that I couldn't get out of my mind; what if, despite all our best efforts, it didn't work? If I committed myself to Max, moved into his house, declared my undying love to him and then it all went horribly wrong. What if we found out that we didn't like each other as much as we thought, or I discovered he had some awful personal traits that I couldn't tolerate. Like snoring. Or cutting his toenails in the bath. Or, more likely, what if he hated the way I left little piles of mess around behind me. I wasn't the tidiest of people, but living on my own meant I could do exactly as I liked when I liked. From what I knew of Max, I suspected he was the neatest of neat freaks and my sluttish tendencies would end up driving him mad.

I was just thinking about dirty saucepans when Max started sniffing loudly in a most unbecoming and unnecessary way.

'What on earth is that disgusting smell?'

I sniffed too, before suddenly remembering. 'Oh no! My rhubarb!'

I dashed out to the kitchen, with Max following me closely behind, and snatched the smoking pan off the heat with a tea towel, looking, in dismay, at the black, gloopy concoction stuck to the bottom.

I swear I heard Max snigger behind me.

He put his arm round my shoulder and peered at the evidence in front of him. 'Hmmm, if it's all right with you, I think I'll give the crumble a miss today.'

I let out a heartfelt sigh. Well, at least now he knew he wasn't inviting a domestic goddess to live with him.

Twenty-Two

'Where do these go, Ellie?'

It was a couple of weeks later and Katy was holding up some clean glasses in her hand, that she'd been polishing conscientiously for the last few minutes with a tea towel.

'All the beer jugs go down here on this shelf beneath the bar.'

After that emotional session in Max's kitchen a few weeks ago with Katy, I'd encouraged Max to sit down with her for a proper chat about her future plans. She'd been adamant that she didn't want to return to Spain and Max had agreed that she could stay in Little Leyton on two conditions. Firstly, that she came up with a proposal as to what she was going to do here - he wouldn't allow her to mooch around at the manor doing nothing. And secondly, that she got her mum's agreement to her staying in the UK, which after lengthy discussions, Katy's mum had agreed to. Apparently, she was very relieved that the whole thing with Katy and her biological father was out in the open and she was keen for a reconciliation with her daughter, even if she was mindful of the fact that it might be some time in coming.

Last week Katy and I had been into town to visit the local

college and to pick up a prospectus. She had decided she wanted to do a business administration and finance course and had all the necessary paperwork now to complete. She was just mulling over a couple of options, but was determined to start her course in the coming academic term. I'd promised her a couple of shifts a week at the pub so she would have some extra spending money while working towards a qualification. In fairness, she'd turned out to be a great little worker, turning up on time and showing enthusiasm for all the tasks given to her, even the less glamorous ones, like mopping up spilt pints of beer. Nothing fazed her and it was good to see her with a new sense of purpose and direction in life. She was a huge hit with the customers too as she always had a smile on her face and would stop to have a chat with anyone who engaged her in conversation.

'What should I do now?' she asked, hanging up the damp tea towel over the radiator. To be honest, I'd been grateful for the extra pair of hands at the pub because for some reason I'd been feeling even more worn out than usual. I put it down to all the drama of the last few weeks catching up with me, and was hopeful that we'd all reached a new level of calm. I'd seen Sasha around the village on a couple of occasions recently, tootling around in her little blue car, and I'd wondered how she was getting on. She couldn't have long to go now until the arrival of her baby. I would have to make an effort to pop in to to see her.

'I think you're all done here, lovely,' I told Katy now. 'You've worked really hard, thank you. You can get off home if you like.'

'Oh, okay. Although... I'd much rather stay for a while if you don't mind.'

I shook my head, I didn't mind at all. I enjoyed having Katy around and she would be good company in the afternoon lull between the end of the lunchtime shift and the beginning of the early evening shift.

'Shall I make us a cup of tea?' she offered, and headed off into the kitchen, coming back later with two full mugs and the biscuit tin. I smiled, as Digby followed her up and down the corridor, ever hopeful that he might be in line for a treat too.

'How's things then, Katy?' I asked, when she plonked herself on a stool next to me.

If she was feeling low in her mood, she wasn't showing it, and today she seemed more than happy to chat. 'Oh fine. I'm feeling a lot better now. And it's so much better now between me and Max. He's been really brilliant. So supportive.'

'Good, well I'm pleased things have worked out. It's always better to clear the air and talk about anything that's troubling you, that way you can avoid any misunderstandings. Although I know,' I said, with a smile, 'that it's easier said than done.'

'Yeah, well at least I'm back on talking terms with Mum. Not that I've really forgiven her yet, but I have spoken to her a couple of times and we text every day.' She shrugged, looking thoughtful. 'I do miss her, you know.'

'You're bound to. She's your mum and she'll always be there for you. This is just a hiccup along the way. You might not think so now, but I bet you'll get over this and your relationship will be even stronger as a result.'

'We'll see,' said Katy, looking wholly unconvinced. 'She did say that she could put me in touch with my biological dad, if I wanted to.'

'Oh really. And how do you feel about that?'

'Not sure,' she said, swinging her legs idly from the heady heights of the stool. 'It would be weird, don't you think? He'd be like a stranger and I don't know if he'd even want to meet up with me. He's probably got his own family now and I might upset the apple cart just turning up one day and saying "hello daddy"!'

She laughed nervously, thinking about it.

'Well you won't know unless you try, and I'm sure there must be discreet ways of going about these things, but I guess that's something for you to think about. There's no hurry is there?'

'No, I suppose not.' She was lost in thought for a moment. 'There was something I asked Mum about though, one thing I really wanted to know.'

'What was that then?' I asked curiously.

'Well I had to find out if Dad had known. It was really important to me. I begged her to tell me the truth. Apparently, Dad had known from the very beginning that I wasn't his, but he insisted on bringing me up as his own. She said how much he adored me, how I was his little princess and how he never once mentioned anything about me not being his child. As far as he was concerned, I was his daughter and he loved me. There was nothing more to it than that.'

My eyes misted over. 'Well that's good, isn't it?'

'Yes, it means so much to me knowing that,' she sighed. 'If he hadn't known the truth and had gone to his grave thinking I was his real child when I wasn't, that would have been terrible. I would have been forever wondering how he would have felt if he'd known the truth. If he might have rejected me and wanted nothing more to do with me.

The fact that he chose to take on the role as my father, and that he loved me so much, well it makes me feel so much happier.' She took a sip from her tea. 'I suppose I got hooked up on the detail, but at the end of the day it doesn't really matter, does it? Dad was the man who was always there for me. The one who looked after me. He was my real dad and nothing can take that away.'

'Aw, Katy, that's so true. I'm so pleased you can see it that way.'

'Yeah, and as for my biological father, well at the moment I'm happy to let things lie. Who knows, maybe in six months or ten years I might feel differently, but for now I just want to put this behind me and move on with my life.'

'That's a good idea. You're only seventeen, you've got your whole life in front of you.'

'Yeah, and I'll be so glad when I'm eighteen so that I can drink legally!' She waved her hands in the air excitedly. 'I CANNOT wait!'

I chuckled, feeling the frustration of her words. To be honest, I'd be pleased about that too. One less underage drinker to worry about! 'Well, not long to go now, but don't wish your life away. It goes quickly enough as it is. And at least you've made some friends in the village now. If this good weather keeps up you'll have a great summer what with all the celebrations to look forward to, and then starting college in the autumn.'

I smiled, realising how pleased I was that Katy would be staying in Little Leyton. I'd miss her terribly if she left now and I knew that Max would feel the same way too.

'I know,' said Katy smiling. 'It's good to have some firm plans. Ooh, did I show you,' she asked, whipping out her phone from her back pocket. 'I've got some film here of The Leyton Boys rehearsing. I just love their music, they're so cool!'

Katy had been spending a lot of time down at Becks' Farm with the band, watching them practise, and generally just hanging out, much to Max's dismay. There was a group of lads and girls who did the same and Katy had quickly become one of the gang.

'Gosh, they are good aren't they?' I said, poring over her phone, watching the group of guys strut their way over a makeshift stage, tapping my foot to their music. 'You would think they were professional to look at them.'

'Well they have had some interest from the record companies and they've got a couple of meetings lined up soon so I reckon they're really going to hit the big time.'

'Oh well that would be exciting. We'd be able to say we knew them before they were famous,' I laughed. 'Just be careful with Ryan. I know you're keen on him, but he's a bit older than you and, well, I don't want you getting hurt.'

'Oh no, it's fine. Ryan and I are just good mates.' Katy flicked her hair back and looked at me wide-eyed. Her casual assertion that she and Ryan were only friends did nothing to assuage my worries. I suspected it was too late for any warnings from me. I could tell by the way Katy's eyes lit up and the way she grew animated every time she mentioned his name that she was already in way too deep. I knew it because I recognised it. The way she spoke about Ryan, the way she lingered over his name and the way a colour flushed in her cheeks, was the same way I spoke and thought about Max.

And I'd been doing an awful lot of thinking about Max

in the last couple of weeks. In fairness, he hadn't asked anymore about me moving in with him. I knew he was letting me take my time to come to a decision. There was part of me that wanted nothing more, but it all seemed so scary and such a big step to take. I'd never lived with a boyfriend before and I certainly didn't want to do anything that might ruin things between us. For now, I was just trying to ignore the elephant in the room.

We were so busy listening to the next track from The Leyton Boys that I didn't hear the front door open. It was only when a shadow fell over the bar and I heard a voice, oh so familiar, that I looked up from Katy's phone.

'Hello stranger, long time no see.'

Still my head took its time working out who it was standing in front of me.

'Johnny!' I stood up, still hardly able to believe that Johnny Tay was actually here. 'You're back,' I said, quite unnecessarily.

'Yeah, I'm back, and it's great to see you, Ells.'

He was just as I remembered him, only bigger somehow, in confidence certainly. His wayward curly hair was worn much longer now and his skin bronzed a deep golden tan. The black T-shirt he wore accentuated defined muscles in his arms and chest that had never been there before.

'Well,' he said, opening his arms out wide. 'Don't I get a hug?'

'Oh Johnny!' I lifted up the bar and ran round the other side to him. He swept me off my feet and swung me around him and I soaked up his lovely familiar scent. 'It's so great to see you. When did you get back?'

'Just. You're my first port of call.' He stood back and

looked all around him. 'Well, the old pub is looking just as I remember it. How are you enjoying being landlady?'

'Oh, it's everything I thought it would be. Hard work, long hours, but lots of fun.'

Johnny had always been one of my staunchest cheerleaders and had encouraged me to take on the pub. Even though he had a vested interest in keeping the pub open – it was his favourite drinking hole and he'd been a regular here ever since he was a teenager – when I'd wavered and questioned my ability to run the pub without Eric being around, Johnny had taken me to one side and told me that I had to do it, that there would be no one better for the job.

'Don't keep me waiting any longer, Ells. I've been away for six months. I'm absolutely gasping for a pint of beer.'

'Oh gosh, of course. Wait there!' I said, bustling back round to the other side of the bar and pulling out a glass jug. 'A pint of the usual then?'

'You remembered!'

'How could I forget,' I said, with a smile.

He waited as I poured the beer, watching my every move, the action seeming to take much longer than usual with Johnny looking on, keen with expectation. 'Oh god, that's so good, even better than I remember,' he said, smacking his lips, after taking a very long glug, almost emptying the glass in one go. 'I have to give it to you, Ellie. You do keep a very good pint of beer.'

High praise indeed from someone like Johnny.

'So,' he said, a questioning smile forming on his lips, 'are you still going out with that smooth-talking, filthy-rich, intensely annoying property developer, Max Golding?'

'Yes, yes, I am.'

'Well that's deeply disappointing, Ellie. I thought you might have got over that little infatuation by now. The bastard! I never did like him.' Johnny was teasing me, but I'd known him long enough to realise that there was an element of truth to his words.

'Johnny, I know you don't mean that. And by the way, I should introduce you, this is Katy, Max's little sister.' I gestured to Katy who'd been avidly watching our conversation ever since Johnny wandered in and now had an amused grin on her face.

'Oh shit! Hi Katy, lovely to meet you,' he said, holding out a hand in greeting. 'You do know I was only kidding about your brother. He's a great guy, a really great guy.'

'Don't worry. As his sister I know just how intensely annoying he can be.' She turned to me. 'Look I'm going to get going now, but I'll see you tomorrow.'

'Yes, you get off. Thanks Katy.'

'Well that wasn't embarrassing at all,' said Johnny once Katy had left. He moved his glass forward on the bar, indicating he was ready for his next drink.

I laughed, and pulled Johnny another pint. He hadn't changed in the slightest. After my initial shock at finding him in my bar, we quickly picked up where we'd left off six months ago, with Johnny telling me tales, amusing and teasing me.

'So was it really amazing?' I asked him. 'Trekking around the world?'

'Yeah, it was good. I got to see so many amazing sights, climbed mountains, saw beautiful sunsets, walked barefoot over glorious remote sandy beaches. I'm really glad I did it.

It took me out of my comfort zone, showed me a whole new side to life I didn't know existed.'

For a moment I was transported to that remote beach imagining how wonderful it would be to feel the sand between my toes and the sun on my back. I couldn't imagine when I would next get a chance to go off on holiday. I promised Mum and Dad I would visit them in Dubai, but the months were rolling past and there was always something on the horizon that kept me behind the bar of The Dog and Duck. Not that I was really complaining. Now the sun was shining in Little Leyton, it was our own tiny bit of paradise in the depths of the English countryside.

'And do you have wanderlust now?' I asked. 'Are you going to disappear off again somewhere new? Or are you back to stay?'

Johnny shrugged. 'Who knows? Back for the immediate future though. Sadly, I need to earn some money again. Besides, it's great to see new cultures and meet new people, but it's just as great to come home again. There's no place quite like the Dog and Duck.'

'Good, I'm pleased to hear it.' I glanced at my watch. It was just before five. Polly would be shutting up shop soon and then she would no doubt come straight round here for her customary after-work tipple. Did she know Johnny was home? And how would she feel coming face to face with the man who'd broken her heart?

'Does Polly know you're back?' I asked, trying to keep the panic from my voice.

'No. I thought I might need some Dutch courage first before telling her,' he said, holding up his glass, with a wry smile. 'I texted and emailed her a couple of times while I was away, but I got the impression she wasn't that keen to hear from me.'

'And you really expected anything else? You broke her heart, Johnny.'

'I didn't mean to. I certainly didn't want to. Things happened fast between us. Maybe too fast. I just needed some space, a chance to get my head together. Hopefully she'll understand that when I get the chance to talk to her.'

I wasn't so sure. Polly had been getting her life back on track these past few weeks. I couldn't bear the thought of her going on a downward spiral now Johnny was back in the village.

Mind you, it was really nothing to do with me. Maybe I should just take a step backwards and let them get on with it. An occupational hazard of being the landlady of the local pub was that it was easy to believe you could take on everyone's problems and solve them. I had to frequently remind myself that wasn't the case.

'Hello young man!' Arthur's face lit up when he came through the door and saw Johnny propping up the bar. 'Back from your travels then?'

'Yeah, I couldn't stay away, Arthur. Let me buy you a pint, and you can tell me what's been happening in the village in my absence.'

'We want to hear what you've been doing, don't we, Ellie?'

I laughed, nodding my head in agreement. As I poured Arthur's pint, he turned away from Johnny for a moment and leaned across the bar to whisper to me.

'That crumble you made me was bloomin' lovely, darling.

Almost as good as my Marge's.' He chuckled. 'I have to say that in case she's listening up there. But, oh, I did enjoy it. If I bring you some more rhubarb sometime would you make me another?'

'Of course, I will,' I said, feeling a huge swell of pride, and a tiny pang of embarrassment. I'd almost cried when I realised I'd scorched Arthur's prize crop and seeing my disappointment, Max had made a mercy dash to the supermarket to buy up their stocks of rhubarb. I knew it wasn't the same as using Arthur's home-grown produce, but it had done the job and next time Arthur would get the real thing as I was determined not to make the same mistake again.

With Johnny now deep in conversation with Arthur, I decided they wouldn't notice if I popped out for a moment so I slipped out the back door and dashed round to Polly's Flowers. The last thing I wanted was for her to get the shock of her life from walking into the pub and coming face to face with Johnny. The front door was locked, the closed sign hanging wonkily inside, and when I banged on the glass, thinking she might be out the back, there was no answer. She'd obviously shut up shop early, but frustratingly she wasn't answering her phone either, so I sent a couple of texts asking her to contact me.

Back next door, the pub was slowly filling up, with everyone making a beeline for Johnny, as he held court, regaling his audience with tales of his foreign adventures. A succession of people came in, all wanting to buy him a drink, so he was well and truly ensconced, and I doubted whether he would get out of the pub much before closing time.

It was much later than when she usually came in that

I heard Polly's distinctive voice trilling through the front door. Luckily Johnny was too preoccupied with his loyal band of followers to notice. If I could just get Polly to one side for a jiffy, tell her the news, then we might be able to avoid any awkward moments between the pair of them. I rushed out from behind the bar, weaving my way through the huddles of people, moving bodies out of the way, until I was standing in front of Polly.

'Oh hi, Ellie,' she said, coming to an abrupt standstill as I stood firmly in her way. She smiled warily, trying to look past me, obviously wondering why she was getting a one-woman welcoming committee from the landlady.

'You're late tonight. I was wondering where you'd got to. Did you receive my texts, I asked you to call me?'

Polly curled up her lip and shook her head. 'No, but then I've not looked at my phone recently.' She gestured with her head behind her and it was only then that I realised she wasn't alone. George Williamson was trailing along after her.

Ah, that would go some way to explaining why her mood was so chipper. Now I came to think of it she'd been spending an awful lot of time with George recently, ever since she'd managed to persuade him to open the summer fete for us. That had been a real coup and all of the committee had been so thrilled that we would be having a famous personality joining us for the day. Maybe she'd signed George up for something more too...

'Come through into the back bar. I've got something I want to tell you,' I said, trying to keep the panic from my voice.

'Oh, that sounds interesting. Well, actually I've got something to tell you too.'

Thankfully, George slipped away to get a round in, leaving us alone for a minute.

'Look, Polly...'

But she didn't give me a chance to finish because she was giddy with excitement and determined to get her news out first.

'Guess what?' Polly grabbed me by the wrists, her face alight with excitement. 'George has offered an amazing prize for the charity auction. A signed hardback copy of each of his books plus the opportunity to have a character named after you in his next book. Can you believe it? You can choose to put in your own name or someone else's. Isn't that great?'

'Yes, well that's brilliant, so very generous, but the thing is...' I spotted George returning with a tray full of drinks, and realised I wasn't going to have time to tell her about Johnny.

'Here you go.' George placed the drinks on the table.

'Polly was just telling me about your amazing donation to the charity ball,' I said, looking over my shoulder and noticing, with a huge sense of relief, Johnny deep in conversation. 'I can't thank you enough, George. It's going to be a hugely popular lot.'

'I hope so, and no problem at all. I've not really had a chance to get involved in village life until now what with all my deadlines so this is my way of making up for that. I'm looking forward to coming along and joining in with all the fun.'

'Oh George, that's so lovely.' Polly threw her arms around George's neck and gave him a friendly kiss on the cheek, leaving him looking gratefully bemused. I suppressed a smile. Clearly I was well overdue a proper catch-up with

Polly. She turned to look at me. 'So, what is it you have to tell me?'

'Oh, it's just that…' I glanced from her to George, weighing up whether I should say something. Perhaps it would be best to leave it; I didn't want to mention anything in front of George. The pub was really busy now, maybe the pair of them would have a quick drink and then slip out again without even bumping into Johnny. But that turned out to be wishful thinking on my part because just then Johnny sauntered past the back bar on his way to the loos.

'Polly!'

She looked up, a quizzical expression on her face, seeing but not actually believing who was standing in front of her. 'Johnny?'

He held up his palms in the air, a big grin on his face. I could have throttled him then for being so squiffy, so full of himself, so certain that Polly would actually be pleased to see him. Johnny may not have noticed the pain and confusion flicker across her features, but I did.

'I'm back Polly.'

'So I can see.' Bless Polly's heart. She said it with a big welcoming smile. From the depths of somewhere she'd gathered her composure and looked Johnny directly in the eye. 'Well, it's great to see you again, Johnny. And looking so well too. Travelling obviously suits you. Oh, I don't suppose you know George. He's recently moved into the village, he's renting Ellie's old place at the moment.'

She placed an arm through George's, gaining confidence from his proximity.

The two men nodded in acknowledgement of each other, but I noticed a flicker of irritation in Johnny's expression.

'Well, no doubt I'll see you around,' said Polly, very clearly bringing their conversation to a close. 'We'll have to catch up sometime.'

Johnny Tay might be back in town after travelling around the world on his adventures, but if he thought Polly had been sitting at home pining for him, just waiting for him to return, then he might have just realised he was sorely mistaken.

Twenty-Three

It was ten days before the summer fair and I was down at Braithwaite Manor, along with Josh and Mary from the committee, firming up on the arrangements for the big day; where exactly the marquee was going to go, what lighting we required, how many portaloos we would have, the placement of the tables and chairs, and confirming numbers with the caterers. Max's gardens were looking stunning today thanks to his small team of landscape gardeners. The lawns were a lush green, striped and perfectly tended and climbing roses in an array of yellow, oranges and reds rambled over the old retaining walls, their sweet delicious scent filling the air. Raised beds were awash with a plethora of old-fashioned flowers, like hollyhocks, delphiniums, foxgloves and mock orange.

'Fancy living in a place like this,' said Mary, looking all around her, before her gaze alighted on the striking Georgian mansion. We'd finished all our summer fair business and were now having a mooch around the gardens, admiring all the hard work that had gone into creating such a beautiful space. We all looked up at the imposing architecture for a moment to appreciate its grandeur.

In truth, I'd been giving a lot of thought to living here.

How amazing would it be? This could be something I woke up to every day, if only I said the word. Most women would jump at such an opportunity so what was holding me back? Fear mainly. It hadn't been that long ago that Sasha had been the lady of the house, well at weekends and holidays anyway, and look what happened there. Perhaps it was an offer Max made to all his girlfriends. For convenience's sake. And if I were to move in would that be the kiss of death for our relationship? I really wasn't brave enough to find out, nor was I ready for that kind of commitment.

'I know, it's stunning, isn't it?' I said, soaking up the beauty of my surroundings. The sun shone high above us, kissing my bare arms and warming the back of my neck. I twisted my hair up in a knot on top of my head, securing it with the band around my wrist, immediately feeling the benefit of a breath of coolness at the top of my shoulders.

'Very generous of Max to allow us to use the grounds,' said Josh. 'It will be the perfect setting for the ball.'

'I just can't wait,' I agreed. 'This year's summer festivities will be the best ever.'

Mary nodded. 'Well, as much as I'd like to spend the entire day here in Max's beautiful grounds I really ought to get back and see Lester. He'll be wanting some lunch.'

'Yes,' Josh glanced at his watch, 'and I should get back and do some work too.'

I said my goodbyes and wandered on down through the garden. Really, I should be getting back to the pub, but another half an hour or so wouldn't matter. It really was too lovely outside. And once I got stuck behind the bar, I knew there'd be little chance of me escaping again. I took a deep breath, inhaling the warm fragrant air. There was so much to see here. I'd been out in these gardens on several occasions, but on each visit there was something new to discover. Another delicate flower coming into bloom, a shrub turning from a dowdy green into a vibrant pink, trees bearing fruit. I walked through the archway cut into the hedge separating the gardens and found myself in the vegetable garden. Lining the gravel pathways was an abundance of lavender, its lilac flowers trailing over onto the path, its gorgeous scent teasing my senses.

Right down at the end of the garden there was a bonfire burning and I noticed someone working, tending the fire. It took only a moment for me to realise it was Max. His distinctive tall and broad frame wasn't easy to miss. Especially today when he had his sleeves rolled up, his white shirt unbuttoned to the waist, his chest smudged with black marks from the heat of the bonfire. He was dragging cut branches from the trees and shrubbery across the ground and tossing them on the fire. Back and forth he went, the sweat pouring off him as he worked. As I approached closer, still keeping out of view, I felt compelled to watch him. His jeans were worn low on his waist, showing a glimpse of black cotton briefs beneath. There was something about the way he worked, single-mindedly with determination and effort, that made me think he wouldn't want to be disturbed. He was lost in his own world. Besides, I'd taken up far too much of his time recently, bombarding him with questions and requests regarding the summer ball, he was probably sick to death of me and the demands of the summer committee. Best leave him to it, I reckoned.

Reluctantly I turned and walked away, but I'd only covered a few steps when I heard Max call out my name.

'Ellie! Where you going?'

I span round to look at him. He'd stopped what he was doing and was stood stock-still, legs wide, one fist on his hips, the other holding his rake upright. His eyes were narrowed against the blinding light of the sun. If only I had a camera to capture the moment, Max in all his earthy glory. Had he known I was there all the time, watching him, transfixed by what he was doing?

He beckoned me over and I wandered down towards him.

'Hello.' I was staring, I knew, unable to take my eyes off him.

He wiped the sweat from his forehead with his arm, appraising me closely. I wondered if he could possibly know the effect each of his movements, so casually executed, had on me.

'You okay, Ellie?' he asked, reaching a hand up to my cheek. 'You look a little... tired?'

Oh terrific. Max looked as though he'd just wandered off a photo-shoot for Hot Hunk of the Year and I looked... washed-out.

'No, I'm fine,' I said brightly, opening my eyes wide, as if that might help. 'I've just been running about all over the place recently. I guess it's catching up with me.'

'Please tell me you weren't going to slip off without coming down to say hello?'

I laughed, underneath the appraisal of his reproachful gaze. 'Well, I could see you were busy. I didn't want to disturb you.'

He threw the rake he'd been holding into a pile of cuttings and grabbed me at the waist, pulling me tightly towards him. My legs swayed beneath me and I hung on tighter to his firm hold.

'Never too busy to see my favourite girl.'

'Really? Don't let Katy hear you say that.'

He laughed. 'Well, you know, you both count as my favourite girls.'

He took my face in his hands and kissed me passionately on the lips, my mouth opening, receptive to his urgent insistent touch. His saltiness on my tongue stirred a longing deep down inside. The flat of his hand sweeping over the curve of my breast and the dip of my waist took me to a point from which I knew there could be no return.

'Come with me.'

Before I had a chance to ask him where, he'd scooped me off my feet and into his arms, carrying me across the overgrown area where he'd been working. He took me behind a large shed that housed the mowers and tools. Putting me down on my feet again, he pushed me against the wooden structure, his arms spread wide either side of me, pinning me beneath his embrace. Not that I had any intention of escaping. My lips reached out for his, wanting more of his kisses, to feel the firm hardness of his body up against mine. I felt light-headed with the heat or desire, I wasn't sure which. All I knew was that I wanted Max with a desperate longing that surprised me with its earthy intensity.

'Should we go back to the house?' I asked, my voice low and breathy, even though I wasn't certain my legs would carry me there.

'No,' he answered forcefully. His hand swept up inside my dress, stroking the top of my thigh, his fingers teasing me as they stroked and massaged my skin, my body buckling to his touch. My hand reached out for the button of his jeans, releasing its hold on his fullness, my hand grasping his erection, his eyes locking with mine before they fluttered closed with desire.

Max was a master of foreplay, but not today, there wasn't time. Both of us were lost to the moment, hungry for each other. He fingers moved beneath the elastic of my knickers, finding the warm soft moistness waiting for him there. I gasped as he pushed his way inside me, my body accepting and longing for him. I moved my hips, lifting my pelvis up against his, to accommodate his body as he drove deeper and faster inside me, every movement of his taking me to a higher peak of pleasure, my arousal fuelling Max's own desire, until I could hold on no longer, my release coming in a heartfelt gasp of pleasure, with Max shuddering to his own release at the same time.

After a tender moment held tight in his arms, he pulled away from me smiling, his gaze devouring me just as greedily as his body had done a moment ago.

'You are a very bad influence, Max Golding.'

'No, you're mistaken. I'm a very good influence, I think you'll find.' He ran his hands through my hair, wrapping strands around his fingers. 'Just think if you were to move in here with me we could have moments like this all the time.'

It was the first time we'd spoken about it since our discussion at the pub, although I'd spent many hours mulling it over in my own mind.

'Oh my goodness, but can you imagine? I'd never get any work done.'

'Oh, sweetheart,' he said whispering in my ear. 'I imagine it all the time.'

Rearranging my dress and tidying my hair back up on top of my head, I laughed his comment away. It was flattering to think that Max was still keen on me moving in with him, but despite how much I adored him, how much I loved his company and the positive effect he had upon my well-being, it still scared me to the very core of my being. Maybe six months down the line I'd feel differently about the situation. Who knew, maybe six months down the life Max would be feeling differently too.

'There's so much going on at the moment; it's such a busy time for us at the pub and then there's Katy to consider, and we've got Stella's christening and the summer fair coming up. It's not the right time, Max.'

He chewed on his lip, smiling, as though he was just humouring me. 'There's no better time,' he replied, 'but look, I'm not going to put any pressure on you. It's up to you. I want you to come and live with me because you want to not because you've been persuaded into it. I'm a patient man. I can wait.'

I allowed myself a wry smile. Max was the least patient person I knew. He went full speed at everything he applied himself to, grabbing anything he wanted there and then with a determined urgency and I had no reason to expect that he was any different in his personal relationships.

'Fancy some lemonade?' he asked me now, turning away and wandering off towards the shed.

'Ooh, yes please.' I went after him, expecting to follow him up to the house to grab a drink but instead he delved around in a cool box in the shed and pulled out a bottle of lemonade, pouring it into two plastic cups. 'How very civilised,' I said, laughing.

I drank the whole lot in one fell swoop, the cold bubbles welcoming and refreshing, revitalising me against the oppressive heat, and I immediately held my cup out to Max so that he could pour me another.

'Come on, let's go and sit down.' Max pulled a tartan check blanket out from a box in the shed and handed it to me, while he carried out the cool box and cups. Leading me through another cutaway, we came to a smaller secluded garden, this one with a round lawn with a bird water fountain at is centre.

'Oh my goodness, the grounds just go on and on. I didn't even know this place existed.'

Max chuckled. 'I call it the secret garden for that very reason. You're honoured, not everyone gets to sample the delights of this little place.'

'I should hope not either,' I said, giggling.

Max shook out the blanket and laid it on the ground, placing the cool box on top, and I sat down beside it on the grass, falling backwards, stretching my arms out to the side, revelling in the sun's warmth.

'Cheese sandwich?'

'What?' I turned to look up at Max, laughing.

'You can have half of my sandwich if you like. If I'd known we'd be having lunch together, I would have prepared a proper picnic. I'm afraid this is all I can offer you.'

'No, don't worry. I'm not even hungry.' My limbs felt heavy and tired from all the earlier exertions, and my head dizzy, from the effects of the sun and Max, I suspected. I would grab something to eat later back at the pub. Now

I just wanted to savour the moment. If I closed my eyes, I felt sure I'd be fast asleep in a matter of minutes. 'Where is everyone today then? It's so quiet down here.'

'The guys have gone off to the cottages to do some work there. Gives me a chance to come down here and get my hands dirty.'

He flashed me a smile as he said it and I had to wonder if he was talking about gardening or something else entirely. He'd lost his shirt altogether now, his strong broad chest glistening under the sun's rays, his long legs stretched out on the grass in front of him with his body supported on one elbow as he looked down at me. I ran my hands over the grass, to take my mind off Max, the short stubbly blades tickling the palms of my hand.

'How's Katy doing?' I asked him.

'Better. She's seems a lot happier in herself these days. I think she's relieved to get everything out in the open. I'm going to see if I can get Mum over for a few days in the summer. Maybe on neutral ground, they can start to rebuild their relationship.'

'Yeah, I guess it will take time.'

'At least she's looking forward now. Thanks to you for the job at the pub. It's been a godsend to her, it's given her a real focus to her week. And then she's got her college course to look forward to in the autumn. You know, I'm really quite pleased that she's sticking around.'

'Oh, me too,' I said smiling. Funny how in such a relatively short space of time and despite all the difficulties, she'd warmed her way into our hearts.

'Things are finally coming right for Katy,' said Max. 'I just hope she doesn't do anything silly in the meantime.'

'How do you mean?'

'Well, she's spending an awful lot of time with that lad, Ryan.' Max grimaced and shook his head. 'I suspect he has something to do with her improved mood too. She's only seventeen. I do hope she's being sensible.'

I laughed. 'Oh, Max, you're sounding like a Victorian father. Katy's very sensible, she's shown us that. Okay, she's had her moments, but then she wouldn't be a normal teenager if she didn't let her hair down occasionally. What is it you're worried about exactly?'

'Well, I know what young men are like, they've only got one thing on their minds and Katy doesn't need any extra challenges right now.'

'Ah right! So you don't fancy being an uncle then?'

'No I most certainly don't,' he said, shuddering. 'I'd definitely be sending her back to Spain if that happened.'

'Have you spoken to her about it?'

'What? Are you kidding? Can you imagine how that conversation would go down?'

'Well look, I can have a word with her if you'd like me to. Nothing too heavy. Just point her in the direction of the Health Centre, so if she does need any help or advice, she knows where to go. But do you know, I expect Katy has it all sussed anyway.'

'That would be perfect.' He rolled over on top of me, grasping my face in his hands. 'You see, this is why I need you in my life, Ellie. You make everything so much easier, so much more manageable.'

'Oh, stop it, you old flatterer you,' I said, pushing him away.

He rolled over onto his back and pulled me over on top

of him, laughing. My hands couldn't help themselves from rolling over the contours of his chest, as he reached up to me and caressed my breasts through the thin fabric of my dress.

'I mean it. It's one of the things I love about you, Ellie. The way you bring people together. I suspect you don't even know you're doing it half the time, but you do it at work, at the pub. And you do it here with me and Katy and my mum. If it wasn't for you, we'd probably all still be at each other's throats.'

'Aw, that's such a sweet thing to say' I said, delighting in the lovely things he was telling me while desperately trying to ignore the tingling sensations his hands were inflicting on my body.

'It's true.' A smile lifted up the corners of his lips. 'And there's something else I love about you, Ellie.'

'Really, what's that?' Him telling me he loved me twice in the last minute or so had probably done more to send me into my current state of meltdown than the magic his touch was weaving.

'Your freckles.'

'Ugh. No,' I said, trying to swipe them away from my face with my hands. The first sign of any sun and my face was covered in those pesky tell-tale sun spots.

'Yeah, they're so cute.'

He pulled my face down to kiss me, and when I came up for breath again, he hooked me with a gaze that drew me into the depths of his soul. Hmm, I couldn't deny the strength of my feelings for him even if I wanted to.

'I love you too, Max.'

Twenty-Four

Later, when I arrived back at the pub, I found the place pretty much deserted. Apart from a small huddle of guys sat on stools at the bar, it was empty. With all the windows open, the cool stone floors and the dark nooks of the centuries old building, it made a welcome retreat from the heat outside. Although it wasn't long before I heard chatter and laughter filtering through from the beer garden.

Our cider festival, a new and what I hoped would become a regular event, had definitely brought the crowds in. The barn in the garden had been transformed with colourful bunting, a makeshift bar had been erected and bales of hay had been dotted around doubling up as tables and chairs and giving a suitably country feel. One morning a couple of weeks ago, Dan and I had sat down in the garden and drawn up our menu for the event and we had sourced over twenty different ciders from local makers and artisan producers from around the country. Judging by the way, Dan and Andy were working flat out in there, pouring cider, with people queuing up to try out the different selections, they were going down a treat.

I picked up a tray and went round the tables collecting the empty glasses, chatting to people on my way. Paul and

Caroline were sat with Josie, Ethan and baby Stella who was in a little cute romper suit and a sun hat, and I couldn't resist stopping for a cuddle. Ethan shuffled up so that I could sit down next to him and gladly handed Stella over to me.

'Now you must promise me you'll be a good girl for your christening next week,' I said, whispering in her ear.

'Ha, I bet she'll scream the place down when Trish pours water over her head,' Ethan joked.

'Well wouldn't you?' said Paul.

'When's your dad getting back, Josie?' I asked.

'Thursday apparently. I can't wait to see him,' she grinned. 'He's going to notice such a big change in Stella.'

He absolutely would. I held Stella up above my head and she gurgled happily at me, her chuckling infectious. She was a proper little girl now, full of joy and mischief. When Eric left, Stella had still been a babe in arms and now she was crawling all over the place, pulling herself up on the furniture and trying out all sorts of sounds, making herself and everyone else laugh in the process.

I wondered too what Eric would think about the other changes that had taken place in Little Leyton, particularly here at the pub. Would he approve of the beers I was serving, the changes we'd made to the beer garden and the events we were running? Never mind the pub guide inspector, the person whose opinion meant the most to me as far as running the pub was concerned was definitely Eric. Hopefully he wouldn't be disappointed in any way.

'Well, as much as I'd like to spend all afternoon cuddling you, young lady, I need to get on.' I kissed Stella lightly on the forehead and handed her back to her dad, her little legs kicking in approval. I picked up my tray and went on my way.

'Hello lovely, how are you?' Betty Masters greeted me from another table. 'Come and sit down for a moment.'

I duly obliged, allowing myself a small smile. This little job was going to take me some time at this rate. Not that it was a problem. I'd arranged for extra bar staff to be on this afternoon anticipating how busy we would be. They were working flat out; Dan and Andy were manning the barn, Gemma and Rich were running the bar indoors, and Katy had just turned up and was doing a grand job of clearing the empties away. Besides, it was part of my role as landlady to give my time to my friends and customers, and I loved to catch up with them all and to hear all their news.

'I don't know if you've seen, but I've left you a little something in the kitchen.'

'Ooh, not my favourite Bakewell tarts?'

'Yes, just a few. Well, I know how much you love them. I was only popping in to drop them off on my way home but seem to have got stuck here,' she said, lifting her head to the sun before taking a sip from her drink. I liked to go across to Betty's Tea Room at least once a week, for my regular fix of coffee and cake, but if I didn't show up for any reason, then Betty would always go out of her way to bring her lovely homemade goodies to me.

'Thank you, Betty. I will definitely slip off later, put my feet up and enjoy one of your special cakes. How are things with you then?'

'Ooh, busy,' she laughed. 'Although I wouldn't have it any other way. The baking for the summer fair has started in earnest. I've already done several batches of scones for the freezer and I shall be baking all of this coming week too in preparation.'

Every year, as well as opening the tea shop on the day of the summer fair, Betty would serve her lovely scones with clotted cream and jam from a stall on the lawn. The day wasn't complete without one of Betty's special cream teas.

'What about you? Are you all ready for the big day?'

'Pretty much. I've organised the staff rotas and ordered my stock in.' This was the first year I was handling the responsibility all on my own and I didn't want to mess up. I had to make sure we wouldn't run out of beer or ice or anything else come to that. As well as our usual selection of beverages, we would be serving jugs of ice-cold Pimms, summer fruit punches and champagne cocktails. It would be one of our busiest days of the year and I wanted to ensure that everything was in place so that there wouldn't be any last-minute hitches. 'I've been down to the manor today and run through the arrangements there, so everything's looking good. I just hope I haven't forgotten anything.'

'Oh, I'm sure you haven't, Ellie. I'm so looking forward to it. And the ball in the evening will be a lovely chance for us to all get together and have a good old knees-up. I think we'll deserve it after all our hard work, don't you?'

'Definitely.'

Betty narrowed her eyes and peered across the bench at me, taking hold of my hand. 'I hope you're not working too hard lovely. You're looking a bit weary. You're not overdoing things, are you?'

Great. The second time today that someone had pointed out how rough I was looking. This morning I'd been in such a rush I'd only had time for a quick coating of eyeliner and a light brush of mascara, and I suspected that had all been wiped clean now after my close encounter with Max.

Note to self: I really needed to take more time with my make-up routine. I longed to be one of those glamorous landladies who always looked perfectly put-together; just done hair, fully made up eyes and vibrant red lipstick, but somehow I never quite managed it. Jeans, T-shirt, barely-there make-up and wild hair was more my style. Thinking about all things perfectly put-together, a picture of Sasha's lovely face flittered into my mind and I wondered how she was doing. I felt a tad guilty realising that I hadn't given her the warmest welcome to the village. When I next had a free moment I'd definitely pop in to see her to say a proper hello.

'No,' I said brightly now to Betty. 'I'm fine. It's nothing that one of your Bakewell tarts won't put right anyway.' I glanced around the garden, feeling inordinately proud that all these people had chosen to come and spend their afternoon in my pub, enjoying my hospitality. It was a feeling you really couldn't beat. 'Well, it's lovely to see you, Betty. I suppose I should get on. I'll catch up with you later,' I said, patting her hand.

I picked up my tray again, and went on my way, actually managing to fill it up with empties this time, and returned it indoors to the kitchen, where I put the dirty glasses into some hot soapy water for washing.

'Thought I spotted you out in the garden.'

'Ooh hello darling, how are you?' I'd just come out of the kitchen and walked straight into Polly who gave me a big hug.

'Yes, good,' she nodded, a big smile on her face. Already the sun had given her a light golden tan and with her high-lighted blonde hair, she looked the absolute picture of health. Much healthier than I did, that was for sure.

I looked over my shoulder and lowered my voice. 'Dare I ask? How's things with Johnny? Or should I say George?' I hadn't had the chance to speak to Polly since that night in the pub because of everything going on with the summer fair preparations.

Polly rolled her eyes. 'It's typical, isn't it? You wait for ages for a man to come along and then two come along together.'

'Like buses?'

'Yeah, exactly. It's okay-ish,' she said, jiggling her hand in the air. 'I've had a chat with Johnny, it was pretty awkward.'

'Yeah?'

'Well it was clear he wanted us to get back together again. Just like that. After six months of doing his own thing, over the other side of the world, he decides he wants to come home and pick up where we left off. As though I've not been doing anything in the intervening time.' She shrugged and we shared a look, one of complete understanding and utter disdain at Johnny's arrogance. 'Yes, I know I've not been doing anything in the intervening time, other than pining over him, but that's really not the point.'

'No, of course, it isn't.'

'Don't get me wrong. I do still have feelings for him, but he hurt me, Ellie. Really hurt me. You know that more than anyone. I don't think I could ever trust him enough to allow him to do something like that to me again.'

'That's understandable.' I went in for another hug because Polly was looking in desperate need of one. I knew exactly what she meant. Part of it was a self-preservation thing. If you didn't let go of your feelings, give yourself one hundred per cent to that other person, then you couldn't be hurt, could you? It was what was holding me back from

Max, although I felt I was on a slippery slope. Grimly hanging on for dear life, but about to go whooshing down the hill until I landed at the bottom with a bump. 'You have to do what feels right for you,' I said, not really feeling qualified to give her advice. 'Who knows, maybe a few weeks down the line and you'll feel differently. So what about George?'

'Oh, George.' She dropped her gaze and actually blushed, like a teenage girl. 'We're just friends,' she said quickly, her face lighting up in a way that it hadn't done when she'd been speaking about Johnny. 'We've been out a couple of times and he's such good company, really entertaining, but...'

'But what?' I prompted her, pleased to see Polly looking like her old self.

'I don't think he's interested in me in that way, you know, romantically. He only came to the village to work and I'm not sure he'll be hanging around for too much longer. Really, we're just friends.'

'Quite good friends though I'm guessing as you managed to persuade him to be our special celebrity. I think his lease on the house runs out in September. I could always ask him if he intends on staying, if you wanted me to.'

'No, don't, I'm sure that will all come out in good time. The summer ball might be an interesting occasion though with both Johnny and George there.' She flicked her hair over her shoulder in a theatrical fashion. 'Oh, what it is to be a woman in demand!'

'Talking of which, I ought to go and do some work. It's madness out there. I'll catch up with you later,' I said, kissing her on the cheek.

Walking out from the cool, dark hallows of the pub, the

bright light of the summer afternoon made me squeeze my eyes tight against the warms rays of the sun. I must have moved a bit too quickly because my head was swirling and my whole body felt otherworldly. A man came towards me who I vaguely recognised, but I was having trouble placing him, not least because my head was still spinning. He looked at me, a concerned expression on his face, before grabbing onto my arms and peering into my eyes.

'Are you all right love?'

Actually now he came to mention it... but I didn't have any time to answer his question. My legs buckled beneath me and I slid down the man's body, only narrowly avoiding landing on a heap on the floor by his quick action in scooping me up into his arms.

I must have come to a few minutes later, as when I opened my eyes I realised I was back inside the pub, lying in an inelegant heap on one of the benches. I found a huddle of worried faces around me and one in particular, Digby, had wheedled his way to the front and was covering me in wet, sloppy kisses.

'Get away,' someone hissed at him.

'No, it's fine. I'm fine,' I said, feeling anything but fine. My head was still swimming and I reached out a hand for Digby, glad of his concern.

'Oh hello.' I looked up at the man who'd gallantly come to my rescue, my brain still trying to make sense of who he was.

'Pork scratchings!' I said, accusingly.

'Ooh dear, she's not making a lot of sense, is she?' said Betty. 'I thought she looked a bit peaky. I said as much when we were outside. Do you think we should call the doctor?'

'No. I'm fine.' I pushed myself up on one arm to look closer at the man. 'You,' I said, pointing the man in the chest. 'You've been in a couple of times. Are you from the Pub Guide?'

'Ah, well, I'm not supposed to say. That information is highly classified,' he said with a knowing smile.

'Ah okay,' I said, slumping back down on the bench. 'Well don't worry, your secret is safe with me. Just please don't mention this little episode in your write-up, will you?'

He laughed and shook his head. 'No, I promise not to. If you're feeling a bit better now, I'll leave you to it. Looks as though you've got plenty of people around to help you.'

'Look, can I get you a drink or something before you go? On the house?'

The man shook his head and looked at me with pity in his eyes. I really hoped he hadn't thought I was bribing him, although at the moment it didn't seem such a bad idea if it might mean a good review. I'd been desperate to make a good impression after all the false starts I'd had with him and now this! I could only imagine what he was thinking about me and my ability to run the pub.

He took a step backwards fading into the small crowd of onlookers and I heard several other voices talking about me as though I wasn't there.

'She needs to get some sleep?'

'Has she been drinking?'

'Perhaps she has a fever.'

I didn't have the energy to refute any of those suggestions, feeling shaky still. I just closed my eyes and let it all wash over me.

'Right, let's get you up to your bedroom.' Dan was the

voice of calm in amidst all the hoo-ha. 'I wonder if you should see the doctor, just to be on the safe side.'

'No, really please don't make a fuss. Just give me five minutes and I'll be back up on my feet. I fainted, that was all.'

'Ellie? What's going on?' A voice cut through the babble. Warm, masculine and wholly familiar. I'd recognise it anywhere, only now, unusually, it was full of concern and anxiety. I opened one eye and winced, seeing Max leaning over me, his dark eyes probing me carefully.

'What are you doing here?'

'A hunch. I had this feeling you weren't quite right.' The white shirt had gone, replaced by a black fitted T-shirt, just as gratifying. 'You've been doing way too much, Ellie. Working here, the hours you've been putting in on this bloody ball. It's not worth it. Not if it's going to make you ill.'

I screwed up my face, disgruntled by Max's dismissal of the summer ball. I was so looking forward to it and it would be absolutely worth it. This was honestly going to be the highlight of my year, well one of them at least.

'Don't be like that,' I grumbled. 'Don't know why everyone's making such a fuss. It was the heat of the sun, that's all.'

'Did you have any lunch?'

'No. I was a little bit distracted over lunchtime if you remember.'

'Right come on,' he said, his tone brooking no argument. He hoisted me up and held out an arm for me to hang on to. 'She'll be fine,' he said, turning to the others who were not quite sure what to make of their landlady having a funny turn. I winced, realising how quickly this little episode would get around to all my regulars.

Upstairs, Max put me into bed with strict instructions

that I wasn't to move and with a promise that he would be back in a few minutes with a cup of tea and a sandwich. To be honest, I wasn't going to argue because I was quite enjoying the fuss Max was making over me. Besides, I felt sure that after a quick nap I'd be feeling much better.

'You see, this is why you need to come and live down at the manor with me. Because then I could keep an eye on you.' Max was back in the bedroom with a tray laden with tea, squash, some fresh fruit salad in a bowl and a ham sandwich. He held his palm to my forehead to check for a temperature and peered into my face as though it might hold the key to some mystery illness.

'For goodness sake, Max, you're making me out to be an invalid. I don't need anyone keeping an eye on me. Really.'

'Someone has to or else you'd be working all hours god sends, running yourself in the ground.' Tenderly, he ran a finger down my cheek.

I sighed contentedly, enjoying the sensation of his touch on my skin, his avid attention fixed firmly upon my face. I sipped at my tea, thinking how I could easily become used to this. Even though it was warm outside, I pulled the covers up to my chin, stretching out my limbs beneath, feeling as though I could fall into a delicious long sleep.

'You know what we should do?' Max went on. 'We should get away for a few days after the ball. Just the two of us. Away from all the distractions of the village. What do you think?'

Most of the time I loved all the distractions of Little Leyton, but I knew where Max was coming from. Sometimes it was good to remind yourself that there was another world going on outside the confines of the village. Maybe that's why I'd been struggling so much recently. The demands of the pub, the summer ball, Katy and Sasha, I'd allowed everything to get on top of me.

I looked up into his dark warm eyes, feeling a huge surge of gratitude for his concern and kindness.

The corners of his mouth turned up in a smile. 'Besides it will be good practise for when you move into the manor.'

Twenty-Five

'Blimey, this place has gone downhill since I was last here!'

It was a couple of days after the cider festival and my rather ignominious fainting fit, and I was back to full fitness. Max had been going slightly OTT making sure I was okay but I'd told him, all I needed was to recharge my batteries. I was just hanging some dried hops tied with lilac ribbon on the oak beams above the bar when I'd heard the front door open.

'Just a moment and I'll be with you,' I'd called, reversing down the step ladder before turning to greet my visitor. 'Eric! You're back!'

'Hello darling. Glad to see you're looking after the old place properly.'

My heart swelled at the sight of my old boss and friend. Eric looked relaxed and tanned as he twisted his head round to view every corner of the pub as though he was seeing it for the first time.

'Gosh, we've all missed you so much. I've been doing what I can here, but do you know this place hasn't been the same without you.'

'I don't believe that for one minute,' he said, laughing.

'And from what I've heard you've been doing a grand job behind the pumps.'

'Really? I hope so. It's been hard work, Eric, but worth every single moment. There have been times when I've thought, crikey what should I do here, and I think to myself what would Eric say? It always helps. Actually, you might not realise it, but you've been with me every step of the way on this adventure.'

'Well I'm pleased I've been of some use, but honestly you don't need my help, Ellie. I can tell that just from looking around me. Great selection of beers, by the way,' he said, eyeing up the specials board.

'Are you going to have one?'

'I'm tempted, but it's a bit early even for me. I'll pop in tonight and we can have a proper catch-up, how about that?'

'Sounds perfect. So what do you think to that gorgeous little granddaughter of yours?'

'Aw, what a peach.' He flapped his hand over his heart, looking immensely proud. 'She's grown up so much since I've been away. Just melts my heart.'

Mine too. And Eric being home gave me a warm glow inside as well. It was almost like old times now with both Johnny and Eric back. They'd shown that however tempting the delights of foreign travel, there was a special pull that Little Leyton held over its villagers that eventually drew you back into its fold, as I knew for myself. Now, if only it would work its magic on Mum and Dad, I thought with a wry smile, and that would be the icing on the cake for a truly magical summer.

Eric spent some time showing me photos of his trip and I gave him a guided tour of the garden, pointing out the changes we'd made, of which he thoroughly approved.

After he left, on his way to visit some friends, I took the opportunity to escape for a while, leaving the pub in the capable hands of Andy. This morning I wanted to pay a visit to one of the newcomers in the village and I'd picked up one of Betty's Victoria sponges specially for the occasion. Hopefully I'd receive a better reception than when I'd last gone on one of these missions, although in fairness I couldn't have known then that the man I was visiting was a successful best-selling novelist who hadn't wanted to be disturbed.

Down at Bluebell Cottages, with Digby sniffing around at my feet, I rapped on the door to the quaint little house. With a cute wooden porch, yellow roses climbing up the struts, and a lucky horseshoe hanging above the front door, it really was a rustic idyll.

After a moment the door was opened by Sasha, whose face lit up at the sight of me.

'Ellie! How lovely to see you.'

Her warm greeting made me realise I hadn't needed to feel apprehensive at all.

'I just wanted to pop in to give you a proper welcome to the village. I've brought you one of Betty's special creations from the tea room. I can highly recommend her cakes.'

'What a lovely thought, come on inside.'

Ever since we'd met Sasha that day, I'd had a niggling sense of guilt over the way I'd reacted to her news. I'd been so overwhelmed by my own concerns, struggling with an array of conflicting emotions, that I'd barely given a thought to how Sasha might be feeling. Learning from Max that she'd been going through her own problems in a relationship that sounded doomed from the start, made me realise just how unthinking and unreasonable I'd been. Now everything had been cleared up it was time to make a fresh start.

The inside of Bluebell Cottage was just as enchanting as its name suggested. With low beams, an open fire place and quarry tiled floor, charm and character oozed from all the period features. Sasha invited me to sit on a chintz sofa, where I soaked up all the folksy decorations: hanging plaited hearts, tapestry cushions and wooden letters spelling out the words LOVE and HOME sitting on the mantelpiece. In the corner was a wicker Moses basket and other baby paraphernalia.

'This is really lovely,' I said, looking all around me as I accepted the mug of coffee she'd made.

'It's cute, isn't it?' Sasha sat down carefully cradling her bump. 'I know I've been very lucky in getting this place. I don't know how long we'll stay here, but it's ideal as a new start.'

'You can't have too much longer to go now?'

'A couple of weeks, although to be honest I'm ready now. I just want the baby to arrive. I'm getting very impatient. Actually, there was something I wanted to say to you. It's a little bit awkward.'

'Oh...' My heart dipped at what Sasha might have to tell me.

'It only occurred to me after I met you and Katy at the shops the other week. It was insensitive of me not to realise. I really hope you don't think I'm treading on your toes, coming back to the village and having Max help me out with the house.'

I laughed gaily as though it was preposterous to think the idea had ever occurred to me. 'No, not at all,' I said, waving a hand around casually, making a big show of side-swiping the thought.

'Max and I are just friends. You do realise that? In fact, that was where our relationship probably went wrong. We were only ever friends and it never really worked for us on a romantic level. He seems really happy now with you.'

'Do you think?' I said, surprised at her directness.

I'd been apprehensive about coming, wondering if it would be difficult talking to Sasha, especially about Max, her ex, my current, and whether it would be better to just skate over the whole issue. I realised pretty quickly, though, that with Sasha it didn't feel in the least bit awkward. She had an honesty and transparency about her that was immediately likeable. I suspected I could ask her anything about her time with Max and she would answer me truthfully. Not that I felt the need to now.

'Oh yes, you can see that just by looking at him. He's much more relaxed these days. That has to be down to you, Ellie.'

'Well it's still early days, but yes, it's going well.' I crossed my fingers and held them up in the air. It didn't hurt to be cautious. 'And what about you and the baby's father?' I ventured, now we were opening up to each other.

Sasha shrugged, a vulnerability flittering over her features. 'He's gone back to his wife. He was separated when I was seeing him and I'd been led to believe that was a permanent state of affairs, but it turns out not to be the case.' She shrugged. 'Me having the baby seems to have worked as a catalyst for them giving their marriage another try. Ha. This isn't what I would have wanted in a million years. Being a single mother. But sometimes life delivers you a curveball and all you can do is go with it.'

'Oh, Sasha, I'm sorry.'

'No, don't be. Honestly. When I first found out I was pregnant, I was devastated. I know it sounds really bad to say that, but I was. This wasn't in my life plan at all, not like this at least. I had so many other things I wanted to do first, but anyway, it happened and now I think it was meant to be. This is my baby and already I love her to the moon and back. All I can do is bring her up the best way I can.'

'Her?' My eyes widened and I jumped on Sasha's casual slip of the tongue.

'Yeah,' she nodded, 'a little girl.'

'Oh Sasha, how lovely,' I said, surprised at how emotional I felt. 'You're going to be a brilliant mum.' No wonder Max had been so keen to help her out. I felt bad now that I'd ever doubted them both in the first place. 'Look you know where I am. I mean it. If you need any help at all then just give me a call.'

'Thanks, Ellie. I appreciate that.'

Sasha got up to see me out when she suddenly clutched hold of her stomach, and looked at me, a confused expression on her face.

'Are you all right?'

'I'm not sure. Just a twinge, probably.'

Only she had another twinge shortly afterwards and then another one and I could tell by the way she held her body, looking down at her bump with a worried expression on her face, that she thought something untoward was going on.

'Perhaps it's those practise contractions you get,' I said, trying to sound as though I knew what I was talking about.

I remembered something vaguely about them when Josie was pregnant.

'Oh god, if this is just a practise then I'm not sure I want to be around when the real thing kicks in.' Sasha ran her hands through her long hair and started blowing, puffing her cheeks out, which I took to be a very bad sign. 'Perhaps I should just... Aargh...' She didn't finish her sentence but instead let out a groan that told us both that this wasn't any practise scenario.

Even more surprising was Digby who howled in response, something he'd never done before, so I knew for sure something here was amiss.

'Isn't a bit early?' I said, desperately trying to ignore what was happening.

'Yes, but you try telling this baby that. Look, I think you're going to have to ring someone, Ellie.'

'Okay,' I said, as we both shuffled back into the house, me panicking that Sasha might give birth in the here and now. What if I fainted again? I'd be no use whatsoever to Sasha then. Taking some deep breaths, as that was one bit of advice for these circumstances that I could remember, I paced up and down, before saying, 'I'll call Max.'

'No, not Max!' Sasha was leaning over the back of the sofa, her face screwed up in discomfort. 'Over there next to the phone is the number of the maternity wing. Phone them. They'll tell us what we should do.' She groaned again and I winced, feeling a referred pain all over my body.

'Yes of course.'

Sasha took over from me, pacing up and down, or rather waddling up and down, taking deep breaths while I made the necessary phone call.

'We need to time your contractions,' I told her after I'd come off the phone, grabbing the pad and pen from the coffee table, as though they might help me take control of the situation. I was feeling hot and sweaty, and totally overcome by the situation, but I couldn't show that to Sasha. Every time she winced, I felt a pain deep down inside. Every time she groaned, I groaned too. Every time she cursed she was never going to have sex again, I pledged the same too. Trust me to choose this afternoon to come and visit. If only I'd come earlier in the week. 'Should I call a friend or your family?' I suggested, trying to remember what Max had told me about her family set-up.

'No, it's fine. There's no one,' she said, shaking her head. Okay, this was going to be fine, the maternity nurse hadn't seemed too concerned. There was absolutely nothing to panic about here. Not yet. 'Although...' she paused, looking down between her legs. 'I think you may need to phone the hospital again. My waters have just broken.'

'Oh no!' I blurted out, trying hard not to pull a disgusted face, and failing. Even Digby turned on his heel and disappeared into the kitchen out of the way. With my phone wedged in the crook of my neck, I followed behind Sasha with a towel that I'd grabbed from the bathroom, mopping up after her. The hospital advised us to get there as soon as we could so I phoned Max straight afterwards – there was no way I was doing this on my own – and was so very relieved to hear his voice when he picked up straight away.

'Max! I'm with Sasha and she's having a baby...'

'Oh, Ellie, we've been through all of this. I thought I...'

'No, no, you don't understand. She's having the baby *now*. Right this minute. I'm at the cottage and I need to get her to the hospital, but I've got Digby here with me. Could you come over and take him back to the pub please.'

'I'm on my way,' he said, sounding so much like a proper all-round superhero that I half expected him to fly in through the window in his cape and knickers, although that was probably just wishful thinking on my part. Thankfully he was only up the road and turned up in his Jeep in a time no self-respecting superhero would be ashamed of, and the relief I felt at his arrival was immense. I so wanted to run into his arms, for him to hold me, to tell me everything would be okay, but I knew now wasn't the time or place. At least the responsibility of Sasha and her baby could be shared now between me and Max.

'Look, get Sasha into the jeep and I'll drive you straight to the hospital, drop you off and then I can take Digby back with me. Unless you want me to go with Sasha?'

'I don't mind.'

We both turned to look at Sasha who was slowly waddling her way out to the jeep.

She paused for breath, supporting her back with her hands. 'Oh, Ellie, would you mind coming with me? Max, you're great and everything, but you wouldn't be my first choice of birthing partner.'

Crikey! Birthing partner? Me?

'Well, that's bloody charming,' he said laughing, looking mightily relieved at being let off the hook. 'I've got my wellies and rubber gloves in the back especially.'

'Er no, thank you. But Ellie, I wasn't thinking, if you need to get back to the pub. I perfectly understand. I'd planned on doing this on my own, so it's not a problem.'

'No, it's absolutely fine,' I said, trying to quash the panic

I felt. 'I'll be with you, if that's what you want.'

Sasha nodded gratefully as she climbed carefully into the Jeep and again I was reminded of her vulnerability at a time when she needed all the love and support around her she could get. I tried to imagine how I might feel about to give birth for the first time; excited, but scared and apprehensive too. And for Sasha it would be especially poignant knowing she couldn't even have the man she loved bear witness to the birth of their baby, to help her through this experience. I knew I was a poor substitute, but there was no way I would let Sasha do this all alone.

'Do you want me to let Peter know?' Max asked, as he steered the Jeep down the lane.

'Um… I don't know. I suppose he should know really, shouldn't he?' An uncertainty clouded Sasha's reply.

'Leave it with me.' Just being in Max's presence brought a calmness and a sense of control to the situation. From the back seat of the car, I glanced up, our eyes meeting in the rear-view mirror and the look of reassurance he gave me warmed my insides. For once he drove slowly and carefully. Usually he went at breakneck speed, throwing the Jeep around the bends in the lane like he was a rally driver while I hung onto the edges of the seat for grim death, but this time he was clearly mindful of Sasha and her special cargo.

At the hospital he pulled up outside the maternity suite and rushed round to open the door for Sasha.

'Let me know as soon as there's any news,' he said, squeezing my hand. 'Good luck, Sasha!' he called, and then whispering in my ear, 'Good luck, Ellie.'

*

It was four a half exhausting, emotional and completely overwrought, hours later – and that was just for me, lord only knows how it was for Sasha – that I was able to ring Max, barely able to get the words out.

'The baby's here, a beautiful little girl, 6lb 3oz, and her name is Ruby Emily.' Whereupon I promptly burst into tears.

'Well done,' Max said, his voice brimming with warm humour, as though I'd single-handedly delivered the baby on my own or given birth myself. 'Are they both okay?'

'Oh yes, they're absolutely fine. The baby has a full head of hair and she's just adorable. I've left Sasha feeding her. Peter's just arrived too, so I'm going to leave them alone together. They reckon she'll be out in the morning.'

Tears engulfed me again. In fairness, being a birth partner to Sasha hadn't been on my to-do list for today. Obviously delivering cakes to newcomers to the village held risks I could never have dreamt of. Still I wouldn't have changed the experience for the world. I had nothing but admiration for Sasha who'd been strong, determined and inspirational, whereas I'd been a wobbly mess, and I felt honoured to have been there for such a life-changing and life-affirming event. Even if I'd been about as much use to her as a chocolate teapot.

'It was just wonderful, Max,' I said, trying my hardest not to sob into his ear.

'Stay there, I'll come and fetch you,' he said, coming to my rescue for the second time in one day.

Twenty-Six

The day of Stella's christening dawned and I spent the morning wrapping the gifts for Stella that Katy and I had chosen on our shopping trip. Afterwards I soaked in a long warm bath, exfoliated and scrubbed everything in sight, put a deep conditioning oil in my hair and while that was working its magic, I kicked back and luxuriated in the bubbles, enjoying a rare moment of calm. Usually, I would be in and out of the shower in a jiffy, so the opportunity to spend some decent time pampering myself was a proper treat. Mind you, today I totally deserved the full princess treatment, it wasn't every day I became a godparent.

I was just drying myself off and changing into my underwear when I heard my name called from downstairs.

'Ellie? Are you there?'

'Come on up, Katy,' I said, wondering why she was here. If I was remembering correctly then she wasn't due in for her shift until later this afternoon. I really hoped she wasn't about to let me down, because with the christening party taking place in the barn I knew we would be in for a really busy shift.

'Oh hiya,' she said, taking in my half-naked body, and not batting an eyelid. 'Sorry, shall I come back some other time?'

'No, you're fine. What is it?' I unwrapped the towel from my head and brushed through my hair.

'Can I come and stay with you?' she asked.

'What? Oh no, please don't tell me you've fallen out with Max again?' The siblings had been getting on brilliantly of late, and with Max agreeing to Katy staying, to attend college here, for what might potentially be a couple of years, I dreaded to think they might have taken a backwards step.

'Yes! I can't believe it. He's only gone and invited Mum and Alan over. They're coming to stay next week.'

'Oh right. Well that's a good thing, isn't it?'

'Eugh no!' Katy shuddered and wrapped her arms around her chest. 'It will be really odd. I just don't know if I want to see Mum yet. Speaking to her on the phone is one thing, but this... How will it make me feel? Looking at her and knowing that she's been lying to me for all these years. It makes me feel ill just thinking about it.'

I put down my mascara wand and twisted round to face her. Today she was wearing cut-off blue jeans and a pink T-shirt. Her hair had grown longer since she'd first arrived, softening her angular features, and her skin had been kissed by the sun, giving her usual pasty complexion a flattering warm glow.

'I can understand how you feel, honestly, but you're going to have to see your mum again at some point and maybe this is the best way. On neutral territory, so to speak.'

I stood up and went across to the window, opening it up to let in some air. It promised to be another warm and sultry day.

'I don't know why he had to go and invite them over in the first place.'

'Well, she's his mum too. Look just approach it with an open mind. Your mum's going to want to heal the rift between you. And Alan too, I reckon, now that a bit of time has passed. Just see how it goes. You're bound to have a few awkward moments, but I bet once you get chatting again, everything will seem much more normal. Plus, it will give you the chance to ask her any questions you might have.'

'I'm dreading it.'

'Oh Katy, I bet you are, but at least there'll be lots going on in the village over the next couple of weeks so you'll all be able to get out of the house and do things together.'

'Terrific!' The sarcasm dripped off her tongue. 'Really, if all gets too much, can I come here please? Do you know, I'd probably be much happier living somewhere like this.' She plonked herself down on my bed and grabbed a cushion to her chest, looking perfectly at home. 'The manor is great and everything, huge and luxurious and all mod cons, but it doesn't feel like home.'

I smiled, knowing exactly what Katy meant. 'Hey, just think how lucky you are. Most people would give their eye teeth to live in a house like that.'

'I know,' she said, screwing up her mouth. 'But... it's just a bit sad up there. And lonely. I feel a bit cut off. All I think it needs is a woman's touch.' A smile lifted the corner of her lips. 'You know what, you should move in up there.'

I faltered for a moment, wondering if Max had mentioned anything to her, but seeing the mischievous glint in her eye, I suspected she was just being her usual provocative self.

'Thank you,' I said, 'but I have a perfectly good home here. Anyway,' I continued, pulling my dress off the hanger on the front of the wardrobe, 'I need to get ready. Will you help?'

It was a simple off-white dress with a pretty floral print that flowed out from the waist to a wide swingy skirt. It was another one of my purchases from my recent shopping trip with Katy. Again, not something I would ordinarily have chosen, but Katy had picked it up and urged me to try it on, and as soon as I slipped it on, I'd known it would be the perfect outfit for today. Light and summery and comfortable. Or so I thought. Now, well I wasn't sure if I'd made a mistake in choosing it. It was much more fitted than I remembered.

'Can you help with the zip?' I asked Katy, as I wriggled into the tight-fitting bodice.

'Here we go,' she said, pulling the two opposing sides of fabric together, physically manhandling me inside the dress. 'Perfect,' she proclaimed, with a smile, but I wasn't sure. I looked at my reflection in the mirror, turning this way and that, and wondered if it wasn't too fussy, too clingy or just not me.

'Maybe I should wear one of my old favourites,' I mused.

'Absolutely not. You look stunning. You have to wear it.' Not wanting to go against Katy's advice, I reluctantly agreed. What was the matter with me? I was so used to wearing jeans and tops all the time, that a dress and heels brought out a crisis of confidence. I examined myself again in the mirror. It would do! I would do. Heck, it would more than do!

A moment later, Katy asked, 'Can I have a hug?' She held out her arms to me, and I was taken aback by her childlike innocence and obvious need for affection.

'There's always time for a hug. Come here,' I said, pulling her into my chest.

'I just want to say a big thanks, Ellie.'

'What for?'

'For being here. For being lovely to me. For being my friend. I wouldn't have got through these last few weeks without you.'

'Aw, Katy, you're like the little sister I never had. You know I'm always here for you. Just promise me you'll give it a really good try with your mum and Alan. It will be much better if you can find a way to make it work.'

'Yeah, I suppose you're right.'

With Katy seemingly in a better mood, she volunteered to walk Digby for me before the start of her shift. Downstairs, I did my customary sweep around the bar, checking everything was in order, before going out into the garden. I'd spent the previous evening decorating the barn and now pink and white gingham check bunting hung across the rafters, pink and silver helium balloons bobbed on the chairs and the long buffet table was covered in sparkling confetti, the plates, cutlery and glasses all in place for today's event. Betty had delivered the two-tiered sponge cake this morning, iced in pink and white, with pink booties on the top layer and Stella's name spelled out in fondant cubes on the silver foil platter. There was some room inside the barn for seating, but I suspected everyone would want to venture outside to make the most of the good weather. I took a step backwards, admiring my handiwork.

'Oh there you are, Ellie. I've been looking for you.' Eric came up alongside me, his gaze taking in my dress and high heels. 'Don't you scrub up well. You look absolutely lovely.

276

My granddaughter doesn't know how lucky she is to have such a special woman as you for her godmother. Anyway, you need to come with me. I have a little surprise for you.'

'Really?' Excitement fluttered in my chest. 'What is it?'

'Well, that would be telling. You'll find out soon enough. Come on,' he said, taking me by the hand and leading me into the snug bar of the pub.

'Hello Ellie darling!'

I took a step backwards, not daring to believe what I was seeing.

'Mum? Dad?' I think I may have squealed, as my feet danced excitedly on the floor. 'Oh my god! I don't believe it. What are you doing here?'

'Well, you didn't really think we'd miss the christening, did you? It's been so hard keeping the secret, but we wanted to make it a surprise for you.'

'Oh my gosh! Only the best surprise ever!' I said, laughing. I ran across to them, tears filling my eyes, as I wrapped my arms around them in a hug. I kept having to look at them to make sure it was really them. 'I can't tell you how happy this makes me, but look what you've done to my make-up,' I said, wiping away smudges of mascara from my cheeks.

Dad laughed and hugged me again. 'You still look beautiful, even with panda eyes.' He wiped away a tear from my cheek. 'Go and get yourself sorted, love, and then we ought to get on our way. There'll be plenty of time later for catching up on all the news.'

The whole day was shaping up to be pretty amazing. Together, we made the short walk to St Cuthbert's church, me walking hand-in-hand with Mum and Dad, gossiping all the way. I'd last seen Mum in the autumn when she'd visited, but I hadn't seen Dad in over a year, so there was lots to talk about. At the church we gathered outside in the grounds, swapping stories, all the guests coming up to Mum and Dad to greet their return. To think that Eric, Johnny, Mum and Dad were all home again in the village, in time for Stella's christening, it was the best thing I could have hoped for. When Max turned up in his Prince of Wales check suit, white shirt and pale blue silk tie, I felt a surge of pride and affection, knowing that he was here for me. He went straight over to my parents, greeting Mum with a wide smile and a hug.

'How lovely to see you again, Veronica.'

Her face lit up, and then even more so when he complimented her on her outfit.

I gave an indulgent smile as Mum blushed, bowled over by Max's charming manner.

Then Max held out his hand firmly and introduced himself to my dad. 'A pleasure to meet you, Mr Browne.'

I'd wondered when Max would get to meet Dad and now it was finally happening. I thought my heart might explode with all the love filling the air this afternoon.

The only person who was entirely underwhelmed by the proceedings was little Stella who grizzled the entire time and had bright red cheeks in expectation of some new teeth arriving, we suspected. During the service I jiggled her in my arms, but she wasn't having any of it, and even when I handed her back to her mum, she still continued grumbling and sobbing, her tears falling onto the beautiful cream lace christening gown that Ethan had worn as a baby. Looking at him now, all six foot four tattooed inches of him, it was quite a stretch of the imagination.

'What is the matter with that child?' whispered Max in my ear, playfully.

'Stop it. She's teething, that's all.'

'Shouldn't they do something with it. Like feed it. Or wind it. Or take it home.'

'It's what babies do,' I said, shaking my head, laughing at him. 'And by the way, she's a her, not an it!'

'In that case, remind me not to sign up for one anytime soon.'

'Behave!' I scolded him gently.

Back at the pub, with Stella changed out of her dad's dress and into a much more comfortable short romper suit, the festivities truly kicked off. Everyone had a glass of champagne, a fresh orange juice, a pint of beer, a cup of tea, or whatever their favourite tipple was and Stella, much happier now, chewing upon a piece of crusty french bread, was happily passed around among the guests.

Dad came up behind me and squeezed me affectionately around the waist. 'It's good to see you looking so well, Ellie. You were looking a bit scrawny when we left for Dubai, but having a bit of meat on your bones suits you.'

'Malc!' Mum chastised him.

'Er, thanks Dad, I think. Did I tell you, Mum, I acted as midwife the other day when Sasha, one of our friends, went into labour unexpectedly. For a moment I thought she was going to have the baby in front of me in her living room. Honestly, it was a bit scary, but Max and I managed to get her to the hospital in time. She has a lovely little girl too now.'

'Goodness me,' said Mum, smiling. 'How lovely! It's all about babies in Little Leyton at the moment. There's bound to be a third, you do realise that. I wonder who it will be.'

Mum's gaze drifted around the garden. 'Ooh look there's Johnny, I must go and say hello to him.'

Standing beside me, Dad and Max were talking about this weekend's Grand Prix and who was likely to win, so I zoned out, my gaze following Mum as she wandered over to the other side of the garden, her words, delivered casually, playing over and over in my head.

There's bound to be a third.

What a daft thing to say! Just superstitious nonsense. I didn't usually believe in that sort of stuff, but for some reason her words struck a chord with me. My hands instinctively went to my belly as a sense of realisation filled every cell of my body.

I'd missed my last period entirely, but it wouldn't have been the first time, and this month, well, I was… late. Everything slowed down in my head as the bits of the puzzle were magnetically drawn together. The evidence: I'd been overwhelmingly tired, as people had so kindly kept pointing out, my emotions were all over the place and, I held up the flute of champagne in my hand that I'd barely touched, looking at it accusingly, my taste for the fizz had all but disappeared. Not to mention my fainting fit, and the struggle I'd had getting into my dress this morning.

The sun flooded the beer garden with its goodwill and people sought shelter under the wide patio umbrellas. Laughter, chatter and bonhomie filled the air, but with every passing second I drifted further away from all the people around me and closed in deeper on myself as I tried to make sense of the dawning realisation inside.

'Oh here she is.' Josie came up and planted a kiss on my cheek. 'Thanks for everything, darling. You've been

brilliant, and all this,' she gestured to the barn, where peo-
ple were helping themselves to the buffet, 'is just perfect.
You've done us proud, really you have. Come on.' She foisted
Stella upon me. 'We need to have some more photos.'

I pulled Stella into my embrace, our cheeks touching, her
hands reaching out for me, little fingers grasping my hair,
her hold surprisingly tight. She filled my arms with her
fullness and something stirred deep down inside, something
instinctual, something I simply couldn't ignore.

'Look at you two,' said Josie, peering into her camera.
'So gorgeous!'

I was still laughing and smiling, going through the
motions, but suddenly I felt detached from the whole proceedings, my mind drifting off to another place entirely.
After the photos, I handed Stella back to her mum and made
my excuses, before wandering off through into the bar.

'Hey, Ellie, where you going?'

I'd slipped off unnoticed, or so I thought, but my heart
slumped hearing Max's voice behind me, just as my hand
reached the knob of the front door. I closed my eyes, not
knowing how I would face him. What could I tell him?

Bugger!

Sasha popped into my head, the parallels to her situation
resonating deep down inside me. She'd been in a new and
exciting relationship, had fallen unexpectedly pregnant, and
her new man had made a hasty retreat. I took a deep breath
and turned round to look into his handsome face, wanting
to tell him my suspicions, but knowing I couldn't.

'Max!' *Oh Max. Why? And looking so bloomin' gorgeous today too. It just wasn't fair.* 'I'm popping out for
some fresh air.'

'Fresh air? You've been in the garden for the last hour.'

'Ha. Yes. No. I need to go and do something. I won't be long. I promise.'

'I'll come with you.' He stepped towards me.

'No!'

His face darkened at my sharp response, his eyes narrowing as he observed me. 'What's wrong, Ellie?'

'Nothing. Nothing's wrong.' *Pull yourself together, Ellie. Act normal. Act as though you haven't just discovered something that could be potentially life-changing.* 'Ten minutes, I promise, and I'll be back.'

Not bothering to wait for Max's reaction, I dashed out. There'd be plenty of time for difficult conversations later. Why I was even going through this charade, I didn't know. Rushing to the shops in the hope that there might somehow be a get out of jail free card? That I might be putting two and two together and getting five? That I might just have gone off on a wild flight of fancy and really it was all a big misunderstanding?

It wouldn't take me long, less than two minutes, or so the packet that was sitting furtively inside the paper bag I'd been clutching all the way home said.

'Did you get what you needed?'

'Oh yes, thank you.'

I span round, taken aback. I'd sneaked a peek through the window as I returned to the pub and confident that all the christening guests were still out the back enjoying the sunshine, I'd been just about to dash upstairs, unnoticed.

Had Max been lying in wait for me? Could he somehow know? No, surely not. This whole episode was playing with my head, making me nervous.

'Good, so are you going to come back to the party?'

'What? Oh yes, just one moment.'

I ran upstairs. Two minutes that's all it would take. I could do the test and get back downstairs again before Josie and her guests had even noticed I was gone. Sitting on my bed, I pulled out the packet from the paper bag, reaching for the instructions. My hands shook as I unfolded the leaflet inside.

'Ellie?'

I heard footsteps at the top of the stairs. Grabbing the box and the papers, I quickly stuffed them behind my pillow just as Max appeared at my bedroom door.

'Sorry, Ellie, but I was worried about you. You're not feeling faint again, are you?'

'No,' I said smiling. I kicked off my heels sharply. 'I was just changing my shoes. These are absolutely killing me.'

It would have to wait until later.

Twenty-Seven

Most of the christening guests had departed, Josie and Ethan had taken Stella home, along with some of their relatives who were staying the night, only a small group including Mum and Dad, Max, Polly, Eric, Paul and Caroline, Betty and her husband, Victoria and Trish Evans, and Johnny had gathered around the long table outside, and looked set to remain there long into the evening. Ordinarily I would have been sat with them, soaking up the atmosphere, engaging in the conversation, making sure my friends had all the drinks they needed. Not this evening though. Ever since the weight of Mum's words had registered with me, I'd felt removed from the whole situation. As though I was watching it all unfold from a distance.

When Max went off to the bar to get another round in, and with my friends and family deep in conversation, I headed upstairs, closing the door shut on my bedroom. I delved beneath my pillow and pulled out the box, looking at it accusingly, as if it was somehow to blame for my predicament. I ripped off all the packaging and threw it to one side. Two minutes that's all, two minutes before I knew for certain my fate. I dashed into the bathroom and came out again shortly afterwards, clutching onto that little stick as though my life depended on it, which it did.

I sat down on the bed, cuddling a cushion to my chest, the answer staring out at me from the little stick. I don't know how long I was sitting there for, lost in my thoughts, but it was Digby who brought me back to the moment, nudging my hand with his wet nose, something he often did when I was thoughtful. Or sad. He looked up at me with those soulful dark brown eyes and emotion welled up inside me.

'Oh Digby, what on earth are we going to do?'

He edged forward and licked my hand.

I'd wanted a baby. One day. Sometime in the future. In my mid-thirties, I'd always imagined. When I had a successful career behind me, a happy marriage, a family home and a dog. Well, one out of four wasn't bad. It was something for the future. Not for now. Not when I'd taken on the pub. I still had so much work to do here. So many plans. The simple truth was I didn't want a baby now. It was completely the wrong time. And what about Max? I couldn't even bear to think about Max. I knew exactly what he thought about babies, he'd made that perfectly clear.

'Ellie, are you in there?'

'Er...' Quickly, I got rid of the evidence, furtively stuffing the test back under the pillow. Before I had a chance to reply, the door flung open and Max stood on the threshold, the same dark expression on his face, that he'd worn earlier. When was that man going to learn some manners?

'Can't you knock before you come barging into my bedroom,' I snapped. 'What is it, Max? What do you want?' I knew I shouldn't be taking it out on him right now, but I just couldn't get a handle on my emotions.

'I was worried about you, that's all.' His expression

softened, concern in his eyes. 'I just came to see that you were okay?'

'I'm fine,' I said, in imminent danger of bursting into tears.

I stood up and pulled the covers over the bed, adjusted the curtains, folded up the towel on my chair, anything to avoid looking at Max. I wasn't ready to talk to him. I still couldn't believe it myself. Maybe only two minutes, but in that time my whole future had shifted. I needed to come to terms with this. To decide what is was I was going to do. There were so many questions fighting for attention in my head. How would I manage the pub *and* bringing up a baby? Could I really carry on as landlady of The Dog and Duck? What would I tell my family and friends? What would my mum say? And most importantly, what on earth was I going to tell Max?

'Come on, Ellie.' He walked closer and I felt the air crushing in on me. 'You haven't been right all day. There's something worrying you, I can tell. What's wrong?'

'Nothing's wrong.' I bristled from his proximity and turned away. 'I just need a bit of time on my own, that's all.'

'I know you better than that.' His hands found my waist and he spun me round, my whole body tensing to his touch. Sensing my reluctance, he quickly removed his hands and took a step backwards. 'Hey, Ellie, what is it?'

'Just leave it, would you? Please, Max. Just go. I really don't want to talk about it now.'

I hated seeing the bewilderment on Max's features. Today was meant to be a special day for making memories. Now I would forever remember Stella's christening for all the wrong reasons.

'If that's what you really want.' He shrugged. 'Is it something I've done?'

I shook my head. 'No.' I just wanted him out so I could have some time to think, to decide what I was going to do next. 'It's nothing. It's just…'

'Hey, what's that?'

My stomach curdled at his words. In what seemed like slow motion, he bent down, reaching out for the discarded wrapping on the floor.

'No, don't!'

But it was too late.

He picked it up, turning it over in his hands, his eyes meeting mine in a moment of recognition and understanding.

'My god,' he said, examining the pieces of paper he had retrieved.

'I've only just found out this afternoon,' I said gazing out of the window. 'I had no idea. Then my mum mentioned something and it was like, *oh my god*. The penny dropped. I was going to tell you Max, honestly I was, I just needed some time to get things straight in my head.'

'Right. I see.'

He'd fallen quiet, clearly taking in the enormity of what I'd just told him, obviously trying to come up with something to say, something to placate me, but I didn't need his sympathy or his false promises. A fire burned within me, my hand instinctively cupping my stomach, something instinctual kicking in.

'Hmm, that would explain things then.'

'What?'

I turned to look at him directly, gauging his reaction. His

dark brown eyes shone intently, the corners of his lips raised in the faintest of smiles.

'It would explain why you've looked so goddamn sexy today.'

'What? You've just found out I'm carrying your baby and that's all you can say.'

He nodded, almost apologetically. 'I've not been able to take my eyes off you. All day long. Now I know why. Every single time I've searched you out, I've been taken aback by how lovely you are. Just how much I love you.' He paused, the intensity of his gaze sending ripples down my spine. 'Look at you,' he said, coming towards me and reaching out a hand to my cheek. 'Your hair is shining, your skin is glowing and, if you don't mind me saying, your tits look absolutely magnificent in that dress. Pregnancy clearly suits you, Ellie.'

I was locked in his gaze, a pulse in my forehead beating furiously. 'Yes, but...' I faltered a moment, wondering whether I should feel insulted or flattered by his comment. I was taken aback too by the fact that Max hadn't turned on his heel and run.

'There are no buts, Ellie.'

'Oh Max. There are plenty of buts. I didn't plan this. It's a complete disaster. I've got so much to do, a pub to run and...'

'You do want to keep our baby?' Max's tone was serious now.

'Yes.' No question. 'It's just...'

'Then it's fine. Absolutely fine. You're overthinking this, Ellie. You know, you can't always plan things down to the tiniest detail. Sometimes you just have to make it up as you go along and go where the journey takes you. And this journey will be a great adventure, can't you see that? You won't be doing this alone. You've got a great support team around you. And you've got me.' He held the top of my arms firmly, looking into my eyes beseechingly.

I wanted to fall into his arms, for him to caress me and tell me everything would be all right. Max would do that for me because he was that type of man. An honourable man, but I was under no illusions, Max hadn't wanted this, any more than I had. It was far too early in our relationship for having babies.

'Oh Max, I appreciate what you're saying, but I don't expect anything from you. This is something that's happened, and I'll deal with it.'

'Come on, Ellie. Stop with the I'm an independent woman and I don't need you in my life crap.' He sounded rattled. 'This has happened to us. And...' he nodded, as though only just considering the enormity of it, 'I don't know about you, but I think it's pretty wonderful.'

I wrapped my arms around my chest not knowing what to think. 'You don't mean that, Max. Only the other week you were saying how you couldn't imagine yourself having children. How relieved you were that it was Sasha in that situation and not you. Look at you today with Stella. You don't even like babies!'

He shrugged, and curled his lip. 'You know something, I'm coming round to them. When that kid stopped grizzling she was pretty cute. And you might not have noticed it but I spent a fair amount of time this afternoon with Stella on my lap having a fairly intense conversation about the merits of the Summer Meadow ale. She agreed it's pretty decent.'

His eyebrows lifted, his dark eyes warm with affection. I couldn't stop myself from smiling.

'Besides, this isn't about Sasha,' he said, reaching out for me, 'and it's not about Stella either. It's about you and me, Ellie. Our baby.'

And that was when I fell into his arms, my head pressed against his chest, tears rolling down my cheeks. He held me tightly, caressing me with his hands and whispering in my ear, telling me everything was going to be okay. At that precise moment, I could actually believe that he might be right.

Twenty-Eight

'Well, why can't we tell anyone? It doesn't make any sense to me.'

It was the morning of the summer fair and I'd been up since five thirty so excited about the day's events ahead. I'd been out in the barn converting it into a beach hut, or at least the next best thing anyway, with nautical bunting in blue and red trailing from the rafters, striped cushions on the seats, and fairy lights decorating the entrance. I'd placed buckets on the tables with sticks of rock and cartons of popcorn inside and big bright beach balls and glass fishing net floats hung in the corners of the room.

'I've explained, Max. Let's just get today over with and then we can tell everyone. Today is all about the summer fete and the ball. I don't want to steal the thunder.'

To be honest, I was totally overwhelmed and delighted by Max's response to all of this. And a little surprised that he hadn't woken up the morning after finding out the news and changed his mind. If anything, with each passing day, he became even more excited at the prospect, coming up with baby names and showing me brochures of buggies and cots. It made me smile, but really I couldn't think very much beyond the summer fair at the moment.

'You're mad. Do you know that? What can be more important than telling everyone about our baby, but if it makes you happy then we'll wait another day. Just makes sense to tell Mum while she's over here.'

'Yes, of course. And I'm desperate to tell my mum too. It will be so exciting and I can't wait to see their reactions, but we can do that tomorrow.' Max's enthusiasm for telling the world our secret warmed my heart. 'So how's things going with your mum and Katy?' I asked, changing the subject.

Max shrugged. 'They're tiptoeing around each other at the moment. They haven't come to blows yet though, so I'm hopeful.'

Just then the front door of the pub flew open and Katy breezed in, her face dropping at seeing Max.

'Ah, talk of the devil,' he said, laughing.

'What are you doing here?'

'Er, I've just come to visit my girlfriend to see if she needs anything doing, that's all. Is that allowed?'

Katy gave him a withering look. I wasn't certain she'd forgiven him yet for inviting her mum and Alan over.

'What would you like me to get started on, Ellie?' she asked, snubbing Max.

'All the glasses in the barn need polishing and setting up on the trays. If you can do that, it will be a great help.'

The pub was a hive of activity this morning, with a constant stream of visitors, people popping in to see if any help was required and others taking a sneaky drink before they started on their jobs for the day.

Eric bustled in through the front door with the local newspaper in his hand. 'Have you seen this, love? You've got a double page spread. It's from the Potter's Pub Guide.'

'Really?' I wondered if that was a good or bad thing. Two whole pages to list my catalogue of faults and the humiliation at having Eric bearing the news.

Everyone huddled around the bar, peering over the paper where a photo of me standing in front of my lovely pub took centre stage. Victoria Evans had popped in earlier in the week and asked for a quick photo to accompany an article she was writing on the summer fair. *Sneaky*!

'Shall I read it out to you?' asked Eric, commanding the attention of everyone. He cleared his throat.

'There's never a dull moment at The Dog and Duck in Little Leyton. Under new management since Eric Cooper, the previous incumbent of twenty years, hung up his tea towels over the pumps for the final time last December, the place has undergone a subtle shift in character and style. The unlikely new custodian is Ellie Browne, a young lady who grew up in the village and who pursued a finance career in London before taking up the reins of the pub. The faded decor has been given a facelift, with new furnishings and paintwork, but the intricate charm of the old-fashioned country pub remains as it ever was. The outdoor area has been transformed into an all-weather oasis, with plentiful seating and patio heaters and cosy blankets for those chilly nights. Always popular with the real ale drinkers in the area, the pub continues to cater for its original customers in supplying a wide range of traditional and craft ales, frequently changing its menu, and running special taster evenings for its customers. But it would be wise not to make the mistake of thinking that The

Dog and Duck only caters for beer drinkers, when the pub has something to offer to almost everyone. Every night of the week sees different groups gathering to participate in their chosen hobbies. The knitting group, the aviation society, a reading group, and French for beginners are just a few of the groups who meet on a regular basis. Along with the open-mic sessions, the weekly quiz and the impromptu sing-alongs, the pub not only acts as a drinking establishment, but also as the warm and welcoming hub to the community. This is what customers say:

"Nothing's too much trouble for the lovely land-lady at The Dog & Duck, she serves great beer in super surroundings, what more could you want?" says regular customer, Jim.

"You won't find a better pub for miles," says Keith.

"The warm and cosy heart to the village," says yet another satisfied customer.

"With five-star beers and a guaranteed five-star welcome from the charming new landlady this pub is a little gem. Highly recommended."'

'He's only gone and given you a Silver award, Ellie,' said Eric, in awe. 'Bloody hell. Took me five years to get my first award.'

'Oh really, Eric.' I squealed, clapping my hands together excitedly, tears filling my eyes at the glowing write-up, and especially at the lovely comments from my customers. 'I'm so relieved. I can't believe it.' I jumped up and threw my arms around Eric's neck, kissing him on the cheek. 'When you left, I was so worried that the pub would go downhill, that our customers wouldn't like me being behind the bar and that they would start drinking elsewhere. The only reason I've picked up this award is because I've followed on from what you've been doing for so long. Everything I've done here I've done with you in mind. I so wanted you to be proud of me.'

'And I am proud of you, Ellie. In fact, I couldn't be prouder. You've done an amazing job.'

'What's all the excitement about?' Mum and Dad appeared from upstairs with Digby in tow. It had been so lovely having them to stay and already I was dreading the time when they would have to leave again.

'Come and have a look at what they're saying about your daughter,' Eric said, fondly.

'See what did I tell you,' said Max, taking me to one side and whispering in my ear. 'You're a superstar, capable of doing anything. And you're carrying my baby. I can't tell you how amazing that makes me feel. Just make sure you don't overdo it today. I know what you're like and I don't want you making yourself ill. If you need me to do anything, then just give me a call.'

'What about the Manor? Do I need to come down and check on all the arrangements for this evening?'

'No, absolutely not. We've got everything under control.'

With Max gone, I wandered over to the window and peered out onto the village green. All the marquees were erected and colourful bunting hung between the lamp posts. Polly must have been extremely busy these last few weeks because the High Street was lined with her distinctive hanging baskets overflowing with a profusion of pink blooms. Although there was another hour to go until the official opening of the fair by our special guest, GG Williamson, already people were milling around the green getting an early view of the stalls, chatting to their friends and neighbours. I could see Paul and Caroline in the distance plus Josie, Ethan and Stella. I was looking forward to catching up with them all later.

Already the pub was filling up, people gravitating outside to the barn where the Pimms and the fruit punches were going down a treat. Andy, Dan, Rich and Gemma were manning the bar, and Eric had volunteered to do a stint too, so I took the opportunity to go and find Katy, to see what she was up to. I spotted her in the garden and smiled. She wasn't a shirker that was for sure. If she didn't have a job to do, then she would find one and now she was whipping around those tables, collecting glasses and returning them to the kitchen, working her little butt off.

'Fancy going over to the green for the opening ceremony?' I asked her.

'Would that be okay?' Her face lit up at the thought of seeing her favourite author.

'Of course. Come on, we'll go together.'

Along with Mum and Dad, we walked across to the green where there was already a big crowd congregating, waiting for our special celebrity to arrive and judging by the large number of people clutching books written by George, I guessed a lot of them had come along purely to see him.

'Oh, Katy, how clever of you thinking of asking George to open the fair. It was the most brilliant idea.'

With a great deal of cheering, George duly did the honours and cut through the pink ribbon tied around the oak tree, announcing that the fair was now open. Immediately the brass band struck up, playing a jaunty tune. Before his queue of waiting fans got to him, I grabbed George by the wrist.

'Mum, Dad, come and say hello to George.'

'Ah, hello! I didn't realise you would be back so soon. Does this mean you'll be wanting me to move out of your house?' he asked, his mouth grimacing.

'Oh no,' said Mum. 'We're just here on holiday for a couple of weeks, staying with Ellie at The Dog & Duck. I hope you're enjoying living at the cottage?'

'It's perfect. I've got so much work done since I've been here, it's been marvellous, and I've made some lovely new friends too. In fact, I was going to ask you, Ellie, if I might extend my tenancy for a couple of months, if that's okay?'

Mum and Dad nodded eagerly.

'Yes, that should be absolutely fine. I'll get the paperwork drawn up and drop it in to you.'

Hmm, I wondered if it was just the peace and quiet keeping George in Little Leyton or whether a certain florist was another reason for George wanting to stay. With his faithful band of fans growing restless and encroaching further around us, we made our excuses and left.

'We'll look forward to seeing you this evening at the ball.'

We were mooching around the tent selling bedding plants when I heard someone call my name. I turned round to see Sasha with the pram.

'Aw, Sasha, how lovely! I'm so glad you came. How's it all going?'

'Good, I think. This is our first trip outside the house, and it took me about two hours to get ready. I don't know how I'm supposed to do that every day.'

Mum laughed. 'Don't worry, love. It does get easier. And, what a beautiful baby you have,' she said, peering into the pram.

Katy took a step closer too, smiling.

'She's gorgeous,' I agreed, 'and I can already see the change in her from when she was born.'

Sasha's face beamed, looking inordinately proud.

We stood around for a good few minutes, just admiring Ruby, cooing over her, at the wonder of her perfectness. It was only a few minutes, but the pleasure it brought us all, I felt sure we could have stood there all afternoon doing the same.

Surreptitiously, my hand went to my tummy. Funny to think that in less than nine months' time I would have a baby of my own. That Ruby and my own child might grow up together, become friends and go to the same school. Mum didn't have an inkling that I was pregnant and nor did Katy. I glanced across at them now, wondering how they would react when they found out the news.

'I'll come and see you soon,' I told Sasha. 'We can have a good old catch-up.' These past few weeks, having the privilege of being Sasha's birth partner, had brought us closer together, and it was funny to think that I might have found a new close friend in Max's ex.

Mum and Dad spotted some friends over by the tent serving the teas and they wandered off towards them, while Katy and I stood by the arena and watched the school-children dancing the maypole.

'Is everything all right with Max?' she asked, out of the blue.

'Yes.' I turned to her. 'Why would you ask that?'

'I've just noticed how peculiar he's being. Whenever I come along he stops talking as though it's something he doesn't want me to know about. I'm also worried that it's something to do with Mum. Another awful secret that they're keeping from me.'

'No, no, it's nothing like that,' I said, quick to reassure her.

She turned to me accusingly. 'Right, so there is something, I just knew it! Why, Ellie? Why do people have to keep secrets from me? I hate it.'

She went to run away, but I quickly grabbed her arm.

'No, don't go, Katy. You've got it all wrong. It doesn't affect you at all, although...' I paused thinking, realising just how much it would affect Katy. Her brother would become a father and that would make her an auntie. With her staying in Little Leyton now, having a baby around would be a big change for her. Max and I hadn't made any firm plans yet regarding our living arrangements, but they would definitely impact on Katy too. I remembered her reaction to Sasha's pregnancy. Would she feel so strongly about mine?

'Just tell me, Ellie. I can't bear it.'

I saw the hurt in her eyes. After everything she'd been through recently, I just couldn't put her through any more. I pulled her away from the arena to a spot where we wouldn't be overheard.

'Look, Katy, you must promise not to tell anyone. Not for the moment. This is between you, me and Max.'

'What is it?' she said, looking genuinely concerned now.

'The thing is… well, I'm not sure how to say this, but…'

Katy's eyes grew wider with each word that I spoke, clearly conjuring up a host of dreadful scenarios.

'I'm pregnant,' I blurted it out quickly, the words just hanging there in the air, resonating in my head. *Wow*! I'd said it, told someone other than Max that I was having a baby and it made me so thrilled to say it aloud. Katy however was looking at me blankly.

'What?'

Oh goodness. Maybe this hadn't been such a good idea after all. I really hoped she wasn't going to kick off just as the fete was getting underway.

'We're having a baby, Katy. It was totally unplanned so we're as shocked as I bet you are. We're just getting our heads around it now.'

'Oh. My. God!' Katy screamed the words so loud, I felt sure the whole of the village green heard her. A sea of heads turned to look at us.

'Shhh,' I scolded her. 'No one's supposed to know.'

'That's amazing! I'm so happy for you. I'm going to be an auntie.' She twirled around on the grass, her hands held out wide.

'Can I take it you're happy about this news then?'

'Oh, it's the best news ever! Does that mean you'll move into the manor? Will you get married first? Can I be your bridesmaid?'

I threw back my head and laughed. 'Too many questions, Katy. Far too many questions.'

Twenty-Nine

Thankfully, due to the sweeping design of my ball gown, it still fitted perfectly, covering up the tiny little bump that was just protruding from my stomach. No one had noticed yet, but I didn't think it would be much longer before my pregnancy would show. Still, after tonight, we'd be able to tell all our friends and family our happy news.

We'd gathered in the barn downstairs at The Dog and Duck for drinks before setting off for the ball. For the first time in weeks I actually fancied an alcoholic drink, but I made do with an orange juice and lemonade instead, pretending it was Bucks Fizz. I don't know if it was the fizziness or the excitement of the occasion, but it hit exactly the right spot, making me light-headed, my whole body feeling as though I was floating high on a cloud.

'Oh look at you,' said Mum, grinning broadly. 'Don't you look beautiful?'

'Like a proper princess,' said Dad, and I wasn't sure if he had some fluff in his eye or if it was something else making them water.

Everyone was dressed up in all their finery, the men in their dinner suits and the women in a variety of sparkly ballgowns and sophisticated cocktail dresses. Some people carried their intricately decorated masks in their hands and others were already wearing theirs. It was hard to imagine that the bunch of scruffians who congregated in the pub on a regular basis could actually look quite so glamorous.

We were just discussing how we ought to make a move when a klaxon sounded outside the pub. Someone went running to the front, and beckoned for us to follow. Hearing the sound of a rumbling engine, we went outside to find Max standing next to a vintage tractor with a trailer, decorated in colourful bunting and with straw bales for us to sit on.

'Your carriage awaits, Madam.' Max bent forward, bowing with an exaggerated flourish.

'Oh my goodness, what is this?'

'Well I didn't think you'd all want to walk down the lanes in your posh gear and high heels,' said Max, laughing. 'So I've laid on some transport. Cinderella will go to the ball.'

His broad frame filled his dinner suit perfectly, the white of his shirt highlighting his lightly tanned skin, the slight shadow of stubble lending him a dangerously sexy air.

'This is perfect,' I said, touched by Max's thoughtful gesture. He'd always been this way but ever since hearing about the baby he'd become even more so.

It was a beautiful summer's evening and we were all laughing, high on the good vibes radiating on the back of that trailer, screeching as the tractor bounced over the bumps in the lane. Within five minutes we were at the manor and we were all eager to disembark and get inside the marquee.

'Doesn't it look amazing?' I whispered to Max.

The big white tent dominated the lawn, and already the sound of excited chatter and laughter filled the air. Cool white fairy lights twinkled in the trees and bushes, creating a magical otherworldly effect. Along the red carpet, tea lights flickered in glass lanterns providing a warm welcome.

'Well, that's all down to your hard work, Ellie. You organised most of this, didn't you?'

I supposed I had, but it hadn't felt like hard work at all. Everything we'd talked about for months, all the meetings at the pub had all been for this one night. Whatever I'd hoped for, the reality of it far exceeded anything I could have imagined. I swept into the marquee on Max's arm, hugging our secret to my chest with a smile, and wafted around the tent, chatting to all my friends, family and neighbours.

'Ellie, you're looking gorgeous?' Polly came dashing across to greet me, dragging George along with her.

I felt the tiniest pang of guilt that I hadn't told my best friends, Polly and Josie, my news, but I knew they'd forgive me my reticence. Tomorrow, everyone would know and I simply couldn't wait.

'So are you!'

Polly was wearing a black sheath dress that showed off her slim figure, her blonde hair swinging in her trademark bob. But there was something else transforming her appearance tonight. A glow in her cheeks and a twinkle in her eye that told me she was feeling positive and happy again, back to the Polly I knew and loved. She shared a glance with George that showed me they were both as smitten as each other.

'Do you know,' said Max, whispering in my ear. 'I wonder if we should make the grand announcement tonight. I could get up on that stage and pronounce it over the megaphone.'

'Don't you dare,' I said, digging him in the chest.

'Why not, Ellie? I want the whole word to know you're having my baby.'

I laughed. 'I want that too, but I want it to be special. To tell people individually. Besides, tonight is all about the food, the booze and the dancing. Come on.'

Sitting at a long banquet table with all my friends and family, I was swept away on a wave of happiness, content enough just to watch all the goings-on around me.

After an exquisite three-course meal, which I was told was absolutely delicious, but which I hardly touched because I was far too excited to eat, the charity auction got under-way, and the level of excitement and noise rose to such a pitch that I thought it might blow the roof of the marquee.

Tim Weston acted as auctioneer and the lots, theatre tickets, weekend breaks, beauty treatments and stadium tours came thick and fast, the amount of money being bid increasing at an alarming rate with each passing lot.

I gasped, amazed by everyone's generosity.

When the prize donated by George Williamson came up for sale a buzz of excitement swept round the tent. I had thought Max might have bid on this lot for Katy, but there was a two-man bidding war going on over the other side of the tent. In the end, to a wild round of applause, the lot went for several hundred pounds.

Over the other side of the table, I caught Katy's eye and she shrugged, disappointment flickering over her features for the briefest moment, before her face lit up with a smile again. I suspected nothing was going to get in the way of her enjoyment tonight. Against all the odds, she was sat between her mum, Rose, and Alan, chattering away excitedly, as if there'd never been any bad feeling between them. Earlier, this evening I'd been introduced to them both and found them perfectly charming.

'It's so lovely to meet you at last,' Rose had told me. 'Katy talks about you all the time. And so does Max, come to that,' she said, giving a knowing smile. 'Really though, I have to thank you for everything you've done for Katy, for being such a good friend to her. I know it hasn't been easy for her these last few months.'

'It's been a pleasure,' I said, meaning it. 'We've loved having her around.'

Now, back in the excitement of the tent, the gavel went down on the last lot, a luxury holiday in Dubai, and a huge cheer erupted in the room. The members of the committee looked around at each other, we'd raised far more money for our charities than we could ever have imagined.

There was a lull in the proceedings when tables and chairs were pushed back to the edges of the tent in readiness for the dancing, and Katy came scooting across the floor towards us.

'The band are just setting up. Squeee! I can't wait. They're going to be brilliant.'

She scooted back off again, and we watched, laughing, as she fluttered around the guys in the band, running errands for them.

'I don't know what's got into that girl. She's been in the best mood today.'

'Ah, probably just excited about the band, I suspect,' suppressing a smile as I remembered Katy's enthusiasm at hearing our news today.

'Katy, over here?' Max beckoned her back across the room and she came running again, looking like the teenager she was. 'I got this for you.' He handed her an envelope and both Katy and I looked at him in surprise.

'What is it?'

'Well, open it and you'll find out.'

Excitedly, she ripped the envelope apart, bits of paper flying in every direction. She gasped pulling out the card inside.

'The GG Williamson prize? But you didn't bid, I was watching you.'

'No, I didn't bid, but someone who works for me did.' His eyes danced with mischievous pleasure. 'Well, it wouldn't have been a surprise otherwise. I hope you like it.'

For the second time that day I saw Katy squeal with delight. 'I love it! I so wanted this, but I didn't want to ask. Thank you so much!' she cried, jumping onto Max's lap and hugging him tight. 'I must go and tell George, he'll be so pleased I got to win. You're the best brother ever, do you know that?'

With Katy dashing off again, Max sat back in his chair and nodded, a satisfied smile on his face.

'Well, it won't last, but it's nice to know I've done something right in that girl's eyes for once.'

'Aw, it's great to see her looking so happy,' I said, taking hold of his hand. 'You know, despite her prickliness at times, she just adores you and all she wants is to please you.'

'Yeah, it's funny, but I'm kind of getting used to her being about the place. It wouldn't be the same without her now. I wonder though how she'll react when she finds out about the baby.'

'Do you know,' I said, smiling, 'I've an inkling she'll be overjoyed at the news.'

Max narrowed his eyes, casting me a questioning glance, but I just laughed his suspicion away.

'Anyway, I couldn't get something for Katy, and not you.'

I looked down at the shiny gold envelope that Max now placed on the table in front of me and I felt my skin prickle in anticipation. Could this day really get any better? I pulled out the card, tears forming in my eyes.

'The luxury holiday in Dubai? You bought that for me?'

'Yes, well you keep saying how much you'd love to go and visit your mum and dad, and this seemed like the perfect opportunity. I know left to your own devices you might never get round to it, and I thought if you're going to go, then you really ought to go soon.' He glanced down putting a protective hand around my bump.

'Oh Max!'

He smiled. 'Come on, let's go outside and get some fresh air,' he said, taking my hand in his. 'It's a beautiful night out there.' Before we left, we stood for a moment, just watching, as people gravitated towards the dance floor at the call of the music. It lifted my heart to see Mum and Dad swaying in each other's arms, so full of joy, and Polly and George getting up close and personal. Eric had been literally left holding baby Stella, while Ethan swept Josie around the floor as though he'd been taking lessons, her face a picture of delight. The return of her dad had definitely given her the boost she'd needed. The other returning wanderer, Johnny, was sitting this one out and instead was sharing tales at the table with Dan and Silke. At Katy's behest, Rose and Alan were even up dancing too. Sasha had decided, perfectly understandably, not to come along tonight, but I was looking forward to filling her in on all the details when I next got to see her. All my friends and family under the same roof on this glorious summer's night, what more could I ask for?

Outside we walked hand in hand along the lit pathway that wound its way down through the gardens, the muted music from the tent serenading us. We both turned to look at the magnificent house highlighted against the night sky and I felt a huge swirl of happiness at being here tonight amongst the people I loved, and most importantly being by the side of the man I loved. I leant into his embrace, feeling his strong arm around my shoulder, certain I was the luckiest woman alive.

'You know you'll have to come and move in at the manor with me now.'

'How come?' I said, playfully.

'Well, this is a perfect place to bring up our family, Ellie, don't you think?'

I let out a soft sigh, feeling a pang of regret for The Dog and Duck, but knowing deep down that Braithwaite Manor was not only where I wanted to raise a baby but where I wanted to live, with the man I loved.

'Just imagine it, Ellie, our children running across the lawns. I can picture them now.'

'Children?' I asked, looking up at him.

'Four, I reckon.'

'Four?' I said, almost choking at the idea, but my mind was already entertaining that thought very nicely.

'Well three then,' he said chuckling. 'We should definitely get married.'

Now it was my turn to laugh.

'Married? That's not even a proper proposal.'

'Fair point,' said Max, wrapping his arms tighter around

me, looking up to the sky in search of answers. 'Maybe we should get engaged first then, how about that?'

'Hmmm, we'll see.'

Up above, the stars could be seen shining brightly over us, a guiding light to our brand new future together.

All I knew was that I felt ready now. Ready to let go. I knew with an unwavering certainty that this was everything I wanted; Max, a home together and our baby.

Everything else was entirely negotiable.

Acknowledgements

Firstly, a huge thanks must go to the fantastic team at Aria. It's such a pleasure to work with you all and your support and encouragement is truly appreciated. In particular, special thanks to Caroline Ridding, to Sarah Ritherdon for her patience, understanding and amazing editorial advice – I really wouldn't have made it here without you – and to Yasemin Turan and Nia Beynon for always being so efficiently helpful in answering my sometimes daft questions. To Jade Craddock for her insightful comments and for the liberal sprinkling of magic dust again.

As always, a big thanks has to go to my lovely family, for being with me every step of the way in the making of this book. Normal service will be resumed soon.

Finally, a special thank you to you, my readers, for picking up this book. It always gives me such a thrill to know that people are reading my work, and hopefully enjoying it too, and your continued support of my writing fills me with gratitude.

Thank you.

Jill xxx